winged creatures

winged creatures

Roy Freirich

ST. MARTIN'S GRIFFIN ❧ NEW YORK

This is a work of fiction. All of the characters, organizations, and events portrayed in this novel are either products of the author's imagination or are used fictitiously.

www.stmartins.com

Library of Congress Cataloging-in-Publication Data

Freirich, Roy.
    Winged creatures / Roy Freirich.—1st ed.
       p. cm.
   ISBN-13: 978-0-312-37895-0
   ISBN-10: 0-312-37895-5
   1. Life change events—Fiction.   2. Psychological fiction.   I. Title.

  PS3606 R448W56   2008
  813' .6—dc22   2007038545

First Edition: January 2008

10 9 8 7 6 5 4 3 2 1

...for a bird of the air will carry your voice, or some winged creature tell the matter...
—Ecclesiastes 10:20

Go, go, go said the bird:
human kind cannot bear very much reality...
—T. S. Eliot, *Four Quartets*

A function of speed and distance, the trajectory of a bullet in its last stages resembles an arc, succumbing over time to the force of gravity.

If the target is at point-blank range, the effect of gravity on the trajectory of the bullet, for all practical purposes, can be described as nil.
—Donald Hank, Ph.D., *Handgun Ballistics*

fledglings ~

Laraby ∾

Distracted is barely the word for Laraby today, because as he exits Carby's Restaurant, pausing outside the little water-stained stucco box of a place with his jumbo "Joe to Go," he wonders if he ever picked up his change. Wait, was there change at all? He hesitates, and then laughs to himself and juggles keys and coffee to hit the auto unlock button on his key ring. His little black Mercedes chirps cheerfully back at him and gives its lights a quick flash, and he climbs in and drives a little fast to his noon shift, down Route 89, along the edge of Hunt Landing and this row of ugly prefab fast-food spots.

He eases up for the underpass beneath I-94—Detroit one way, Ypsilanti the other—in case that rookie Michigan highway patrolman with his parka too big is waiting again just the other side, with his heater going and a coffee of his own, and maybe a crossword puzzle, or worse, his radar gun up and ready.

Laraby's late now, two, three minutes, no big deal, but it's the principle, especially when your father was chief attending and founding partner; you don't want staff saying you're taking advantage of the fact week one of ER residency, which they will in a heartbeat, from the aides to the honchos and old hands who worked with Laraby senior.

In the hospital lot, Laraby glides into his new spot, farthest from the entrance but still first row, there beside the big sedans of the surgical chiefs and administrators. He climbs out with his coffee, shutting the door behind him, liking the pricey solid sound of perfectly designed latches meeting and catching, all machined to within millimeter tolerances.

Inside, he clips along and has almost gained the stairwell when Chief of Emergency Surgery Travis Carlson rounds the corridor corner, spots him, and slows. Preternaturally tanned and tall, Carlson looks twenty years younger than he is, nowhere near old enough to have been Laraby's dad's colleague and founding partner in the Hunt Landing Medical LLC. Carlson stands with the big-boned, laconic bearing of a Midwestern duffer nicely settled into his own, for this is his turf beyond any need to prove it to anyone, ever, from whence his easy confidence and boundless good humor.

"Bruce, I'm hearing good things." Carlson's smile as he pauses is bland and obligatory, his mind probably already on the weekend.

"Well, I had a Scout knife-cut that needed suturing, and a broken leg to ship up to orthopedics. No rocket science."

"Good hand, so far." Rolex glinting, Carlson half-lifts a hand in an absent wave as he strolls off.

Approaching the ER nurses' station, Laraby has planned a quick busy smile and an offhand greeting, friendly enough but not particularly inviting, since "give 'em an inch, they'll take a mile" has been his observation of conversation with these girls. They are a stiff-coifed, whippet-thin Ypsilanti housewife with a prematurely aged face, and a borderline obese black commuter from West Detroit with a big booming laugh and a ready smirk. In a word, trouble. Their chatter is littered with the pop culture vernacular of the times, "girlfriend" and "bad hair day" and "talk to the hand," punctuated with the whoops and high-fives endlessly recycled on so many "reality" television shows, with their adolescent dramas of rejection and loyalty and betrayal.

Today they're standing in the waiting area, among a hushed crowd bunched before the big black wall-mounted television, and curiosity stops Laraby and draws him closer as the crowd shifts and murmurs, and a few hands flutter to a few mouths to stifle gasps.

Laraby feels that prickly burst of tension at the thought that some giant catastrophe has again befallen us all, with its immediate toll of human flesh and blood, and the days and weeks and months that presumably follow, of layers of shock and grief and their potentially irrevocable aftereffects. He presses in, trying to see around the big hair of one of the temp girls from HR.

From outside, even now Laraby can hear the *thwok thwok* of a helicopter and the crazed sirens dopplering off down distant county roads, and he guesses his beeper will be paging him within the minute.

On the TV's little screen Laraby can make out squad cars pulled up at haphazard angles, doors left open. SWAT cops in Kevlar inch along an exterior wall of a stucco-and-glass fast-food restaurant, and his eyes narrow in astonishment to read "Carby's," right there in those balloon-style letters above the entrance of the place, same as those across the white plastic of the take-out coffee cup still warm in his hand.

For a second Laraby lets himself wonder if it's even the same restaurant, and how anyone could tell them apart anyway, since these franchise joints are built to uniform corporate specs, and half the time not more than a few miles apart. But of course it's the same place, and whatever misfortune unfolds within could just as likely have befallen him, if he had arrived there a few moments later, or if he had chosen to go back to check on his change.

On TV now the cops stop, their backs flat against the salmon-colored water-stained stucco, seemingly unwilling to move past a window where they can be seen by whoever is inside.

The frame pans sideways to focus on a woman in the near foreground, with a complicated-looking hairdo, hamming it up into a microphone with an urgent hushed breathiness: "Police arrived just over ten minutes ago, Stu, but they're still unsure at this point whether they have a random shooting or a robbery or a hostage situation in the making. All that's clear at this point is that shots have been fired, one man has escaped out the back and is now talking to police, who continue to study their options as this drama continues to unfold—"

Suddenly, from inside the restaurant, three gunshots sound in rapid succession, trebly and tinny, but still loud enough to crackle the TV's little speaker. *Blamm, blamm, blam!* The reporter flinches, crouching. The frame lurches sideways and drops, displaying a dim jerky square of sidewalk.

Bits of disconnected whispered speech leak from the edges of the screen: ". . . camera . . ." ". . . no, don't know . . ." ". . . wait . . ."

The frame readjusts to provide a tilted distant view of Carby's front double doors, with just the top of the back of the reporter's hair in the foreground as she faces toward the scene, crouched or kneeling beside what's probably their remote van.

Across the lot, the cops continue inching along the water-stained exterior wall toward the door, and now a klaxon fire alarm blares, a maddening metallic grinding sound. And *blammm!* another gunshot. A pause. And then yet another. And then silence, during which nothing and no one moves.

One cop counts down from three to one on his fingers, takes a step, and flings open the glass front door and then flattens himself back against the wall again, his short little riot shotgun held vertically, barrel practically against his ear. He waits a beat, and then he and a second cop launch themselves through the open doorway.

The third cop hesitates, pale, his back still pressed to the stucco. But when this one tries to step through, he simply stops, sinking to his knees as if in prayer, as *pfft,* the feed goes dead and the screen goes black, and then flickery with flashes of white noise.

A woman next to Laraby murmurs "Oh, my God" just as he feels the vibration of his pager in his pants pocket, and starts to run down the short bright hallway for the scrub room.

First GSWs are bound to give pause, Laraby knows this as he paces the OR anteroom moments later, scrubbed and gloved, but still he goes blank with his heart skittering and sinking as they wheel in three gurneys, rushing and shouting. Laraby stares at the shreds of red sport jacket on the upper thorax case that's bleeding out too fast, and at the chalk white inert face of the head wound and wads of bloody compresses the EMTs apply for pressure, but it's the glimpse of tan windbreaker under the plastic sheet of the DOA that sucks the air out of his lungs when third-year surgical resident Howland, following fast behind, says: "Shooter, lost him on the way. Let's move."

In the OR, it's as if time stretches and gaps as Laraby's focus narrows to a centimeter of shredded bone and stringy leaking vessels, and then another centimeter after another of the same, too many and far worse than he's ever seen as an ER intern, and then in a sudden panicky burst his focus expands to the room itself and the squeak of foam-soled shoes on linoleum and the intermittent tones of the monitors. Suddenly, he wants to sob out loud; his hands keep getting lost so quickly in the bloom of blood rising from the opened chest of the second critical from Carby's restaurant. Bullets have smashed through ribs, and the resultant splinters have perforated key arteries, and Laraby has been suturing against all hope, since by now the patient's blood gas levels, most important the level of oxygen in his blood, have for more than twenty minutes been lower than life-supporting.

Undeterred, Laraby continues to try to save the slick, inert red lump of muscle in his hands. The steady tone of the flat-lined EKG harmonizes with the tone of the flat-lined EEG: a chord, a chorus, a consensus.

More blood blinds Laraby, flooding the surgical field. His first patient, the guy in jeans whitened with drywall dust, was pretty much gone, with a shot-out brain stem, and now this one hemorrhages internally so fast Laraby can barely make out the thick tree of vessels that branches from the man's dead heart. He finishes resecting and clamping a shot coronary artery, and blinks against the glare stinging his eyes, and even though the RN mops and irrigates and turns momentarily to

7

check the flat-lined monitors, it all seems far away, because the scalpel in Laraby's hand has somehow gently edged the limp aorta, and a thin needlelike stream of blood sprays momentarily, and then subsides.

"Uhhh . . . looks like a bone frag got the aorta," Laraby says, to anybody. "I gotta clamp. Maybe . . . just . . ." His voice fades, with all hope against hope.

Dan Howland turns back from the irrigation machine he has been adjusting and shakes his head at all the bleeding. "Whichever, whatever. Not enough clamps in the world, Bru."

Laraby keeps on, clamping and suturing pieces that become more pieces as he joins them to other pieces of useless tissue, split apart and gaping from the bone splinters broken off by the bullets that pierced the upper thorax.

He sutures and sutures and the RN is watching and mopping and looking at him kind of questioningly for Laraby doesn't know how long, but hey, it's her problem. He's fine with trying as hard as he can for this guy who ended up here, out of nowhere, for no reason.

But finally he's holding a red soggy mess of dead human muscle in his hand and it's time for the TOD and the sheet over the head and his sweaty rubber gloves to come off. He rips away the mask stinking of his own dry mouth, gasping at air, and a small flash catches his eye, a wink of light from the gold cuff-button of the razored red sport jacket dangling down the side of the gurney.

Howland clucks sympathetically at the chart as Laraby heads out. He follows him into the scrub room, shaking his big handsome horse face ruefully. "Hell of a week to start ER, pal. But you definitely went the extra mile. Defib, breather, attempted suturing. Carlson wouldn't have."

Laraby slams the tap on, blasting water into the sink. All the chatter about chart review for the HMO, mandated to pare down unnecessary procedures, all the little caveats buried in the welcome aboard glad-handing, all of it comes back to him now. Well, fuck them.

He looks Howland right in the face. "Hey, Dan, you got something to say, try English."

He shrugs, Mr. Casual, Cool Breeze. "Nada. But *he* might, so I'd keep the chart short 'n' sweet. Either way, you gave it definitely the best—"

"Yeah. Better, best, bested." Laraby slams off the tap and grabs a paper towel.

Howland shrugs. "Families out there." He looks over his clipboard. "Realtor, Aaron Hagen, wife and daughter. Other guy, first in? Local contractor, single dad, two daughters."

Laraby has to make sure. "Tan windbreaker? Who was that one?"

Howland, "The DOA? Shooter, forget it. So, who do you want?"

Laraby doesn't think it over. He simply knows, without understanding it, that somehow these dead are his failures, that everyone knows it, and that their families are owed his apology and atonement, if there is any at all to be had. "I got it. I just need to change and take a minute."

Howland imitates concern. "You sure? Because—"

"Got it."

Howland lifts an eyebrow, fine with him, as Laraby walks.

In his tiny office, Bruce Laraby sits behind his desk, idly humming, staring off. Before him lays an unruly pile of condolence cards, and behind him there are arrangements of white lilies, their smell gone cloying over the blurry week since his dad's funeral.

So what is the point? he wonders. The temporary little healings, the brief reprieves—in the end how ineffectual against the looming separation and absence, how vain and ridiculous, basically. Because when the tissue won't hold a clamp or suture, all the hard-won skill in the world shines like counterfeit coin, all the love and admiration and esteem of his wife and colleagues are stolen gifts.

If Laraby had thought ER a chance to prove otherwise, today laid any such hopes to rest. Doubts linger, nag, and finally loom: is it all a losing battle, or is *he* losing the battle?

The nurses rankle him the most, really—catty, opinionated amateurs who never say a word but second-guess you with a glance that lingers too long, or a purposeful look away. Bitches, let's face it. The talk all happens behind your back, easy to spot in the way conversation turns stiff when Laraby steps up to the RN station for a coffee, and then stalls altogether as he steps away again, until he's presumed out of earshot. These halls are like high school, filled with the whispered subterfuge of betrayals and the sting of ridicule, all the vicious innuendo of adolescent politics.

Suddenly a fury wells up in Laraby and overwhelms him, until his own pulse is a roar in his ears and his arm is sweeping across the meaningless idiotic litter on his desk, sending papers and cards fluttering and paperweight plunging. And then he sits there, blinking in the stillness, looking down at the floor and the broken framed photo of him and his dad in their med coats, arms around each other, smiling up at nothing.

The Children ∼

Sixteen-year-old, mousy Anne Hagen sits in a molded plastic chair in the waiting area beside her year-younger friend Jimmy while a bunch of paramedics and cops mill around, sipping coffees and murmuring and basically trying not to stare at them. Since they were led from Carby's restaurant, they have been given blankets and little waxy Dixie cups of water, and have been asked again and again if they want more, but now Anne has a moment to look around and check off the seconds as the second hand on the big wall clock does, and then she sees the soundless picture of a minister and the church or whatever on TV for a moment before looking over at the potted plants and wondering if they're real. And then the colors, Anne has read that the paint colors in hospitals and military facilities and jails are chosen on purpose to make people feel calm or hopeful or whatever.

And dopey Jimmy has said not a single word, fine. But when they

take him into a room he looks so small, his eyes wanting to keep looking into hers as they lead him in. For reassurance? As if they meant
any harm. As if they could do any that hadn't been done already.

She just stares flatly back at him, giving him nothing to say. To
anyone.

She turns and stares at the TV again, which now shows the minister walking across a stage in his blue suit and kind of silly hair with his
hands in the air, beneath a giant stained-glass window. People in the
TV audience have their eyes closed, but their mouths move like what
Jimmy said to do, reciting something that, because the sound is off,
no one can hear. Except maybe God, after all.

Now Anne's mother, Doris, is rushing down the hall toward her, a
blur of tears and smudged makeup, from her busy morning shopping
or "straightening up" or vacation planning or checkbook balancing,
Anne is never really sure. The cops and paramedics and ER people
step back, respectful, as Anne stands from her plastic chair and opens
her arms. Anne and her mom embrace, and Doris lets out a long
shuddering kind of sigh as they sway there, "Thank God. Thank
God."

The hospital staff and emergency people around them glance and
look away and Anne knows mostly that the world has shifted; she has
become the subject of questions and stares and curiosity that feel like
a new kind of space she can now finally expand to fill, like a kind of
opportunity. Dry-eyed, she lifts her head slightly, almost proudly. And
she pats her mother's back like a child's, and finally speaks: "You cry,
Mom."

Her mother clings more tightly, her eyes squeezed shut. "You too,
baby. It's all we can do. And wait."

Over her mother's shoulder, Anne's eyes meet a paramedic's, and
he looks away, embarrassed.

And behind him Anne notices Lori and Sue Carline, two girls from
the grade above hers, standing there wide-eyed and pale with dread,
and Anne guesses now that the tall dead guy in the ball cap and
goatee and dusty jeans was their dad, some kind of construction

builder, if she remembers, and his daughters have been called or driven here from the school. These Carline sisters were never her friends, in their slutty crop tops and eyeliner, they were always the princesses of the phony popular Quad Squad, whispering and rolling their eyes, giggling or pitilessly judging. Which isn't to say she isn't sorry their dad is dead, so she opens her arms and hugs them, too, and lets them cry. Which they do in big showy gulping sobs. And now her own mom, too, because her husband is dead, though she doesn't know it yet.

Which is when for whatever reason she begins to notice so many other things at the same time: the orderlies and nurses pretending not to look, that cashier girl who worked behind the Carby's counter blatantly staring, the salmon-colored plastic chairs and dentist office music chiming softly from those little round speakers in the gray white ceiling.

And then across the hall she sees the cross over the door of the little hospital chapel and she knows for sure now, what she needs to do: to ask God above to let her deepest wish for the absolute final truth rise up.

When the doctor in his clean blue scrubs with his sad look steps up from nowhere to tell them what she already knows, it's like a silence falls over everything because she forgets to listen to sounds, because at the beginning of her mother's uncontrollable crying her mother's mouth forms at first what really looks like an ugly smile, which twists as tears run from her eyes like she's been slapped, down over her face, which has become so pale in some places and reddish in others.

Anne spreads her arms wide once more, to her mother and her grief, and to the Carline sisters and theirs, to everyone's, because it's always right to respond to the needs of others, after all, especially at times like these.

And when she opens her eyes again there's a small dark man in glasses a few feet away, with a clipboard and colored papers, watching her, waiting, for what God only knows.

In the chilly little exam room, on the wax paper under the fluorescent lights that make her eyes ache, she creases a "Five Stages of Grief" brochure, while the small dark county psychologist guy, Ron Abler, sits on a stool and stares at her through his smudgy glasses, with his too-intense look and clipboard and his low voice making sounds that must be words, but that add up to nothing that can possibly change anything that has happened or ever will: "The way you've been a comfort to everyone, Anne, we're all grateful to you. But we're concerned, too, and we want you to know how sorry we are for what you've been through, and for what you and your mom will go through . . ."

Anne looks at him straight on, clear and direct, because eyes that have seen what she has can be almost judging, and her voice can slowly whisper, "We'll go through what . . . God intended. Knowing that makes it easier."

Abler shouldn't stare so much, but he does. "Some people don't have that belief to help them. It's good you do, Anne, but—"

"Belief? God wants a witness."

Now he tilts his head, Mr. Curious. "Pardon me?"

"When God wants a witness, he touches one. Wakes them. To see it. To see us through to forgiveness." Dare you, dare you to doubt me, she thinks.

He pauses but still doesn't look away. "You've been through something terrible, Anne. I don't know how you feel about it, and probably you don't, either. And that's the way it should be right now. But at some point you'll want to figure it out, so you can stop thinking about it so much. When you want to figure out how you feel about what happened, will you talk with me?"

"I pray for that."

Pray for which, he probably wonders, which is fine, because at least she knows for sure. If she ever figures anything out, he'll be the last on earth to know, whether there's ever a prayer from her lips to

His ears, from here to eternity and back, or not a single one, ever at all.

He watches another moment, like he's waiting, which he can all he wants, for a miracle, forever, no matter to her, before he stands and puts on the sad face and says, "Anne, your dad loved you, you know that, and he always knew you loved him, too, so much, so if you feel worried about that in any way, please . . ."

Now she can smile at him. "Never worried, not afraid, not with faith in the truth."

Again the stare. "We're going to give your mom something to give you to help you sleep. I want you to come back in and see me after you're rested. I'm so sorry for everything, Anne. Do you feel okay about going home?"

Imagining the answer, her bedspread, her posters, her CDs, the square of light that is her window to their square little backyard: "Going home? I do. Feel okay?"

"Yes."

". . . Yes."

❧

Jimmy watches this nurse who won't stop moving around, all evasive action, nervous and overweight with choppy hair and lots of little earrings, shoving the stool into a corner of the little exam room with a squeaking noise, yanking the cord to the rattling blinds to lower the light.

"You wanna blanket? They turn that air up in here and between you and me I wouldn't say no to one sometimes myself."

Her smile is so wide. Is it kind? Or demanding? What does she want?

Which is when the short dark guy in the glasses comes in too quick and busy with his frontal approach and his semicovert agenda of observation and reconnaissance. The guy checks his clipboard and looks at the nurse, reading her name tag, "Hi . . . Julie. Thanks so much. We'll be just a few minutes in here."

So she blinks at him a second and then gives a quick little nod and leaves.

The guy's hand comes out fast, but his voice is carefully low and easy. "Jimmy? Hi, I'm Ron Abler. I'm working for the county, to talk to everyone who was there in the restaurant, and see how they're feeling."

His hand looks small and pink for a guy's, and it hangs there until he blinks and slowly pulls it back and leans against the base cabinet, with a sad little smile: "Okay. The doctor who examined you thinks we should maybe get to know each other. Maybe talk a little, though I hear you're not saying much. Will you talk to me? How are you feeling?"

Exposed redoubts cannot be defended without losses, Jimmy thinks. Cannot.

"Will you shake your head yes or no?"

Bits of color flash between the blinds, the hissing sound of traffic.

Abler stages another probing maneuver: "Will you write down your answers if I ask you a few questions?"

This is where stillness is key, where any movement can reveal key strategic factors.

Finally Abler goes to the door and motions for the nurse to reenter and stand by, and as she does, he retreats out into the bright hall where Mom and Dad sit in their parkas in those plastic bucket chairs lining the scuffed wall. They look up, suspicious, as he approaches, with his hand out again.

The wax paper on the exam table crackles with every move, like something burning, and the nurse is grinning again: "You sure I can't getcha Coke or something?"

No answers here, because any information will be a wedge to get more, until it all comes out at once, unstoppable, which can't be allowed. And so there can be no direct contact with anyone now, with any of these people who must fail to make him speak or otherwise communicate any hard intelligence about his or Anne's current or past positions, relative to themselves or anyone else.

Through the partly open exam room door he sees his parents looking blankly down at the card in Abler's uplifted hand, until finally his mom reaches out and takes it. The loyalty of allies can shift in any conflict; supporters may betray and sue for separate peace, leaving you vulnerable, without alternative fallback or adequate means of escape.

Beyond them, through an open door of another exam room, there's that last guy, big and pale, with sideburns, who wore the short-sleeved white shirt and tried to run or who knows maybe even jump the gunman but got shot. He doesn't look so bad off, more like an ambulatory casualty; an intern or resident or doctor murmurs to him as he stitches up what looks like just a cut on the guy's forehead, no big deal. But suddenly the guy goes still, completely, with his eyes staring off, as if at something only he can see.

And when the intern or whatever leaves, this big guy waits a second before sliding his legs over the side of the gurney and letting his feet touch down. And then he walks in little steps, barely lifting his feet, soundlessly out of the room in his street pants and blue hospital gown, out onto the oatmeal-colored linoleum of the hall, like a ghost no one else sees. And now the even weirder thing happens: the guy hesitates and turns back to somehow wink, impossibly, down the hall and through the half-opened exam room door, right at Jimmy. And then he puts a finger to his lips, *shhh,* and shuffles slowly on out of view.

The wax paper crackles again beneath Jimmy, and he chokes down a sudden thick sob of desire to simply and completely disappear, too, from the gazes of all these eyes trying to appear so sorrowful and kindly inquiring, when they are all in fact about gathering data for their own fields of operations and objectives.

What can they need to know that can be of any use now, that they could possibly understand?

Cover, stealth, camouflage, diversions: none of them work once they have you. Silence is the only option, which he knows well that Anne will demand, to protect the truest memory of all.

Charlie ～

Forty-eight-year-old driving instructor Charlie Archenault knows he's shot but that it's not bad because even though what happens after that is far away, he can still see it. Blurry, no sound, but he sees it.

Charlie thinks, are we gamblers? Only every time we get out of bed, use a hair dryer, toaster, garbage disposal, take a bite of food, cross a street on foot, never mind get in a car, in which Charlie happens to know more people die every year than servicemen in the entire Vietnam war, thanks very much.

The first guy on the floor, luck was not with him. Or the Realtor guy in the red sportcoat with the two kids under his table. But the counter girl in the kitchen, the cook, they made it.

And Charlie thinks, I wish my luck on my daughter most of all, on my wife, on everybody. If it can truly be.

In his exam room, he's still holding his discount coupon and claim ticket, and the intern is sewing up the cut the bullet made in the side of his forehead, and he knows he's more fortunate than even the ones who weren't shot. Because what are the odds of, first, being there; second, getting shot at; and then on top of those two, it's a graze wound you walk away from?

The intern steps out and now Charlie's waiting for a last once-over from some guy they say is from the county who will talk with everybody from Carby's. But what's he gonna tell Charlie to make him feel better than he does right now? Because fortune smiles on him. From ear to ear.

And he needs to smile back.

His feet are funny, and the idea makes him chuckle, because his tingling feet make him a little dizzy as they take him out of his exam room and down the short hall, past another exam room where the goofy kid who wore the camo jacket and was under the table with the girl now sits, and past him and everybody to the empty elevator. Faces seem synchronized as they turn away at the last moment, to regard other faces that turn away or look elsewhere to let him pass unnoticed, always the best way.

The doors slip closed and Charlie looks at the beige scuffed paint and hears the swell of tinny orchestral strings leaking like gas from a round little ceiling speaker. The floor drops and Charlie smiles down at it and puts a hand on the wall, making sure it's dropping, too.

Now the elevator doors slide open with a loud *ding!* and a sigh like an exhalation, revealing bright fluorescent glare on linoleum first, and then as Charlie's eyes adjust, the stacked boxes of cafeteria and housekeeping provisions that line this basement service corridor of Hunt Landing Memorial. Linens, laundry, food, like a hotel, Charlie thinks. *You can check out anytime you want, but you can never leave.*

What's that from, he wonders momentarily, and then the question itself brings Liz Taylor to mind, blowsy and boozy with her cigarette dangling in that movie where Richard Burton plays a professor and she's asking the same thing—what's that from? And Richard Burton with the bags under his eyes and sad cardigan goes to the storage room or whatever and takes down his rifle.

But ahead right now, in fact, there's a security guard bending at a drinking fountain, and Charlie checks out the guy's gun as he passes. The handle is all he can see, protruding from the holster, heavy and black with etched crosshatching for a better grip, though on TV they always hold a pistol two-handed now. When did that start up, anyway? Because for sure in the old detective or cowboy movies they could hold it just fine and shoot plenty straight with one hand, thanks much, without all the self-important panicky drama you see now.

Charlie chuckles to himself, and heads over to a service entrance. And then he shuffles right out into the glare, pale blue paper hospital gown over pants.

Outside on the sidewalk it's bright enough to blink, the sky so white Charlie feels like laughing. So he does. And he walks on past a knot of people on the sidewalk gaping at a big screen through a TV store window, and he stops to look over their shoulders at the reporter standing in front of Carby's, which is now surrounded by that yellow tape exactly like you see on TV. She's pretty much a looker, with her eyes shining with excitement and her glossy lips moving, but Charlie can't hear anything.

A skinny kid with long hair does a dim double take at Charlie's bandaged head and then at his hospital gown draped over his pants. Charlie looks down at his clothes, too, and then back at the kid, whose gaze has been dragged back to the bright square of glass and the soundless colorful images there.

Charlie crosses the street and then stops to look in his pockets. And finds car keys. And a wallet.

And up ahead there's a sign—TRUDELL CYCLING—beneath an art deco–style winged bicycle wheel. Charlie lets out a strange manic giggle and heads for it, keeping his head perfectly still on his neck, afraid to blink or breathe for fear the sign may retreat into some endless distance like a mirage in the desert, or simply disappear.

When the owner, in those Spandex or Lycra or whatever neon bike shorts, stabs his register to ring up the "Cyclists Do It Longer!" T-shirt Charlie has tried on and opted to buy and wear out of the shop, a bell goes off, making Charlie flinch and step back, fast.

The guy shuts the noise off and shakes his head in smiling wonderment. He points to a sign: FREE GIFT EVERY 100TH CUSTOMER!

Charlie blinks at him, stunned again into slowness by the sudden noise and quick pace of events, one after another with no time to catch up.

The owner grabs a plastic helmet and hands it over, eyeing Charlie's bandage. "It was gonna be a racing seat, but you look like maybe you could use this. Good to go, or you wanna bag?"

As Charlie shuffles along with his helmet, a gleam on the sidewalk catches his eye, and as he bends to pick up the quarter he feels his blood pounding in his temples. He straightens and stares down at the coin shining dimly in his palm, eagle wings outspread, not a bearer bond for a zillion dollars or brick of gold bullion or envelope of diamonds, but a sign of signs to come, certainly.

He giggles and gives it a toss, watching it turn in the sunlight. He catches it, and slaps it onto the back of his hand: tails. Which by itself means nothing, unless he tosses again and gets tails. Which he does. And again, tails.

And again, but he fumbles the catch and it falls onto the sidewalk, rolling a little ways, round and round on its edge, finally landing— tails, of course, which is when all the facts arrange themselves into a kind of elegant clarity, which suggests and finally demands a plan, which couldn't be simpler or plainer to see, really.

Charlie pulls out his wallet: empty. But up ahead, no worries, there's a bank, a redbrick building with white faux Colonial trim just a half block down the shadowless street.

Though a few passersby glance at the big bandage on his forehead, he knows his smile reassures them that he is really very lucky, and that they are, too. Everyone is, basically, who is still alive and not too dumb to realize it, to see or ignore or even miss the vivid flash and blur of weekday traffic, or the leafless winter trees with their gnarled branches gripping at the sky, today as blank and white as Styrofoam.

Carla ∾

To Carby's Restaurant cashier, twenty-two-year-old Carla, sitting here alone in the far corner of the general admittance waiting area feels like a waste of time. Maybe she should just leave and let them take care of the ones who need it? Sorry as she is that those guys all got shot, she doesn't have a scratch, and if time could be rewound like in some movie and those moments lived again like life as usual, that would suit her to a "T," but who wouldn't it, come to think.

But now, funny enough, that big strange guy, who had the discount coupon and wore the white short-sleeved shirt and also got shot, walks past the window with a thick bandage on his forehead, out by the parking lot and down the sidewalk, pausing to look around at trees and sky as if he's never seen either in his life before. And then he just wanders on, turning a corner he peeks around first, moving out of sight.

Carla's gaze returns and travels the room and slows at a tall pale but definitely good-looking doctor in clean scrubs. Him? From Carby's, strange enough it is, the distracted rushed guy in good shoes with the coffee to go and the nice thoughtless flash of smile. No smile now, though, as he approaches the teenage girl who was there and what must be her family.

But bad as she feels for that girl? Sorry but she just seems a little bit too brave and above it all and in charge of everything. Meanwhile the lady who must be her mom and those other two girls, who act like but don't look like her sisters, put on a scene because let's face it, everyone thinks they're all so important, all the time, always.

Carla looks away, she shouldn't be staring, she knows, and so she looks over at the wall-mounted TV, where a cop has turned up the sound so all can hear a reporter standing in front of what must be this hospital, who looks into the camera and says in a hushed serious voice, "Police now say they may never find a motive for what they're calling a random shooting-suicide here in Hunt Landing. Meanwhile, we have word that doctors have examined and are due to release three uninjured victims, pending counseling, while the struggle to save two men listed as critical continues—"

"Awful," a woman's voice intones to anyone, and Carla turns to see her, elegantly middle aged, in expensive clothes and a cast on her arm, just now sitting in one of the molded plastic seats nearby. Her shoes are made of some sort of woven leather, and her lipstick shines darkly and expensively, matching her purse.

"I know. I was—"

Bleeep, bleeee-eeeep. The woman yanks up her cell phone, and her voice sounds polite but also tired and bored. "Hello?" She stands and paces away toward the entrance doors, her shiny little phone pressed to her ear, and a peal of showy laughter escapes her as she steps out.

Carla sighs and shifts in her hard chair, looking around again. On one magazine cover that anorexic actress and her country-singer boyfriend dance on a beach. President Bush looks stern on another, but his wife has a nice smile. The fluorescent lights send flat squares of glare shimmering off the linoleum.

On the television now, slim elderly people trade high-fives and shake their heads fondly at one another, and then the news show logo reappears with that big urgent theme music when suddenly a nurse is there, flicking the TV off, glancing back apologetically at Carla, and then rolling her eyes at the other nurse behind the reception desk who shouldn't have allowed the TV to be on at all, who of course shrugs back as if to say "not my job."

Slowly, the ache in the small of her back from too much time on her feet begins to throb, but the police and paramedics have insisted every single person in the restaurant get admitted and examined and then discharged, just in case someone could be shot and not know it, apparently.

Suddenly a short dark man is there, blocking her view with his clipboard and stack of brochures, blinking behind smudged glasses, holding out his hand. "Ms. Davenport? I'm with the County Mental Health Department? Ron Abler. Just checking on everyone from the scene. You're the cashier?"

She stares at his hand, then at his face. "Mental health?" She looks at his rubber-soled loafers, his rumpled chinos and polo shirt, and asks, "A doctor?"

He retracts his hand. "Ms. Davenport, no. But the hospital consults with us in these cases."

He hands her a card and a brochure. Carla looks down at the brochure: "Victims of Violence."

Abler clears his throat. "Now this brochure details what you may experience in the next few weeks: loss of sleep, appetite, maybe you'll remember more than you want to, maybe—"

Carla blinks at him. "Wait now. They've got this printed up before? In case something like that happens? And you give these out afterward?"

"These aren't important. It's that if you need to talk you can."

She glances down at his chinos and tennis shoes again. "To . . . you?"

When Carla tries her cheap little cell phone it's dead, what else, and she sighs into the lobby pay phone, listening to the endless busy signal she's gotten yet again, trying to call Jenn to tell her she's okay, to be sure that Davy's okay. She hangs up and paces in a little circle of frustration. You'd think Jenn would have call waiting, much as she likes to talk, and about nothing or anything, anytime, to anyone, even narrating a TV show she's watching for God's sake. Carla has heard her do it.

Then why wait? Good-bye to nobody, thanks for nothing, Carla stalks out, already discharged with her "Victims of Violence" brochure, good to go.

Out near the circular drive just outside the entrance, that lady TV reporter Carla has seen on the local news and her crew spot her in her red-and-white-striped Carby's blouse and step up. With a nod to a fat camera guy in a snorkel parka, the reporter smiles at Carla all friendly and sympathetic and turns to the camera, which must be running now because she talks into it, "We're here outside Hunt Landing Memorial Hospital, Bob, interviewing the families of victims and survivors of today's tragic shootings at local Carby's Restaurant."

She turns to face Carla. "Miss? Do you work at Carby's Restaurant? Were you at the scene?"

For a tiny second, Carla thinks who Bob is, remembering him as the local or "east midstate area" anchor, a guy with a kind of modified spiky haircut like they have now who is always cracking lame jokes, trying to end one story and introduce another. But she's ready to answer and let everybody know, for sure: "I was there, yes. I work the register."

The woman leans in, intent. "But you're not hurt? Did you lose any family or friends, anyone close?"

Carla's mouth opens and closes and opens but nothing comes out until, "No, I'm . . . fine. Okay. No one, but . . . but I did try to call out. On a cell? To—"

But the cameraman is interrupting, "Jane, the Carline girls . . ." and already swinging his camera away as the woman reporter and her crew turn, having spotted the Carlines exiting the wide glass doors of the hospital.

Stung, Carla stands there alone, watching them all trailing their cords and cables, jostling one another for room as they surround those two girls who must be the Carline girls, who else, with their streaky faces and stunned blinking eyes, in their low-rise jeans and hoodies under quilted parkas. Carla glances down as if for the first time at her striped red-and-white Carby's Restaurant shirt and realizes she hates it, because why shouldn't she and who wouldn't, anyway.

pigeons ~

The Children ～

Later in a darkness in which nothing exists but faint sounds from some distant disconnected elsewhere, Anne hears first the sounds of soft weeping and unintelligible whispering. And then, sudden enough to stop a heart, there's that sharp quick cracking sound that echoes. And again. And without mercy, again, loud enough to make you wince and want to close your eyes or keep them closed if they already were.

Brrr, brrr, a phone rings, softly but insistently, in some other next room, in some other faraway place.

And then there is the unmistakable, tiny, almost inconsequential sound, a hard metallic *click.*

But it's her dream of the klaxon fire alarm next, the metallic endless unvarying *BRRRRIIING* echoing in her memory, that brings her eyes slowly open to see that she is in her own silent room and bed, alone finally, without having to say anything more to anyone for a while. She can take her time and look around and remember each thing one at a time: the Justin poster, her CDs and laminate desk and iMac computer with the Dilbert her dad gave her stuck on the side of the monitor, her mirrored sliding closet doors giving back the curtained windows and

27

weak light leaking from their edges just above her as she lies in bed in the late afternoon, like she's sick and that's why she's home from school.

Above her the ceiling is bumpy, with that hard foam stuff like in all the places built when this one was, and the dimness makes the bumps look big like cottage cheese, which she remembers is what they call it anyway so it makes sense.

She turns her head to look at the wall next to her and the paint is bumpy, too, from the nap of the roller as it goes on, she knows, because she helped her dad paint it a year ago this coming Easter. She dabbed his shirt with the finish brush, leaving a little glot of the Navajo White, and he chased her around with his roller, cackling like some insane monster of paint, PaintMan, which was pretty funny. Mom looked in on them with her funny smile, which can be sort of sad and hopeful-looking, and you wonder does she feel left out, but then she goes back to the kitchen or the den to straighten up there like always and she seemed fine anyway.

Dad was always saying "coat of paint," because in his work of selling houses this was the instant way to "up the curb appeal" and get "top dollar." But most of all Anne loved it when he flipped up the collar of his Red Carpet jacket, and spun around in place like Huey Lewis, one of his favorite singers, and landed on a knee, wailing on an air guitar or into an imaginary mic, Mr. Red Carpet Realtor RockStar.

He's always making her laugh, though, it's almost like a contest where she tries not to and so he tries harder and harder, like they have on that TV show with the contestant in the chair and the comedian jumping around, he's always jumping around, making fun of anyone, even of himself trying to sell houses to "idiot lookie-loos," crossing his eyes and in a goofy voice saying stuff like "school district resale zoning permit contingencies, baby! Solar air, radiant heat!"

And then the time when—

A small shadow worries the edge of light leaking from her curtains, a brief flutter of dimness just outside. Anne goes still, and then draws back her covers and sits up in her flannel nightgown, staring.

It's like God, Anne knows that. The Father who holds her hand and comforts her, so that she can testify as she must to that day and the life that ended with it, from the beautiful ordinary early minutes before everything began to happen to them.

When they sit down with their food, her look goes sly and she sneaks a french fry off her dad's plate and he fake-slaps her hand, laughing, it's a ritual. But of course then Jimmy has to totally filch one from her plate but she grabs it back.

And of course he has to say, "You'd let Howard." The big loudmouth.

And Anne's dad hears that and goes, "Howard again. Who is Howard?"

So her face is beyond red again. If she ever gets some goods on Jimmy, don't ask her to keep a secret.

And Jimmy won't shut up now as usual: "Howard Howard Howard! Mr. Rich Lowell Heights, Lexus-driving grunge poser and pathetic slave to all-around juvenile delinquent Mitch, whose forehead I just happened to splatter at paintball last weekend—"

Anne rolls her eyes. "Shut up! God!" She makes the cross sign, warding off all evil lameness as Jimmy makes his eyes round and clutches his heart in mock shock.

Even though he can be fun sometimes in a silly way, enough is too much. Jimmy's like some dopey kid brother, really, since grade school when they rode the same bus from Pointe Hills to Hunt Grammar and she smacked Mitch Heinfer in the head with her book bag when he wouldn't stop picking on Jimmy, who didn't deserve it.

But let's face it, he's a year behind her and smart as he is, and even though they IM, he's also loud and too goofy and it doesn't help. Not on campus, anyway, when Traci and Lori and Sue and the Quad Squad walk by her table with their books and lunch trays and hear him braying like a donkey with his eyes crossed, or talking with another accent, which he'll do for days at a time, from cowboy, to east Indian, to New Jersey mafioso, pretty funny sometimes, actually.

Nearby, a kind of funny old guy in a short-sleeved white dress shirt

*goes by with a jumbo cup, and a tall older guy in jeans and work boots
steps up to the counter to order, but for some reason starts to turn his
head to look behind him.*

The birds in the yard that Dad kept in cages are dirty, and when she
crosses the dead lawn and dirty snow in her bare feet, drawn by their
cooing, she sees their red eyes and filthy wings and scrabbling sharp
talons.

Her dad kept them, her dad who hid her under the table and saved
her from the man with the gun, Dad who held her hand.

The pigeons seem frightened, restless, rising in bursts of fluttering
to land again and again in their rusty cages.

Anne closes her eyes, swaying slightly, knowing that the father who
protects us is the truest father of all, and—

"Anne?"

Her mom is there, staring, wide-eyed, frightened by her daughter's
strangeness.

Anne stares back, also wide-eyed, manic. "God saw it all, Mama.
And he wanted me to, also. To tell. How brave Daddy was when he
died. How brave—"

Doris steps closer, a hand reaching to reassure. "Anne, honey, what
is it? What do you want to do? Let's get you back into bed. We've got
something to help you sleep."

Anne flinches away. "Sleep? But they have to know. Everyone has
to know."

Doris steps in to wrap her arms around her unyielding daughter,
who simply goes still as she stares wide-eyed again at the wire cages,
at the pigeons flapping and folding their tattered wings, waiting.

As evening darkens the yard and the day beyond her window, lit by
the flickering blue light of her little TV, Anne stares at a fundamental-
ist Christian show, *The 700 Club,* dazed and entranced by the motion
and bright colors, the rhythms of speech and the audience applause,

which has a sound almost like surf, louder and fainter, over and over. The minister wears the same light blue suit with that sort of Wayne Newton pompadourish big-in-front hairstyle, but behind him on the stage there are some musicians with guitars and at drums who have cute hair and dress pretty cool.

The minister swaggers around now, locking and unlocking a knee, twitching a shoulder to the rhythm of his speech with big showy drawn-out syllables, which Anne narrows her eyes at: "For prayers are winged things, flying high enough to reach the gates of heaven—"

She aims the remote, muting him, and tries it out in a whisper: "Gates of heaven . . ."

Now a call-and-response develops as Anne turns the sound on again, just loud enough to hear the guy and for her to whisper back "Strong enough to forgive. . . ."

"Witnessing God's will . . ." The minister seems to stare out at her with beady birdy black eyes as he minces across the stage with a hand in the air.

Raspy, barely audible, Anne repeats back: "Witnessing . . ."

Suddenly a footstep sounds in the hall, a muffled tentative approach, and Anne quickly flicks off the television and lies still, while her mother cracks her bedroom door and peeks in at the silent darkness. And then softly closes the door again.

Back in his small cluttered little bedroom, Jimmy's mom has lowered the shades and it's dim and chilly somehow, though he knows the heat is plenty turned up. He shivers slightly and averts his eyes from his mother's hopeful look as he sits on the edge of the bed in his white briefs, on the quilted red-and-white-plaid coverlet.

His mom, Lydia, smiles through teary eyes. "Honey, do you want to . . . rest awhile? And maybe we'll talk later? Is that okay, or . . ."

Already slipping meekly into bed, avoiding her look, he nods quickly because he knows she may not leave at all without acknowledgment of some small communication, of messages sent and received, and when she quietly retreats he lets his breath expand to more fully fill his lungs, finally, since he is alone and can almost really breathe again now.

He looks slowly around the room, recalling each detail only at the moment he sees it, as if the recognition were déjà vu, his real memory turned ghostly.

The marksmanship trophy is a stranger's, until it comes back to him how Danny Naughton was the better shot but choked in the last round of competition to let him win that day: drizzling, with the smell of the wet hay behind the targets and the muddy grass on the firing line and the report of the rifles sharp and small in the cold air.

His first-person Play Station 2 shooter games lie in a crooked stack beside the player and his little TV, but he has finished them all and knows every dark corridor of every level, every mortal danger behind every door, a sad joke now to ever imagine.

He looks quickly away, his eyes scouring the dim room for something safe. His gaze slides off the picture of his brother, Michael, and him with 30.06s and buckshot ducks hanging limply from their hands, and then slips quickly from their crooked smiles and narrowed eyes to the framed tight shot of Michael in his dress blues and medals with the little plaque and inscription about Michael's day at Al Khafji during the Iraq War. *For outstanding bravery in the service of . . .*

His eyes wander to the window beside it, closed, sealing him seemingly forever inside this airless ugly place smelling of sweat and sleeplessness.

When he climbs out of bed and peeks out through the gap between the tartan curtain and the sill, it's like some kind of reconnaissance, though noncovert, the eerie way Danny Wocek and Bill Elmeier and Chuck Carso are standing in the early darkness there outside Jimmy's house on the curb with their book packs, staring. Year-younger neighbor Doug Kelsig and two of his friends ride up on their bikes now, too, gum-chewing and murmuring to stop and also stare and slowly fall silent, slack-jawed.

Jimmy thinks for a second that it's about dying and that because he has been closer to it than anybody they know, they have this kind of awe of him and his house. He clings to that, a good and safe reason that doesn't make him feel hot with worry and shame and fear.

Because everyone knows. From the wall photo of them hunting with a dead duck hanging from each hand, his brother who fought at Al Khafji in Iraq stares at him, too, because he knows, just like his dad stared too long at him in the backseat of their car when they pulled up in the drive coming home from the hospital. Because he knows, too.

But wait, that's crazy, because no one was there but Anne, who is keeping his secret, if she is, only because he is keeping hers. Which he has to, his position to defend if he is really her friend, and if he believes in anything or anyone at all, ever.

On the leatherette or Naugahyde or whatever seat next to him Anne's leg is almost touching his, and when he nabs a french fry from her plate the way she just did from her dad's, she acts PO'd, her big imitation of deeply irritated, but so what and what girl doesn't? It's all good, because the truth is they IM all hours, which no one happens to know, which is their own secret. Her clandestine communications form a sort of complaint blog, of casual whining. "It was so hot in assembly, thought I was gonna faint," or "OMG, Sophie Marcus is a total b," or even sometimes questions for his opinion, once: "Is Dave Trevas really smart?" Not much, but she's there in her room, in her socks and Old Navy pants and a T, typing letters that form words that are meant for him to see and to answer. There must be moments when she has just typed and pressed send, when she is still, watching the IM window, waiting for his answer, maybe wondering what he will say, and in those moments she's his in the best way to want and to love, to have the same thought or just smile at the same thing at the same time, secretly.

In the den, down the hall from Jimmy's room, the TV lights his mom and dad, Lydia and Bob, in their twin black Naugahyde recliners, both big chairs close and crowding the center of the room in the viewing "sweet spot," since wider angles tend to wash out the image on the rear-projection TV.

Over the years this den has become a depository of carelessly displayed memorabilia, mostly of Bob's sports and fishing and hunting victories, but along the short stretch of wall a shrine of sorts commemorates the memory of their eldest, Jimmy's brother, Michael, where Bob has hung a black-framed photo of him in full marine dress uniform, with a winged medal draped over a top corner, dangling, just above the legend: "Lt. Michael David Jaspersen, for Distinguished Service, Al Khafji, Iraq, February 19, 2003."

Across the room on their TV, the anchorman has a little square window in the upper-right showing the Carline girls behind him, as he shamelessly grandstands, ". . . though the case remains open, our sources tell us the police are all but certain the investigation will reveal this tragedy to be yet another random act of violence . . ."

Lydia glances warily down the hall, then at Bob, whose eyes never leave the TV as he blandly reassures, "Out like a light, last I looked." Then, an afterthought: "All like the man said. Keep him home, quiet, and he'll talk when he's ready."

Carla ~

Carla's late as she finally climbs out of her car and hurries up to the peeling little house and bangs on the door, because Jenn's doorbell has forever been busted and her part-time supposed electrician boyfriend Bill just too lazy or too dumb to fix it.

With her usual dish towel and cigarette, Jenn lets her in right away, standing aside wide-eyed. "My God, Carla. You drove here?"

Carla hurries right by and picks up Davy, who's lying on the sofa in his blanket, crying, of course. The room is hot and smells of unidentifiable old food lying out on the kitchen bar top on paper plates and the TV is blaring a hair color commercial. Jennifer crosses her arms in front of her as if she's cold.

Carla doesn't look at her, cooing down at Davy: "Hi, little man. Hi, you."

Davy fidgets and cries, not quite loudly, but still red-faced, in good lungfuls with little gasps in between. Carla glances over at Jenn: "Waited forever for a bus from the hospital, back to my car."

Jenn stares. "Hospital? But you're okay? We saw it. Thank God you're okay. We didn't know where to call to even find out. I said the police but Bill said no, it's best to wait for word in these situations. You saw it? I think about those poor families and I . . . just . . ."

Carla pats Davy's back, trying to hush him. "I guess I did. I even tried 911, but . . . they never got it anyway, and—"

". . . can't help but, you know, think, I mean what if it were my Danny in there . . . it's all so . . . so . . . so you're okay? I mean, he didn't—"

"No, I'm okay. I mean, maybe I feel a little—"

"Thank God is what. They had those girls on TV, whose fathers died? But you don't have a scratch. Thank God." Jenn seems a little out of breath, her face a little out of control, as if she were unable to choose between expressions of concern or awe.

"Yeah." Carla studies Davy again, his fitful crying, his jerking little hands. "Shhh, shh. What's wrong with you?"

"He's been a little, like, colicky?"

Carla puts her face in his, making her eyes big. "You. Little Colicky Man. Hello Mr. Cross Colicky Man. Hello, you. Shhh."

Davy quiets, and smiles wonderingly up at her. And for a moment she smiles back, and the two of them are right as rain, like when he always lights up when she comes to get him after her shift. Carla worries that the smell from the grill is all over her, some trace of that burned liquid smoke stuff, but it has never seemed to bother Davy, though today his nose is reddish around the nostrils and his breath has a tiny phlegmy catch in it when he lets it out.

Carla looks at Jenn, suddenly wanting nothing more than to be out of there with Davy and back in her own apartment with her Pine-Soled kitchen and a clean fabric-softened sheet in his crib. "So—"

"Go on. We'll settle later."

"Tomorrow. Sure. Thanks." Carla lowers Davy to her hip and glances around the room for his plastic blue-and-white bunnybaby bag. She spots it under a Safeway paper sack of half-unpacked groceries on one of Jenn's barstools, and juggles Davy to slip it free.

"Tomorrow? Honey, Carby's won't be open, they . . ." Her voice trails off as she stares closely at Carla.

Carla stops. "Yeah. Jeeze. That's right. So—"

"Just call us. Whenever. Okay? We'll take him anytime."

"Okay. But—"

"It's okay."

They say if babies are tired enough they'll sleep at a hockey game or a rock concert, though Carla would never put Davy through it to see, so when she flips on her scuffed white little Toshiba TV in the "living area" of her second-floor courtyard studio, she keeps it turned down so Davy can sleep through.

The local news is just coming on with its picture-in-picture segues and sparkling logos and chuckling announcers, and in a square behind this one Carla sees the girl Anne supporting her weeping mom with an arm around her. Those two other girls who lost their dad stand in the near background, dazed, faces red and streaky with tears and snot, and as the announcer makes his face sad, Carla stabs the remote volume to hear ". . . families of local building contractor Henry Carline and Realtor Aaron Hagen for the loss they've suffered. Our thoughts are with them today as they so bravely struggle to cope . . ."

Carla sits forward on her little futon, elbows on knees, watching this showboat scene of these girls, almost *proud* for God's sake, preening in the middle of all that attention, as if any of them did the slightest thing other than be related to somebody who got killed. And you can tell they come from money besides, with their choppy hair and their backpack-style purses and perfect jeans.

From his crib, Davy begins to cry. Little hitches, sharp breaths, and then the squall. Which hits a level that she swears is like a needle in her last nerve tonight, and then of course it climbs higher, stretching out like it could hang there all day, pressing on your eyes and hunching up your shoulders.

Carla shuts her eyes against the sound and sits there. She will sigh and stand and cross the room to him, she will, and she knows this as she sits there, his voice calling to her across space, across any distance, always.

She's a little breathless, shrugging quickly out of her parka and hanging it on the coatrack in back, smoothing her uniform, and stepping back behind the order counter—good thing because her first customer is just a coffee-to-go, a guy she's never seen before, in a hurry but in nice clothes and who has a nice smile and kind eyes and maybe even notices her. Then she has a tiny break between him and the next one who's looking up at the menu, and so she quickly dials the landline to get Jenn, her so-called babysitter, just wanting to say a quick hi to Davy, which annoys Jenn because of course Carla was just there dropping him not ten minutes ago. Jenn sighs and holds the phone to Davy, and his mouthy breath and gurgling make Carla smile. "Hi baby you! Hello! Can you hear Mommy?" and then she has to go, there's the guy who wants to order, but Jenn doesn't get back on the line and Carla is stuck with little Davy going gooo, gooo on the phone and she has to hang up on him, because Jenn is hypnotized by some commercial on TV or—God knows why— just too flaky to come back to take the phone from Davy and hang it up.

New customer hands her a coupon and she thinks he thinks she thinks it's, you know, tacky or something, but really she's still mad at Jenn and Carla knows that's what he sees. He's older, sideburns and a tiny earring, but a short-sleeved white shirt like a supermarket manager or something. And he asks if the iced tea has sugar already in it. Which is a little funny, because Carby's isn't exactly for the health-food set, tell the truth.

The guy get his tea, finds a booth, and this other tall guy—looks like a carpenter or a builder in dusty jeans and heavy boots—he steps up and just starts to order as somebody steps in behind, next up, rush starting.

Laraby ~

Seat reclined, Laraby lies back in his car, watching the blank dimming sky, listening to himself breathe as drizzle descends on his driveway and onto the grounds of his brick Tudor home, one of the oldest in the original Hartford Estates tract of Hunt Landing. Damp makes the ice on the limbs of the mature oaks and maples go *tick, tick, tick.* The engine of his little Mercedes losing heat goes *tick, tick, tick,* as if it were all a giant clock counting down the seconds to the next patient's death. Powerless to prevent it, he has struggled through the levels: denial, anger, bargaining, and acceptance, to attain his current Zenlike serenity—here Laraby conjures a list—in the face of, in spite of, perhaps courageously meeting the sad reality of the inalterable, the inexorable, or maybe just simply the inevitable.

He shakes his head at himself, straightens his seat back, and climbs out into the cold.

Inside, his wife, Jan, gets up from her drafting table at the sound of his entrance and hurries over, studying him with a faint sad smile.

That gawky, perennially pale Bruce Laraby married a beautiful woman remains a defining fact of his life. Jan Laraby has the long, lithe bodily grace of an athletic Michigan college girl, and soft symmetrical features quick to brighten with laughter, but behind the unspoiled sweetness of her demeanor she possesses an intelligence sharp and tireless enough to cofound and successfully manage her own architectural firm. The house plans on her drafting table are hers, for their future home, already half-constructed on a woodsy hillside lot a few miles away.

Laraby turns away from her just long enough to set down keys and medical bag, and then steps inside her arms and wants nothing so much as to finally let out the endless exhalation of frustration and regret that has been bottled in him too long. But once he starts, fear and doubt will infect her, too, like a virus, and even then he would not be able to stop, ever, so there can quite simply be no starting.

Jan pulls away a little, peering at him. "You okay?"

He glances away as he shrugs out of his overcoat and hangs it in the foyer guest closet, with its polished wooden hangers in a row, and the warm smell of cedar. "Sure."

"I caught the four o'clock news. I'm so sorry, honey."

He moves into the living room, suddenly oddly lost. Should he sit or stand, cross to the window or hesitate there by the fireplace mantel? He looks around the room. "Won't be the last long day."

She follows him in with her kind quizzical smile that he doesn't really want to see, not at first. "Not like that. First week, ER? And just after your dad. God, it must have been—"

"It's fine. It's just . . . I was there."

"Honey?"

"Carby's. Just before it all . . . I got a coffee to go, on my way in."

"You . . . my God . . ."

He doesn't want to go on, but there is simply no one else to tell. "Twenty minutes later, they wheel 'em in. Shooter, another guy, both gone, and the one I saw, guy in a red jacket, DOA pretty much. If I knew then what I know now, as they say. Man, to be right place, right time."

She touches his arm. "Well, you have been, and you are, for so many. You—"

"Pour me a Scotch?" He turns away, shrugging out of his sport jacket.

She hesitates. "You go on up and lie down for an hour before dinner. I'll bring it."

Upstairs, Laraby sits on the edge of his bed, numb, staring at nothing as the first silence of this unending day reaches him and his eyes close, for the briefest of moments.

Change in hand, there was change, turning away with a thoughtless smile at the counter girl, away and starting across the dining room floor to the big bright doors with his coffee to go, Laraby blinks at a tiny flash, a wink of light from a gold button on the red sport coat cuff of a man sitting with laughing teenagers.

And on past and out the door to every place else.

He hears Jan's footsteps and arranges his features into a weary smile as she enters with his drink.

"Thanks."

"You're welcome." He goes still, as if at the sound of his own words returned to him faintly, like an echo of a memory, as she sits beside him and touches his hand.

Charlie ~

The doorbell is ringing and Charlie's wife, Kathy Archenault, has to juggle little Beth into her high chair and set her cereal bowl down out of reach before she can hurry through the foyer to swing open the door to a sallow-faced thin man in his fifties, in a tired raincoat and an unfashionable narrow knit tie.

The man holds up a badge, almost sorrowfully. "Mrs. Archenault?"

Kathy won't step back. Because even if Charlie has been to that lunch place that's been on the news all day, he wouldn't have been today, and the only reason she can't reach him and that he hasn't called is because he has had car or student trouble during a class.

But she does step back, suddenly hot and weak, because she has already seen enough blaring, hysterical television news and waited an hour too long before she started calling.

"Oh God, it's been on the news. I haven't heard from him since before lunch, he goes there sometimes, but not always—"

Cavalis quickly reassures, "He's okay. He was there at Carby's, then treated at Memorial for a minor laceration to the head. Not serious. He would've been discharged right away if he hadn't walked."

She shakes her head, confused. "He had some errands, and a student. Maybe he stopped for lunch, but . . . he left? He was . . . what?"

Kathy gives a panicky look back into the living room, trying to glimpse Beth.

Cavalis shifts his features into a concerned, confidential look, slipping his wallet and badge back into his putty-colored raincoat. "He was there, he gave his name, but then he left."

"But he's okay?"

"That's what the admittance report says. Does he have a cell? Did you try that?"

Her fear seems to spread out into the gaps, into the disconnection she hears in the man's words, but she laughs, incredulous, wondering. "Of course, it's where it always is, right on the foyer table. So . . . where? Where is he?"

"We're hoping you'll tell us as soon as you find out." He lets the statement hang, and she hesitates at the small assumptions, that she would be first to know, and that he would be next to hear, if Charlie has somehow become crazy or lost or afraid enough to disappear.

Now he holds out his card, just like a television detective following a lead. "And we'll do the same. Thank you, Mrs. Archenault, and I'm sorry."

Too many possibilities crowd Kathy's imagination, fragments of thoughts that splinter away as quickly as they occur, and she's a little dazed and slow to reach out and take the man's card.

Uncomprehending, she watches him walk away as darkness and a drizzle begins with a soft damp gust, falling on the mud and the last dirty snow along her street.

⁂

At Carby's Restaurant, a patrol car blocks the parking lot entrance from Route 84, and sawhorse barricades and yellow crime scene tape cordon the area from the ten or so bystanders in parkas or under umbrellas gathered there on the sidewalk, gawking and murmuring, a few adding flowers or candles that won't stay lit to the makeshift shrine that's sprung up on a patch of dirty sidewalk. Inside a patrol car, the officer on security detail runs the defroster and wipers intermittently, to clear the windshield and cut the chill.

No matter, because Charlie approaches Carby's from the rear service road, where police have left the parking lot's alternate exit essentially unguarded. Carrying a large manila envelope, he shuffles between the few remaining parked cars and unlocks and climbs into his early model Taurus.

He pulls slowly out of the lot via the rear exit, and turns again to head for Route 84, as if to leave this town and the day behind him.

Okay, not bad, nobody at the counter before him standing there waiting until his turn to figure out what he wants. Charlie looks around; at a booth there are two teenaged kids he doesn't know, a guy and a girl, and what looks to be one's dad in a Red Carpet Realtor sport jacket, but none of his students are there, he's happy to see, so he has a little privacy and can stare off at nothing and scarf a Special without having to see anyone notice him and decide if they really had to talk him or not.

He checks his watch. In fact, Charlie has a kid to pick up in an hour, a stoner, pretty much, who once showed up red-eyed and stinking of pot smoke and thought he would learn merging and lane-changing out on 84, surrounded by big rigs and SUVs. Traffic court or insurance-company mandated, his students are usually serving time behind the wheel for one big bad moving violation too many, as condition-of-parole on felonies or property damage cases, or trade-offs for DUIs bargained down to exhibition speeding. Then there are the simply flunked-out from the high school program, like most of his younger students, going the private school remedial route to the holy grail of teendom—the license.

He glances up at the big backlit plastic menu up over and behind the counter, but he already knows he's there for the Special, and he already knows he shouldn't—Kathy says he's getting a gut, and she packed him a Yoplait and a knockoff Atkins bar today, and since they had Beth money can become an issue. His uncle Kevin may have died last year and left him the twenty thousand and change from (ironically enough) a car accident settlement, but a windfall like that won't come again from anywhere else at his age, and so the dollars do bear watching. It's the impulses that hurt you, the way they add up: calories, carbs, and cash. The latter being why he's here, ad-section clipping in hand, thanks much.

He steps up to the counter girl with dark hair and sharp eyes who's making baby talk into the phone, forever. She finally hangs up and Charlie orders and hands her his discount coupon and exact change. She totals him up quick, no wasted moves, gives him the discount price and his coupon back for next time, with a sly little sideways smile. A gift, an apology? Well, hey, there you go, evidence of kindness and consideration in the world, after all, where and when you least expect it.

Charlie grabs his jumbo cup and fixes his iced tea at the drink island and finds a booth to himself as the guy behind him—tall, tired-looking in dusty jeans and a Peterbilt ball cap—steps up to order and somebody else lines up behind.

Along the wide freeway eastward, Charlie hums to himself as the day goes dark and he drives, one hand in the manila envelope on his lap, caressing the fresh stiff hundred-dollar bills inside.

A double-decker semi blasts by, tires hissing like snakes on the wet pavement, hauling shiny new Chryslers. Charlie starts, and then smiles at the deco-looking stylized winged logo on the backs of these cars. He laughs, shaking his head. And accelerates to stay behind.

And then he cranks up the radio and nods his head side to side to some generic banal pop tune, all airy tinkly bells and bass and crackly drums, layers of girl voices breathy with teasing sexual suggestion, "uh-*uh,* uh-*uh, oh nono*" and Charlie can practically see her, swaying across the stage with her hands in the air in her tight top and low-slung jeans, navel jewelry flashing like all the girl singers have now on TV, on that reality tryout show or even on MTV, in the videos where they change the image with the beat so fast it's just glimpses of things probably not half as sexy if you saw them longer, "uh-*uh,* uh-*uh, oh nono.*"

Charlie joins in with a skinny flat falsetto, lifting his hand high to drum along on the steering wheel as he drives east, deeper into the night.

crows ❧

The Children ~

Cradling flowers in her lap, Doris shivers at the chill wind gushing through the trees of Hunt Landing Cemetery, those firs and bare-limbed old oaks planted more than a half-century ago, when the town first grew large enough to support such a business.

Faces blotchy with tears and the cold, she and Anne and another hundred or so townspeople have gathered in black to sit in folding chairs or stand by her husband's resting place.

She glances farther up the low hill, where a backhoe grinds away, smoothing the muddy apron of residential building contractor Hank Carline's grave. A tarp still covers the piles of sod, ready to be tamped down to take root in time for spring a few weeks away.

Doris sees the sky above them all is filled with gust-driven cumuli, flat-bottomed and towering, golden in the late winter sun, and she senses a shift into silence and looks surprised to see Anne stand and turn her face to this light as she addresses the crowd in a quavering voice: "Who was . . . my father? An example of the kind of faith we need most, when we are afraid and tempted—by doubts, or guilt, or hatred. . . ."

Red and swollen with exhaustion, Doris's eyes narrow in wonder that shy Anne has stood. Worry takes hold as her daughter's odd speech wanders and turns florid with the mixed metaphors of storefront fundamentalism: "So let the Lord lead us on, to fly high enough to . . . reach the gates of heaven, and let Him judge us and my father, who gave his life for mine and Jimmy Jaspersen's, my father who . . . hid us and held on to my hand, smiling. Witnessing God's will."

Doris stares as fear for her daughter overtakes and finally overwhelms these moments of grief she planned to give herself. She knows well how far apart she and Anne have allowed themselves to drift, not that they have been estranged exactly, but Aaron was always happy to be adored and let Doris deliver the hard news. She has seen her daughter roll her eyes at her like any teenaged girl at limits set, criticisms levied, responsibilities recalled. Otherwise, their talk has always skirted weightiness, and now Doris can only marvel at how easily the distances can grow in a single household, stretching into a bearable awkwardness that all simply take for granted. And now this. How far is too far away to reach?

Anne's smile is turned skyward, beatific. ". . . the courage God gave him to save us . . . and us to witness and to somehow . . . forgive."

Doris winces, despite herself. God, witness? They had taken Anne to church once or twice when she was little, to the big modern stucco Presbyterian with its blond-wood pews and colored pools of light from the stained-glass nave, but she had been completely bored by it and she and Aaron had never pushed, by no means devout themselves, soon to drop these visits altogether, no regrets.

And forgiveness? Anne was a girl who kept careful track of the endless slights of classmates who seemed to always choose her for a brief blissful while and then drop her to move on to the richer, the prettier, the more effortlessly popular. The conversational snub, the forgotten invitation, the shoulder turned—Anne held each up triumphantly, proof of the injustices she suffered at the hands of the phony, the shallow and self-obsessed, the blindly conformist. Hurt turned to anger, Doris knows, but now it all seems a lifetime ago.

The ceremony breaks up with brief murmured consolations, somber nods and handshakes. Doris knows these deaths make a story of everyone's relationship to the dead and the circumstances of their death, but today she watches her neighbors acknowledge one another as fleetingly as they can, before fleeing back to their own lives to wonder at the times they had eaten at Carby's, or waved to Hank Carline in his utility truck, or bantered with Aaron Hagen over adjustable mortgage rates and debt-to-equity ratios on the street in front of his Red Carpet office.

For a moment Anne and her mother stand like an island of silence in this crowd, stunned in a sudden respite, when Doris sees Sue Carline approaching. Suddenly Anne steps forward and embraces Sue fiercely. "Kneel with me, Sue. Right now. Let's be as brave as our fathers. Let's pray to be strong enough . . . to forgive."

Doris can only say her daughter's name, like a question, "Anne?"

Sue stutters, frightened, trying to free herself. "I know I want to, Anne, but—"

Sue's mom hovers a few feet away, wringing her hands. "Susie, honey, do you—"

But Anne herself kneels, eyes shining as people gather and stop and watch, an eddy in the crowd, their faces quizzical at first and then pained as they think they understand. Anne grabs both of Sue's hands and looks up into her face. "Your father was so brave, too. It's what he'd want. I know that. God knows that."

A few spectators look away, embarrassed. Sue's mom looks at Doris, questioning, but Doris cannot take her eyes from Anne, lost in her own fear for her daughter, rising up in her like a sour-tasting sickness.

Sue's eyes flicker helplessly from her own mom to Anne and back, and finally she, too, kneels. Another woman, homely and massive in a quilted green parka, joins them and they reach out and clasp each other's hands, swaying, eyes closed, trembling.

Doris shuts her own eyes, fear and shame vying. When she opens them, a cold gust sweeps the hillside cemetery as a great cloud crosses the sun. For a brief moment they are all in shadow, and then in beautiful light again, almost unimaginable.

Now the crowd seems to part, revealing Bob and Lydia Jaspersen with Jimmy, whose eyes dart from side to side at the faces staring at him.

Anne lets go of Sue's hands and stands and smiles at Jimmy, ghastly.

Doris watches helplessly as Jimmy, mile-a-minute chatterbox Jimmy, whom she has known for so long as Anne's best friend, backs up a step, afraid. He looks around again, panic growing. His dad puts a hand on his shoulder that makes him flinch: "It's okay. It's Anne. You know Anne."

Even in the cold Anne looks feverish, wide-eyed, tendrils of damp hair stuck to her neck, with a vaguely mottled look Doris has seen when Anne had flu so bad in seventh grade.

Anne steps forward again. "Jimmy knows me. Jimmy and I are Witnesses. To all of it. Aren't we? Witnesses to love and . . . and bravery we should all be proud of."

Jimmy looks at the ground and swallows hard. He nods slowly, and his mom takes his hand, squinting at Anne, not liking it at all. She offers, "We just wanted to say how sorry we are. Maybe we should—"

Anne keeps the smile on. "Thank God one of us can testify. Thank God."

Lydia lowers her chin and gazes flatly back. "We do. Every day we thank God." Her eyes find Doris's, and Doris looks away, trying to keep her tears from spilling.

"I'll testify for him, Mrs. Jaspersen," Anne reassures. "You don't need to worry. And don't you worry, Jimmy. I'll tell it. No one will forget. Ever."

❦

At funeral's end, in their late-model dual-cab pickup, Jimmy's parents light cigarettes with long exhalations of relief. Bob turns around to look at Jimmy in the little rear seat, a measured gaze that doesn't really invite an answer to his question: "Okay, Jimbo?"

In the cramped backseat, Jimmy tears his eyes from the graves to face his father. He nods. His father stares at him wordlessly, a moment too long before turning back, to pull out onto the cemetery service road and drive them home.

Jimmy stares out the glass at their town as they pass by the weedy, trash-strewn lots bordering the bright new minimall and supermarket, on their way through the "old" downtown with its one-story brick buildings built fast during World War Two, when the ammunition factory brought boom times to the area, at least for a little while, when the whole country was united against enemies with plenty of bullets of their own.

Laraby ❧

After the service for these total strangers who had so suddenly become patients, Laraby extends his hand quickly to firmly grasp the hands his neighbors offer, the Johanssens and Meyers and Petersens and Smiths, and townspeople whose names he should maybe know but can't remember, can't really be expected to remember, as they pause to softly commiserate.

"You did all you could. Thank you."

"Thank you, Dr. Laraby. God bless."

His weak smile flashes and quickly fades between each greeting. Jan clutches his arm, nodding her thanks. As the well-wishers turn away, she studies her husband, with sympathy, and a trace of curiosity. "Sweet. Those people are sweet to think of you."

Laraby looks off at the trees, strangely abashed. "Yeah."

"Don't you think so?" She peers at him with her concerned, quizzical womanly smile.

"No, I do. Yes."

He glances off toward a grave in the distance, the headstone new, the sod Technicolor green.

Jan follows his gaze. "He knows, too. He knows how hard you tried for those people. Same as he would have."

He nods as if convinced. But no, never the same as Dad would have, never, because Laraby senior was nothing if not handy with the impromptu unorthodox procedure in the crunch, the eleventh-hour Hail Mary pass: a jury-rigged temporary stent or bypass, a drain or a suture never meant to last, a workaround until the monitors stopped blaring and more permanent fixes could be contemplated and performed. And they were, so often, that in his late years whispers trailed him in the hallways of the hospital, the man with the legendary touch, with the unconscious beautiful moves of a gifted athlete, the on-the-fly grace notes of a jazz great.

Laraby knows it, with certainty plain as dread and as every day as chronic baseline pain: his method is nothing if not dim pedestrian deduction, plodding, decision-tree driven, boring and by the blessed boring book. Ideas will not of a sudden occur, lightning will not strike, nothing will come to him out of the blue, he will not shoot from the hip.

Which is not to say, ever, that no one will ever be his to save, that no difference can be made by sheer will and effort, dexterity from devotion to training, all to achieve and maintain the skills of a true craftsman, qualities in short enough supply, in way too many physicians, thank you very much.

And timing, of course, plays a role, as it must. To be right place, right time, ready with the knowledge to use the right tools at hand, when the symptoms present and tell the story, to be the right person and be there to hear it, at the right moment, when it's told. To be right, in short, and more often than not, is all that's really asked here, not so much. When did it become so much?

The crowd of townspeople seems to thin and ebb, as many find their cars on the gravel access road by this field of stones. Sunlight comes and goes, falling in patches between larger monuments and mausoleums. The wind turns bitter in a gust and Laraby feels himself nearly shiver and Jan's faint smile and lovely eyes on him as she takes his arm, and they start toward the black cars waiting.

Carla ~

For Carla, the funeral of these Carby's customers touches a nameless buried grief for herself, as if it were her own service and she were truly sorry to be dead. But as the service concludes and townspeople return to their cars and their homes and their lives, Carla slows and stops, with Davy swaddled and squirming in her arms, to hear the awed whispering that surrounds Anne as Jimmy's parents lead him away.

She starts back to her car, but stops, because she sees him there, in a group of older and richer people, the doctor from the hospital, shyly being greeted by a few neighbors or patients, or families of. The woman who must be his wife is chic, for sure, in a dark really almost plain dress, but she's tall and sleek enough to pull off that kind of simple, and make it look completely on purpose. She takes the doctor's arm and leads him off toward the cars and he seems distracted and sad, but who wouldn't be? These were probably his patients, at least for the minutes they had left. What's that like, to hold those lives in your hands, to have the courage and compassion to try to save them? You have to be a kind person first, few enough of those around to begin with, and then you have to be intelligent, so there's a rare combination, the lottery, pretty much.

"Carla?"

She turns to see a face from her bad barhopping days, back when she was pretending to attend Hunt Landing Junior College, before she had Davy. In his torn leather jacket, Zack is a smirky twenty-three-year-old with a faint mustache and an eighties coke-dealer ponytail, to Carla a total waste of space then as likely as now.

He lifts an eyebrow, Mr. Suave 'n' Debonair: "Big crowd. But I bet half didn't even know the Hagen guy. Or Hank Carline. Least I worked for him once."

"Well, I cleaned their tables and took orders when they came in. They'd know me to see me, I guess."

Zack barely knows enough not to chuckle as he says, "Not anymore." He nods toward Davy, who giggles and reaches up a hand. "So, this yours?"

Carla just nods as she grabs Davy's little hand back.

Zack shifts his weight foot to foot, rubbing his hands together against the cold. "So . . . you came down here, too, huh?"

Carla shifts Davy in her arms and looks away. "I got a right to wish them well, as much as the next person."

He hears none of this, subtly ogling her. "Ever gonna let me buy you that beer down at Closkey's? Looks like ya could do with one."

She simply stares at him, disbelief to disgust, shaking her head. Zack shrugs as he moves off: "Whoa. No biggie, no biggie. See ya around. Carly."

Back at home, Carla has already forgotten about Zack and what a creep he is; she's opened the folding doors to her Pullman kitchen and stands there staring absently down at a pot on the stove, water boiling around Davy's bottle as he cries in fitful ragged sobs from his crib.

Carby's is closed again today, and will open again whenever, if at all, Carla guesses. But why think about that yet, until she knows it won't, or it will, or when, either way, since it isn't up to her and there's nothing she can do about it anyway.

She pulls a hard-boiled egg from her refrigerator and shuts the door, fluttering the diploma she has hung under a fruit magnet: "Carla Davenport Has Completed a Course in Parenting, YMCA, August 1998."

Beside it, under another magnet, hangs Carla's infant CPR course accreditation. She glances at these, remembering the folding chairs and old linoleum and fluorescent lighting of the Y and the other moms there with their husbands, some of them looking a little dragged along, to be honest.

Carla moves slowly in a fog of lost sleep, since Davy has been so cranky and the unending hours have stretched to include new and unhappy emotions that take Carla by surprise—annoyance, impatience—but also a fiercer love made desperate by some vague unnamable fear, pressing in like some unseen weight from everywhere at once.

And still he makes that cranky sad sound that makes her feel bad, but why should it? It's his sweet innocent need for her and hers to answer, always, because she does love him so.

Carla lifts him from his crib, and then finds herself hugging him closely, compressing the little heft of his body in a surge of weepy joy.

Because he is her little man who needs her.

Charlie ∾

Eyes blurry with exhaustion, Kathy Archenault could be studying a ransom note, a terminal diagnosis, or a jury's verdict, but it's her little silver Panasonic phone machine on her foyer table she's staring at as Detective Cavalis's weary voice plays back, tinny and sharply digital from the cheap speaker: "…confirmed he left before being debriefed by the county psychologist. So, please, if you have any idea of a reason he might have had for taking off, it may help us locate him—"

Idea of a reason. Like what? A secret identity involving a clandestine arms or drug deal? As likely as adultery. Kathy knows Charlie is probably even less interesting than he looks, but she's always felt luckier than most to have his deepest loyalty and his uncomplicated love. The interesting men were the narcissists, she knows this from her year at college and all the preening towering intellects and aesthetes she ran across, all of them experts at rationalizing their basest self-interests and moving on to other "life experiences."

But Charlie? No. No "idea of a reason he might have had for taking off." Which has always been among the best of reasons to love him. Or have loved him.

✳

This is some jazzy look, with all the semi-seventies mirror, faux marble, and pseudo-gold faucets and spigots. Charlie's seen it in Vegas and Atlantic City, a kind of lowest common denominator Trumpy glitz that makes a junket low-roller feel like a bit of a whale when he first swings through the glass doors into the big action.

Charlie steps to the sink and bends to splash water on his face. A dark little attendant, Filipino maybe, not young, hovers as Charlie peels off his bandage and replaces it with Band-Aids from a counter crowded with Wrigley's and Life Savers and tiny paper cups for mouthwash.

Charlie meets the man's eye, checks the name tag: "Angelo."

Charlie laughs and slips a stiff new twenty-dollar bill onto the tip plate. Points at the man with a snap of his fingers and a wink: "Bought high, sold low, my whole life. I am *due,* my man." And then he even sings a jazzy bar of melody and twitches a hip one way and a hand the other: ". . . someone to watch over me . . ."

Charlie shoves out the door and into the numbing blast of dim lights and noise: in a dark lounge by the cluttered bar a mullet-headed singer in a string tie sits at an electric piano mangling a tune Charlie thinks he likes—U2 of all things, "Beautiful Day"—with an awful smile and short jaunty chords. But hey, why not and why shouldn't it be, whatever the rest of the words sometimes a song just sticks, with a big lifting chorus that makes you want to pump a fist and join in, or sometimes it's one you wish you never heard that just won't go away, like it or not.

For a moment Charlie stands motionless, like a man on a ledge, before some cold vastness too enormous to contemplate, so he won't and why should he, because there's the little chrome ball racing around a roulette wheel, and *clatta-clatta-clatta,* round and round the big spin goes, plectrum clicking in and out of the payoff slots, battling the hiss and sputter of cards shuffled and the muffled clatter of coins spilling from slots like a reward, one that can and should be his, finally, for so many years of the careful and straight and narrow, for looking both ways and steering and braking and guarding our safety.

sparrows ∼

Laraby ～

Borderless blinding glare fills Laraby's dream, as his white-haired dad, Don Laraby, appears out of the brightness to stand in crisp tennis attire, behind a tall chain-link fence on a green tennis court. He hesitates, and tosses the ball high with a practiced flick for the serve, a toss that balances at its apex like a small beautiful spinning planet. But his look turns puzzled, as he suddenly clutches his chest and sinks to one knee. His other hand reaches out, grasping at nothing, his eyes finally filling with fear. The other yellow Penn tennis ball he has been holding slips from his grasp and bounces away, as if pursuing the first. His Prince graphite racket clatters against the HardTru, lifts a bit back into the air, clatters noiselessly down again.

On the next court, Laraby turns to see his dying father, mere yards away, the chain-link fence parceling the space between them into diamond-shapes. Around him, others shout soundlessly, already in motion. But Laraby's frozen in place, just staring, his own heartbeat pounding hot in his ears, repeating again and again as inexorably as this moment that returns to him so often, ruining sleep.

Laraby's eyes snap open. He lies there in his bed beside his lovely, sleeping wife, listening to the stillness. And then, with a minimum of moves, he climbs out of bed, heading into the hall in his boxers and T.

In the kitchen, Laraby runs the tap, fills a glass, and drinks deeply, blinking out the bay window at the dull sky. Movement catches his eye, and he sees it, struggling there against the sill: a white winter moth, blind, dying. Laraby takes a wineglass and traps it there, but the phone suddenly rings *bbrrr, brr* and Laraby leaves it to step to the opposite counter to snap up the little cordless handset before it can wake Jan.

"Hello?" He almost whispers, and then finds his voice, "Debrief, at ten? Sure. Yes. Thanks."

He slowly replaces the phone in its charger, standing motionless, as if listening for some far-off sound, fainter than a thought, so faint it has already disappeared.

At work, it feels like a second first day all over again as Laraby pushes through the glass doors with his attaché into admittance and on past the nurse's station, where of course the chatter gaps and slows and starts up again, brighter and chirpier as the nurses pretend to suddenly notice and greet him as if surprised, "Oh! Hi, Dr. Laraby!" and "Morning!"

Laraby gives his little smile and wave and continues to the glassed-in conference room for the ER incident debrief with his dad's colleagues and Hunt Landing Medical LLC partners, Drs. Carlson and Gretchensky.

Laraby enters, his eyes darting, a strained smile flashing as he greets the two men.

Gretchensky in fact resembles Carlson, nearly as tall and inexplicably fit. Both wear Polo shirts beneath cashmere sport jackets, and big gold Rolexes, but Gretchensky is paler, a fine blotch of sun-damaged epidermis reddening his neck, from golfing weekends back in the presunblock days, before anybody knew.

The routine pleasantries include a lingering handshake and good eye contact, all meant to effectively and briefly convey sympathy and concern for Laraby's loss of his dad.

Laraby's slowed by his admiration for the utter smoothness of these two, so he double takes a little as Gretchensky sits and gets right down to business: "So I'm looking at the rep: you triaged the ambulatories right to the county psychologist? Which left you with . . ." He lets his voice trail off here, leading.

Laraby lowers himself into a chair across the big maple table. "A brain stem wound, also triaged. While I worked the chest wound case."

Gretchensky grunts, shaking his head, showing off his hundred-dollar razor cut. "Bad hand." He sips coffee from a mug, and Laraby wishes he had some, glancing around for any.

Carlson interjects for Laraby. "Not too good. So the chest wound—you irrigated, attempted suturing. Hopeful moves, understood. But once the blood gas stayed bad, the EEG levels would've been par for the course. And then the atropine and open massage?"

Laraby looks from one to the other, wondering if he's heard a recitation of his report as mere verification, or as questioning of its contents.

Carlson barrels along, "No one's saying the patient had DNR written all over him, but the chances of him being viable . . . Even your old man couldn't have pulled him through—"

"Not a prayer, really." Gretchensky shakes his head some more. "But I'm sure we can still find some stats to support us."

Laraby blinks, trying to follow. "Prayer? Support us against what?"

Carlson puts his hands up, all innocence and too much reassurance, "Hey, Bruce, hello? This is all just to check off the debrief box in the incident report, okay? Standard HMO triplicate hell on a high-profile ER case like this—so they can think nothing's left to chance."

Laraby smiles wanly, though he wants only to shout the question *What isn't left to chance?* No matter how we stent and clamp and bypass, pin and plate, prescribe and irradiate, there will always be the anomalies of the molecular, lottery of congenital defects or missed diagnoses, unaccountable eddy of microscopic metastases in the blood—all the infinite uncountable permutations of what may come to be, down to the moments where the separate trajectories of lives converge, or only threaten to, and then in fact simply miss one another completely and forever, like a customer and a killer in a restaurant.

The Children ~

Anne's eyes follow the motion of all birds now, the shadowy flittings that seem to vanish, the passage of whole flocks in silhouettes against the white sky, the burst from winter limb to limb of raucous crows.

In heavy sweaters this morning Anne and her mother, Doris, sit on the scruffy bank of Tompkins River Park, on a car blanket spread over a dry patch among the mud and weeds. Doris has assembled their little picnic—little bologna sandwiches and store-bought potato salad—but now wonders if the "grieving and bonding opportunity" aspect of this outing doesn't appear ridiculously obvious and overly calculated.

Anne seems slightly dazed, with a new small spacey beat between any question and her answer, and a tendency to stare off with a fond sad smile.

Doris sees her daughter has retreated into a performance, and one that doesn't bear up under study, since glances and halting conversations have at best been all they've shared. She understands that "sharing" is the last impulse; every death of a loved one takes root in us at its own pace, which we yearn only and desperately to protect, but she cannot allow her daughter this, or herself, if they are to truly move on together as any kind of family.

So she looks around and finds something to offer up. "Your father and I used to come here. Back when we were in school. Hasn't changed a bit. Though they could put a new coat on those tables, and those grills are a little rusty. But they were back then, too, I guess."

Anne takes a quick furtive glance at her mom. "Back . . . when Dad fought against Vietnam?"

Doris studies her daughter. "Honey, did you misunderstand? He fought against the *war* in Vietnam. Organized a march at school, gave out some leaflets."

Anne looks a little panicky, fingers compulsively kneading the rough blanket beneath her hands. "To . . . spread the truth. Which God knows."

Doris watches her daughter, letting a brief pause gather silence before, "Honey, your father and I, we were glad when you wanted to go to Sunday school with the other kids. But it was fine with us when you stopped going, too. Honey . . ."

Anne gazes straight at her mother now, wide-eyed, frightening: "We're tested. That's what this is. Don't doubt anything now. Be brave when you take the hand of your father."

Doris's eyes fill and she shakes her head at Anne, at her own heart breaking at the depth of her daughter's grief, too deep for either of them to touch: "I know you want to forgive, but forgiveness is hard. First, there's hatred—I'm sorry, baby, but there's a lot of it. Doesn't it make you angry, what happened, honey? At all? Don't you miss Dad?"

Anne's gaze is fixed, impenetrable. "Don't doubt anything now."

Doris reaches her hand out. "Honey?"

"Don't, Mom. You can be stronger than that. The doubts and temptations and the nightmares can fly away the way they came. Don't look at them. That's what they want."

"Oh, sweetheart." She grabs her daughter.

Anne submits limply, not responding, looking instead over her mother's shoulder at a flock of ragged winter sparrows, wheeling overhead. Suddenly, fearfully, "Come with me, Mom. Come quick now." She stands and tries to pull her mother to her feet.

"Anne, honey, what?" Doris stands.

"Come with me, Mom. Come." Anne starts to pull her mother across the muddy dead weeds toward the shallow dark water. "Be baptized in the name of our Lord, Mom. Let's just do it, now. For Him, so he knows you have no doubt in your heart. So He knows you believe in what's true—"

Doris pulls back. "Stop it, Anne. Stop this right now!"

A tug of war ensues as Anne keeps pulling. "Now, Mom. For me, for Dad! For all of us!"

Calf-deep in the freezing water, Doris yanks her arm from her daughter's grip, stumbling back onto the bank. Anne staggers off until she's waist deep and raises her arms to the sky, her eyes closed, ecstasy on her face.

On hands and knees, gasping, Doris stares at her daughter, shocked.

Anne tilts her head back, not looking at her mom, because it's better not to. Shall we gather at the river, that's the question, whatever it means, that's what the song asks before they dunk some quivering wide-eyed cracker in that phony tank on TV with the diorama behind it of Technicolor Bible desert landscape, but this will do, freezing as it is, cold enough to shock into stopping the talk, talk, talk, coming at her nonstop from Mom.

As the water tugs at her clothes and she sways, Anne opens her eyes to look into the sky.

There are birds, black and blurred, a flock of sparrows or whichever still fly around in the winter, wheeling away over the trees toward the edge of the white sky.

But there's one still there, a sparrow for sure, a foot away, pecking with tiny jerky moves at a patch of dirty snow, while Anne watches from just the other side of the glass window, from under their Carby's restaurant table, as she grips her father's hand.

The bird seems to pause to look back, directly at her.

And then the sparrow takes off, joining the flock turning one way and then another in the sky. The birds change direction together, like they're synchronized, again and again, like they're trying to get away from something she can't see, that maybe they can't either but they somehow know is just behind them, always.

At her ear now, Anne hears Jimmy's whisper, papery sounds on his warm faint breath, a secret meant only for her, and which only she can hear.

✑

All through their silent breakfast, Jimmy Jaspersen tries not to keep looking out the kitchen window at the chain-link fence that guards their little concrete side patio, not much of a perimeter. But all is quiet, except for the small sounds Jimmy considers and categorizes as typical: the chewing and sipping and the scrape of fork and knife on Fiestaware, the grandfather clock ticking like an endless mechanical heartbeat, or a bomb, Jimmy thinks, a trigger-delayed device in a movie with a count-down and a wise-cracking hero holding the blue wire and the white wire and a pair of cutters.

His mom looks at him, and when he looks back she quickly averts her eyes, glistening with tears. Which is all he needs, his mom to be crying all the time when he has swallowed every word he could possibly say about everything, to find a way not to.

His dad has joined in his silence, but not as any last place of safety, Jimmy knows, but as always the right way to meet tragedy and what comes after, the less drama the better. To him, it's all that self-pity that's girlish and ridiculous, the whole daytime TV pop-psychology recovered-memory hullabaloo of hurt feelings and the unheard cry for love and the endless public hand-wringing recovery from same. So then they invented "tough-love," a phrase his dad can't stand and believes is just fake lip-service discipline and pseudoaccountability that only insults the real things, added to injury.

Jimmy knows nothing if not his dad on the subject; they have sat before the TV and Jimmy has heard him mock the nonstop ceremonies of self-congratulation that follow any job accomplished these days, to him all part of the same new fearful coddling of the "inner child" who needs elaborate praise for every toilet training success, finger-painting, or passing report card. Inner baby, more like it. Just the beginning: doing what's expected now gets you an award celebration:

firemen who don't cut and run get plaques, cops who make a bust get an award. And you hate to think it, but every widow or widower is always "brave" or "courageous" or "strong" for simply going on with their life, instead of choosing a handful of pills and a dry-cleaning bag tied over their head, or a small caliber bullet upward through the roof of the mouth into the braincase.

Lydia rises from the table, turning her face quickly away as she steps to the sink to rinse the dirty dishes and load the dishwasher. Jimmy watches his dad glance at her and give a tiny sigh over the extra leeway he thinks you have to give women. In his silence, Jimmy isn't asking for that leeway, but of course his dad couldn't know that, and in fact probably thinks him a complete girl baby for demanding it, which is why he barely glances at him, or when he does, lets his look last too long, flat and judging.

So when the phone rings and Bob gets up and steps into the living room to answer it there, Jimmy lets out a long-held breath of relief.

❧

The children always rate the follow-up first; adults get triaged more often than not, resources being what they are, or aren't, more to the point. So psychologist Ron Abler runs the heater in his Yugo, case notes spread on his lap, cell to ear, to start to get a lay of the land and a sense of the resistance. His tiny cubicle in the County Building is surrounded by whining Human Resources Department employees, underpaid to underpay everyone else, and Abler can focus better on these calls alone out here in the parking lot.

He's waited the requisite few days for these kids to reestablish some trust in their own familiar worlds, and now he must win the trust of the parents to gain entrance at all, to only begin to encounter the layers of denial and dread that always surround a secret, whatever it may be. And there is always a secret.

Tonight he can't miss the dry impatience in Bob Jaspersen's voice, as Jaspersen cuts him off in midintroduction. "I know who you are."

Abler plunges ahead. "How's Jimmy? I'm just calling to follow up, and hoping maybe I could swing by to—"

"Well, he could talk any day, like you said yourself in the hospital . . ." To Abler it sounds like the man is pitching his voice low, to avoid being overheard, ". . . and we can't have any visits on our medical records now. We're up for a family policy at my job—"

Abler feels like Jaspersen may hang up suddenly, and so interjects, now or never, to reassure again: "I understand, Mr. Jaspersen, but this is part of a free program funded by the county, no insurance required, so no one needs to see any records."

"Or like you said, he could come around ten minutes from now, all on his own, and talk a blue streak. And then there wouldn't be any records for anyone to see at all, would there?"

Abler lets out a sigh. "Mr. Jaspersen—"

"Let's just give him a few days to see what's what. Thanks again for calling now."

Abler hears the soft click and dial tone. He smiles ruefully out his windshield and folds his little cell.

Charlie ~

Busted.

The blackjack dealer wears a sting tie and green vest, a Powatan Thunderbird Casino name tag STU, and has dyed black hair and a strange little mustache from the 1920 movie matinee idol days, when barbers trimmed them pencil-thin, leaving a gap of naked skin between the blunt-cut hairs and the upper lip that looks just too white to Charlie. He can't stop staring and the distraction makes him late scuffing the table with his fingertips for another card.

Charlie knows the dealer, too, is probably not too crazy about being stared at, especially by some guy with a bunch of Band-Aids on his head who has maybe had one too many Powatan Punches, and so he tries to reassure with casual patter, "Stu, hey, whereya from?"

Stu's glance is quick and flat as he deals another hand to Charlie, his sole customer at this twenty-five-dollar-minimum table, midweek, mid-day. "Chicago."

"Chicago! Wow!" Charlie has no idea why he says this as he touches his first card, a three, with just a fingertip. He scratches at the felt and the guy flips him a nine, so what else, he scratches again, and of course Stu shoots him a queen and he busts for like the tenth time in a row.

The bored dealer scoops up Charlie's cards and his twenty-five-dollar bet, but Charlie has gone still, staring.

Across the room, winged neon dice flash blue and green, sus-pended from a dark featureless ceiling, reflected in endless mirrors, and for Charlie these flashing colors and shapes make the moment a door that somehow opens as if to reveal a future of spectacular for-tune that has always been reserved for him.

His lips form a dazed loopy smile as he stands, slipping the dealer some chips from his bucket and a word of false contrition as he floats by: "Sorry. But I fear I must follow my fate wherever it may lead me. As must we all. Peace, out."

The din of the gaming floor rises as the crowd swells, middle-aged marrieds strolling and squinting at the table minimums, husbands cupping chips and hesitating, some underaged kids groping each other while they feed the slots. Overwrought piped pop Muzak, Ce-line Dion or Faith Hill or someone like her, battles the clatter of coins and the stickman's patter, "Hard ways, eight! No field, no field," as the aisles jam up with folks stunned into slowness by the noise and lights and money.

A gaggle of big-haired west state girls press forward with their weekend boyfriends in baggy jeans and polo shirts, and Charlie eyes a girl, kind of a looker, watching with innocent greedy curiosity, at-tracted to the stack of black chips. Behind her a bent-up old guy rolls a toothpick between his lips, his eyes swollen and bland behind smudged glasses, and you wonder, which is lucky, which isn't? For

Charlie, standing now at the dice table in this ugly suburban Indian gaming casino, every outcome must have an omen.

He tilts back his head again to take in the neon wings that blink back and forth, suspended like a mobile over the dice table area, and then he pulls out a slip of paper from a pocket, staring at it as if at a clue, a piece of a puzzle, the key to a code.

Charlie has his iced tea in one hand and his coupon in the other as he moves on past the booth with the kids and guy, maybe their dad, in the reddish sport coat. There's a clean booth here, well, crumbs on the seats, always, but Charlie gives it a quick swipe with his napkin and slides in as a sudden sharp noise stops everything at once and the room just shifts, everything in it, the light and the shapes, brighter all at once and broken into pictures and sounds that make no sense.

Carla ~

Across the bright dining area, hidden in the kitchen behind the open door of a utility closet, Carla stares out through the mesh grille of this door at all she can see of the customers in the restaurant: the head and shoulders of the guy in the red sport coat sitting still at his booth, the shy funny guy in the white short-sleeved shirt with his coupon at his own table, and the shot construction worker–looking man, down flat and bleeding, motionless. And also the shadow of the gunman falling across the food counter as he crosses the room toward the drink island, his breathing heavy, like somebody who's been lugging boxes or stacking shelves.

Distantly, a phone is ringing, softly but insistently, *brrr, brrr.*

Holding Davy as he fusses, Carla sits in the same plastic chair this evening, in the same Hunt Landing Memorial ER waiting room with its fake ferns and soundless TV, gazing off absently across the scuffed linoleum as a shadow crosses her vision and, "Carla. . . . Davenport?"

Badly startled, Carla looks up at the admittance nurse, a skinny middle-aged lady in pink scrubs and reading glasses on a rhinestone chain, holding a clipboard busy with yellow Post-its.

Carla meets Dr. Bruce Laraby shyly. He's educated and from money, for sure, and though pale and a little in a hurry like in Carby's, his forearms look strong and lean and his eyes are a nice light blue and look straight at you, like he may even remember or like your face. He's busy right away, with the hand-washing and the plastic gloves and adjusting the big light that shines down on the exam table, but his quick glance comes with a little smile, which is nice, too.

Of course now Davy has gone quieter, snuffling and staring around big-eyed, and Carla's afraid that Dr. Laraby will think she's a worrywort or a drama queen for bringing him in at all. But Davy *has* been crying, to beat the band, long squalls of ragged quivering cries that start up again just when you think he's exhausted himself. Last night she went up and down the list and back again: diaper, bathing, formula, burping, rocking, holding, swaddling, even plugging in her old humidifier in case his sinuses were raw. And then the retired, divorced leering security guard next door bangs on her wall. And she ends up with a pillow around her head, curled into a ball against the endless shrieking.

Laraby leans over Davy and prods him gently, here and there. "Hey, mister fella. How you, how you, big guy?"

Anyone can see he'd be a great dad if he isn't one already, which of course he must be, how could he not? So she doesn't ask the question, is in fact biting her tongue when his eyes flick up at her with that little sleepy sympathetic smile.

"Colic'll try anybody's patience. Get whatever sleep you can, give him the medication on schedule until it's gone. And don't go out of your mind. Nothing life-threatening here."

Carla grins. "I'll try not. And thanks." Her eyes drift lower, to his lips still faintly smiling. "Thanks for—"

"Be sure and let your regular pediatrician know you were in."

Carla hesitates almost imperceptibly. "Okay. Will do." She gathers Davy up, reaching for his diaper bag and bottle.

"Take care now." And he is gone, but with a blurry bright afterimage left on the inside of her eyelids, like you get from a flash snapshot.

Outside the exam room, on the way past admittance, another nurse stops Carla and Davy on their way out, but this one is young and nice, with a smart haircut and pink scrubs. "Oh my God, is he cute?" she exclaims, eyes wide and a hand fluttering to her mouth, open in amazement.

Carla slows, stops. "Thanks. I sure think so."

"Everything okay?"

"Colic." Carla almost shrugs to indicate it's no big deal, but thinks better, because the truth is it'll try anybody's patience, after all.

"Oh no. The worst. You may go nuts before he's done with it."

Carla's smile turns grateful, surprised. "Well, I'm sure gonna try not."

The empty space between these women beckons them both, and they each step nearer, the nurse now pointing: "That is the sweetest little diaper bag. With those bunnies? The sweetest."

Flattered, Carla looks down at her plastic baby-blue and white bag. "Kroll's. On sale. Last one. Can you believe it?"

"Hardly. With what they get nowadays." Laughter, bell-like.

For a brief moment, Carla can only stand there smiling with unaccustomed, earnest gladness at the pleasantries of a stranger.

"Well. Good luck. Bye, bye, little fella. God, is he cute?"

Ding! Behind Carla, the nurse's elevator arrives.

"Thanks. Bye now." Carla's smile and fond look linger as she turns away, letting a hand hover in the air behind her as a casual wave goodbye.

Exiting the entrance lobby, Carla holds Davy tightly, smiling to herself, her face reddened as if she's blushing, flushed and hectic from so much kind regard.

She looks down at little Davy and reassures. "But not as nice as you! Acts like he never seen me, but still . . . nice."

He lifts his tiny hand toward her.

caduceus ⟿

The Children ~

Dusk falls quickly across the late winter fields of Hunt Landing, to the Pointe Hills tract of low one-story homes where shadows lengthen to touch and finally join under eaves and across yards to become night.

As Lydia Jaspersen washes dishes, to Bob the jerky motions of her shoulders say she's working up a snit. And sure enough, "I think we should let the man see him."

At their Formica table, Bob sips his beer. He shrugs. "Guy's not a doctor, see his card? Give it time, Jimmy'll come around."

Over the rocky course of their marriage, she's seen too much of her husband's stubborn hoping that bad news will go away by itself. The failed leech field in the backyard stank for months before he would admit it, and he ignored the pain in his shoulder until the rotator cuff finally gave. But this is Jimmy, so she presses, "But when?"

His voice comes back fast. "I don't know. You don't know. Even that guy didn't know. No one does, okay?"

"Okay? What's okay? Jimmy's sitting in there and he's ours to keep well, like it or not. And he's stuck in some kind of nightmare so bad he can't talk to anybody."

"What do you want me to do, Lydee?"

She stacks the dishwasher, rattling the dishes, jamming the silverware into the holder, unwilling to turn and face him. "Let the man come and speak to him. That's all."

Bob stands and holds up his index finger, for nobody's benefit. "One: he's not a doctor. And two: you think Jimmy's gonna say squat to him when we can't even get a peep, you got another think comin'. And what's more: I got a month before we all go on the medical policy at the shop. They have to put us on. But they find out I got a son anybody can call crazy, and they'll let me go rather than pay the doctor bills. It'll be my job."

Now she turns, braving the trump card of his sole financial support and the scorn and belittling of her that too often goes with it. Today she can't let it be enough to shut her up. "Your *job*? This is Jimmy's future."

"Which won't be worth much without clothes on his back and food on the table."

Before she can stop the words, they're out of her mouth, what she barely knew she was thinking: "They let you go, maybe I'll get something. Maybe—"

Bob slaps her, a quick fast sting. Not really hard, but she lifts her hand to her face, her mouth open in shock as she stands there, blinking in disbelief.

They have crossed a new threshold together, and she has no idea if they can find their way back.

Bob shakes his head at her, disappointed that she has backed him into such a corner, where such a thing is not only possible but likely from any man with human limits to patience.

He walks from the kitchen, leaving her in the stillness to listen to the sounds of the house, the *drip drip* of the leaking faucet, the click and hum of the refrigerator, the sighing of the pipes.

❧

Jimmy circles his room, padding silently in bare feet, passing the pictures of his brother, Michael, and himself, his Linkin Park and Live

posters, his twin bed on the scuffed fake-wood frame, his white particleboard desk, and round again. His eyes dart, covering the field, iden-
tifying each object as belonging where it is, as having always been
there, each surface as familiar after all.

From the kitchen the muffled rise and fall of his parents murmuring has ended abruptly, nothing new there either, and his father's
heavy rushed footfalls along the hall signal a retreat, but maybe this
time it's to regroup, before a bigger offensive, since the stakes of
battle have risen, and he's become the battlefield.

Jimmy knows his mother is still in the kitchen, arms around herself, turned to the spotless sink and the little window that looks out
on the dark street. He listens but there's no dull blare from the TV, or
whine of the belt sander from the garage workbench; aggrieved silence has fallen like a pall, which is new.

There are PS2 shooters where he's tossed grenades, same bunker
hall, same enemy, different result. Shrapnel of same size and shape
from the same explosion achieves separate trajectories, like those atoms
from a linear accelerator through X-ray plates, in that experiment
where just watching it changes the outcome. He can change outcomes.

He gives his shut door a furtive glance and slowly types into his
black-and-silver HP desktop computer. Anne and he have always
instant messaged, who doesn't, but now in his sworn silence these words
are his best hope to reach her, though so many of their meanings have
changed. Jimmy knows that even with the little distinctions and hair-
splitting and niggling like they have in debating, factual truth and lies
have always lain at opposite ends of a landscape of ideas he imagines,
with the forces of one massing against the forces of the other in an open
battle for domination, like some Napoleonic or Civil War reenactment.

He thinks of English class, where Mrs. Lubner told them the
Greek philosopher Aristotle thought fiction was truer, but does that
mean lies? Or just that some made-up stories can contain more reality
somehow than actual events can, or a history of them?

In Anne's room, on her TV now, beneath an enormous stained-glass winged angel that may be descending to earth or rising up to heaven, the minister lifts his hands, one knee twitching, his voice clinging lovingly to the syllables: "Be *proud* when you take the hand of thy Father and let him smile upon you—be *proud.*"

Sitting on the edge of her bed, Anne watches, intent. Her lips part with a small breath as she tries out the word: "Proud . . ."

Suddenly, *bliiing!* The cheerful Microsoft XP bell-like "notification" rings out from her computer.

She blinks in surprise, her mouth gone slack as she crosses to her cluttered desk and her computer screen, reading the instant message there from Jimmy:

> MAYBE JUST BECAUSE SOMETHING HAPPENS
> DOESN'T MEAN IT'S TRUE.

Anne takes a step back, afraid. Her arms go around herself, as if against the idea of any other truth but the truth, which brings a prickling sensation like a shock up her spine and makes her heart ache and race and her breath catch in her lungs. Because truth is always more than facts, which can lie. And so she will bear Witness.

Bling! Another IM arrives from Jimmy, and she imagines him pecking slowly at his keyboard, unaware his "Caps Lock" is on and his message shouts like some fanatic's chat room or thread flame:

> MY MOM KEEPS CRYING MY DAD HATES ME—THAT
> MAN ALBER FROM THE HOSPITAL CALLED.

Anne sits now and types furiously, answering him with her own shouting, right back:

> THAT MAN ABLER IS SENT TO TEMPT US ALL INTO
> ANGER AND HATRED AND GRIEF. DO NOT SEE HIM. DO

Suddenly, again, *bling!* The little IM bell goes off on Anne's computer
and she stops typing, staring at the IM window, where a new message
has arrived, from elsewhere, which has never happened:

R U Ok?—HWRD60.

She stands and backs up a step, almost fleeing, not ready at all to face
Howard or anyone else from school, where a comeback that falls flat
or colors that don't work can dog her through the hallways for a week
before anybody forgets, or until someone else does something lame
enough to distract.

Bliiinng! Another IM:

Hey A—miss U—Lori324

Bliinng! Another:

u don't no us but we luv u!!

Anne paces a tight little circle, her breathing becoming rapid and
shallow, face flushed as *bliiinnng! bliinng!* The cheery little bells go
off as more instant messages arrive, greetings and kind wishes requir-
ing answers that probably should be heartfelt and unpretentious but
kind of clever, too.

And then slowly, little by little, one bell at a time, her panic gives
way to a kind of wonder, at the opportunity she has been given to be
conspicuous, in fact to be finally, properly, fittingly pitied, once and
for all.

In her silent kitchen, Doris wipes a tear away, flipping through the broad stiff pages of a photo album. It's all Anne and Aaron, Anne and Aaron. A & A playing basketball. A & A at paintball. A & A in a water fight. In each there's a hopeful light in Anne's eyes for her clowning preening father, a sweet heartbreaking teenaged crush that Doris knew flattered Aaron's aging male vanity, as it is with so many fathers and daughters.

She happens on one of the few of herself, smiling faintly, her pink face and pale hair blending into the pastels of her own decor. A picture of a ridiculous woman, who simply believed too much: that her color choices or her cooking or her furniture upholstery ever mattered to anyone.

She turns the page, and a card falls out:

QUALITY TIME AWARD—WORLD'S COOLEST DAD.

Carla ∼

As Carla sits immobile on her unmade futon, night sounds reach her: the distant yapping of a chained dog, a car door slamming, an engine revving. A fly buzzes nearby, and she absently waves it away.

In the kitchen, across the restaurant behind the counter, Carla has slipped between an open utility closet door and a wall and watches Hans the cook, big fat Swede in his usual greasy apron, flatten himself on the floor under the counter. He begins to crawl. Their eyes meet, ever so briefly, and his are so frightened as they dart back and forth that they look like they're vibrating.

Carla turns her eyes from his, seeing as she does her cell phone, just a short reach across open space, there on a nearby utility shelf.

She sighs and dials her cordless phone, which she has been absently holding, and brings it to her ear.

The *brr, brr* of ringing sounds sharp and digital, and the click of someone answering makes her flinch a little, as if surprised. "Mom? Hi."

On a brief, barely audible wave of static: "Carly?"

"Hi, Ma."

"That's you?"

"Yeah, Ma."

She hears the scratchy click of her mother lighting a cigarette, and her noisy peevish exhalation: "Well, my God."

"How are ya?"

"Oh, good enough."

"How's the knee, Ma?"

"Well, it's been dry, Carla, so good enough. If I keep to my pills and leave the weeds grow in the yard."

A small hesitation. "How's Dad? Is he there?"

"Well, he's . . . he's sleeping."

"It's just nine o' clock, Ma."

Another noisy exhalation, quick with impatience: "You know your dad. He works so hard."

"You okay, Ma?"

"Why, Carly, now why wouldn't I be?"

"Okay, okay, Ma."

"Now are you still keeping up with those junior college courses? And your boyfriend, Steve, is it? How is he? Any plans for you two?"

Carla closes her eyes briefly. "Everything's great, Ma."

"Well, isn't that wonderful for you?"

Carla tenses, the muscles in her neck contracting as if she is cringing, trying to make herself small. "Ma? You know what happened?"

But there is the sound of ice cubes clattering in a glass and "Well, there's your father, now. I guess the phone woke him."

Carla hesitates, a silence her mother won't fill. "Okay, Ma. You take care."

"Bye now." *Click.*

"Bye," Carla repeats to no one. She hangs up, staring off, numb.

Softly at first, from his crib there against the wall, little Davy begins to cry. Quickly growing louder. And louder.

Carla grabs the TV remote, flicks it on. On her little screen a sporty German car is climbing mountain switchbacks in the rain, engine whining, the narrator's voice smooth and smug. She presses the volume button, louder, and a little speaker-cone symbol and "progress strip" appears on the bottom of her little TV's screen.

Tiny Davy continues to cry, fists balled, red-faced.

Carla just keeps on pressing the remote, until the TV is blaring, crackling and rattling, drowning Davy out as she stares off, unseeing.

Charlie ∼

When the dice sail through the air, time seems to stretch out as the various possible results arrange themselves into a series of alternatives, from the least likely to the most probable, the present to the future. But are they really totally random in that moment, at the top of the curve of the dice's flight? Right in that exact millisecond?

Each toss is a test, sure, but do the odds stack up, so that with every craps we're just more due for the seven, or do the odds start from zero with every roll? Charlie would like to ask the stickman (Oscar, from "Ol' Nawlins!" per his name tag), a doughy-looking redheaded guy with seemingly lashless eyes, but he worries Oscar will miss a field payoff or short somebody's odds and both will be in Dutch with the stern-looking fat pit boss with the bulge of jowl practically hiding his shirt collar. Besides, the question is academic, thanks anyway, because a crowd surrounds Charlie now—wide-hipped wives in big earrings and elfin hairdos nudging in, some beery balding retirees from the RV set—because Charlie has either come-out-roll won or made his point so much more often than not that he and the twenty-odd-thousand dollars' worth of chips he has in the rail now present a spectacle.

Drunk, Charlie worshipfully lays a thousand-dollar orange chip on the pass line and steals the boxman's chatter: "Comin' out! Seven-yo! Saaame . . . *shooter*!"

He gives a confiding grin and a salute to old Oskie, who looks resolutely elsewhere as he slides the dice along with his stick.

Charlie grabs them. No patter, no preamble, he lets them fly with a careless upward fling of trust. They arc up high-pop style and land near each other, muffled little impacts in the crowd's hush, as one barely rolls to show a six, and the other teeters on a spilled chip and lands with nice suspenseful slowness to reveal the one.

The crowd erupts with pumped fists, high-fives, laughter. Charlie stands there, blinking, and the moment seems to recur as the same fists pump the air, and again and again laughter bursts from the crowd when the dice land and Charlie makes another point, a tough hard four or an improbable ten, after a run of field and odds winners that lasted so long some of the doubters took down their odds bets. Tough luck, winning is not for the faint of heart, no pain no gain.

As the boxman slides over his stack of winnings, the first to include a gray five-thousand-dollar chip, Charlie licks his fingers, runs them down his cheeks for tear slicks, and puts a hand over his heart to address the faithful: "I'd guess first of all I'd like to thank God for keeping me safe and guiding my hand to this wonderful opportunity to provide the best for me and my loved ones, as should we all! Thanks, Big Guy! And I'd like to give a special shout out to my fans, who have been with me from the get and have made all this possible!"

Beside him, a miniskirted fifty-year-old waitress holds a tray of drinks, and he turns to her with elaborate regard: "How you doing? Good? Good. I'm fine. So I guess we're fine and good. And there are two kinds of people in this world, those who are, and those who aren't. Fine and good."

The boxman catches the look from the pit boss and he clears his throat at Charlie. "Sir . . ."

Charlie puts a finger to his lips, winks and lays four black hundred-dollar chips on the pass line. He tosses the dice away in that careless high arc of his, and spins to grab a drink from the waitress's tray.

"Yo-leven, winner 'leven."

Charlie ignores him, moving a hundred-dollar chip with agonizing slowness through space toward the waitress's tray, as his fans roar laughter.

The gawky pale teenage girl is laughing as Charlie carries his iced tea past her booth. In a Red Carpet Realty jacket, guy who must be her father blows a straw wrapper at her. She blushes, laughing, and blows her own straw wrapper back at him, as her nerdy-looking friend in the camo jacket shakes his head at the whole childish display.

BLAM! BLAMMM!! BLAM!

Three spent shells land on the littered linoleum. Beside them, the guy in dusty jeans and the Peterbilt baseball cap and goatee lands, already comatose, bouncing slightly with the impact, blood oozing from his head.

At his table, Charlie spills his iced tea, looking across at the booth by the big window where the kid in the camo jacket quickly pushes his girlfriend down. Still holding her Coke, she slides under the table with him. Opposite them, in his Red Carpet or whatever Realty sport coat, light-haired guy who must be her father goes to follow but—click—there's the unmistakable sound of a pistol being cocked and the gunman, everyday-looking in chinos and a tan windbreaker, is turned away right toward the guy.

The guy just freezes, knowing he's too late. He sits there, not breathing, afraid to look up.

"Seven, winner seven," Oskie pronounces, his eyebrows beetling up and down, stick moving to grab the dice and slide them back across over the green felt. Did Charlie throw them, when? Must be, because they slide over more chips, odds and half for a backed-up pass bet, or short-changing, who even knows, and there's a funny gap where Charlie stares at the stacks and everyone stares at him, and then he reaches down to accept what must be his, because it isn't anyone else's.

Laraby ∽

End of shift, Laraby changes out of his scrubs under the fluorescent lights, sitting on a low bench between the rows of metal lockers. He has always loved this place, where his dad brought him sometimes as a child and he watched the smirky kidding of doctors just off their shifts, and admired the loose unconscious grace of these big men so secure in their skill and their place in the world.

All sharp jerky moves, he yanks open his locker and tugs off his lab coat and pale blue scrub shirt. Colleague and associate Dr. Dan Howland looks on and then away with a faintly amused, supercilious expression that Laraby would basically like to smash as he tries to explain to the endlessly smug, passive-aggressive prick. "Why does it piss me off? Because at the end of the day it isn't about the size of your dick or your IRA, but about how many lives you save. And Carlson's not asking whether I could've saved them, he's questioning fucking procedure."

"Hey, Bruce, come on. You got a shot-out thoracic artery, a brain-stem wound—nobody's going to ask whether you could've pulled them through. These were showy cases. And you knew when you opted for ER you'd be under a microscope."

Laraby hesitates, and then sighs as he sees himself through the other's eyes, prissy, thin-skinned. "Yeah. You're right. You know what this is? It's first-year resident drama-queen crap."

Howland smirks and holds up his hands, palms out, all wide-eyed innocence, as usual. "Hey, didn't say it, buddy."

Chastised, Laraby's anger shrinks to a small enduring ember, and by the time he's home, it's mostly forgotten. In the oak-floored den, he sits on their oversized tweedy Kreiss sectional, staring vacantly at CNN on their big HD LCD. Lately he has been a little surprised by the number and quality of their possessions, as if a stranger to his own good fortune, and he takes in the silky nub of the upholstery and the flickerless HD image off the satellite dish with a kind of treacly gratitude that tonight edges on guilt.

Surrounded by fabric swatches and tile samples, Jan thumbs through an interior design magazine. She slaps a page. "Know what I'm thinking? I've spec'd out the bearing load in the entranceway a little high, so maybe river slate would work, not too busy, but color matched?"

No response. Laraby's not seeing CNN, but staring at their TV itself, entranced by the smooth matte black of its edges, the perfectly sized row of green LEDs, for power, cable card, input. The key success of its design is pricey simplicity, the sleek aerodynamic thinness of so large an object, which tonight Laraby suddenly feels they are so blessed to possess.

"Honey?" Jan puts down the magazine, goes and sits in his lap, and kisses his face. "You know what? You battle disease, I'll pick the fabrics, okay?"

When Laraby's eyes meet hers, they're shining. "I couldn't battle anything without you, you know that?" For a brief scared heartbeat he wonders if it's true.

Jan gives him her wry look. "Oh, I don't know, Dr. Laraby, didn't you perform a tonsillectomy or two before we sent out the invitations? Successfully?"

"Luck."

She smiles at him, shaking her head.

Jan's migraines have been infrequent, but tonight one arrives an hour after dinner and sends her clawing through the master bath medicine cabinet, before the pain makes her too impatient and frustrated to remember where she left the aspirin. Haste makes her clumsy and she knocks a few pill bottles off the narrow shelf into the sink, with a mild clatter that draws an inquiring look from Laraby, peering around the bathroom door frame to ask, "You okay?"

She hesitates there, leaning on the sink with both hands, closing her eyes against the bloom of pain beginning to throb behind her eyes.

"Migraine?" Laraby steps in and peers at her closely. She nods, wincing. It has been months since her last, and Laraby had thought she had it beat by laying off the coffee and increasing her aerobic regimen on the big Precor elliptical machines at the gym.

"Forget the aspirin, I'll give you the Molodil. Worked like a charm last time."

In his study, he hesitates over his medical bag, touching the winged serpent, the caduceus symbol there, thinking for a second for some reason of the Hippocratic oath, the key tenet "do no harm," pausing as at a thought that occurs and slips away, before he can name or recall it. He digs out a sample pack.

Jan is lying on the bed when he returns, a washcloth folded over her eyes.

He sits on the bed beside her, taking her hand and slipping the tiny pill into her palm. "It's a sublingual, remember? Just let it dissolve under your tongue."

She slips it into her mouth and lies there, holding his hand, unseeing.

In the hushed darkness of their bedroom, as they quietly make love, sweetly, gently, even somewhat demurely, behind closed eyes Laraby remembers her as he first slept with her, seemingly all legs and eyelashes, a doll-like mythically feminine object that fit his best adolescent sexual fantasies and had him shuddering with urgency. The memory stirs him now, but calmly, confidently, and tonight her gratitude and admiration hint at a submissiveness that also adds fuel, a luxurious overabundance, in fact, a reservoir that feels so deep and wide as to be boundless, for hours if need be, but then why hours when she is already sighing fretfully and arching her back and reaching to so gently touch and help him finish, so desirous of his pleasure that it would be cruel to deprive her. But he does, conveying the power of his control as he tightens his grip on her wrist and shifts unexpectedly to sweeten their friction and bring a gasp to her lips again and again. Her need drives her against him and tugs so firmly at the root of his that his breaths come faster and shallower, matching hers as they finally finish together, eyes shut tight, clinging.

They drift awhile, and he opens his eyes to see hers, watching him fondly. He smiles. "Feeling better?"

"Like a miracle. You're a genius."

Laraby chuckles. "You think?"

"Nothing less."

He shuts his eyes again, letting her praise wash over him without demurral or equivocation, letting it into himself and holding it there, as long as he can believe it.

And then Laraby measures her breaths and opens his eyes again to see his lovely wife asleep, and he slips silently from the bed into his boxer shorts and down the short hall to his study.

The stillness of the house and the night seems to gather around him and the small pool of light from his laptop screen, as he searches his Physician's Desk Reference CD-ROM, and reads the result: "Molodil: for treatment of migraine. May cause vascular constriction."

He thinks for a moment. And then types. He gives a small furtive glance over his shoulder, and presses return. Appearing on his screen now: "Statrophine: for treatment of vascular constriction." And among the contraindications, "May cause migraine."

He leans forward, eyes narrowing at the three words near his cursor. "May cause migraine."

furies ~

Carla ～

In the pedes exam room again, Carla winces, wringing her hands while Davy squalls nonstop as Dr. Laraby gently prods his doughy white little body.

"What's wrong with him?" Carla asks softly, careful not to sound panicky.

"Not sure. Let's try a bottle."

Carla hesitates almost imperceptibly and reaches into her diaper bag to pull out a bottle of formula. She hands it to Laraby.

He tries feeding Davy, and to both their surprise he stops crying immediately and sucks hungrily on the bottle.

Laraby's look is glad first, as he chuckles. "Hungry man. We have a hungry man. You fed him last when?"

Quickly, her arms crossing in front of her, "What I said. Few hours ago. Barely took it."

"Anything unusual about the way you . . . prepared the formula?"

For an odd beat, they look blankly at each other, neither seeming to breathe. And then she shakes her head, because what is he saying? That she gave Davy something unusual?

"Not that there would be, of course," he reassures. "Well, I don't see running tests as long as he's alert and has this kind of appetite. There's no outward sign of illness here, Carla."

She lets her shoulders relax, suddenly aware that she has held them so tightly, to the point of aching. But just as quickly another small fear begins, because what is there left to say to him then? Nothing, and less if he's forgotten how they met, or is pretending to. She starts out, "Well, but . . ."

Laraby watches her with a curious smile.

"That's . . . that's great to hear." It's what she must say, hopefully said quickly enough.

Laraby has already gone back to his clipboard, flipping a page. "But I think you should get yourself a regular pediatrician, Carla. There are free clinics if insurance is a problem. We'll give you the list."

Carla knows it's way true that Davy should have his own doctor by now, so she offers her only excuse, and more conversation. "I took that parenting course at the Y. And he's never had one thing wrong."

His head is still bowed as he studies the charts or whatever on his clipboard. "I understand. But it's still best. Meanwhile, let's just try and keep to a very regular feeding schedule."

"Will do."

He looks up with a wan smile right into her eyes. "And then see if you don't get more sleep. Don't want to see those pretty eyes red and tired-looking."

Has he noticed her eyes? Carla smiles shyly, blushing. "No. Yeah. Thanks. Thank you, Dr. Laraby."

Leaving, it's as if she holds her breath until she's outside the hospital. As she exits, holding Davy, she pauses halfway down the broad steps, and looks fondly back up at the building. And lets out her long-held breath as if relieved somehow, finally, of all of it: of television and Davy crying and her neighbor banging on the wall and her mother so mean on the telephone, the dogs yapping and cars screeching off to drunken laughter and bottles breaking.

Later Carla laughs out loud at a *Friends* rerun, that blond ditzy Lisa Kudrow cracks her up every time because her dimness has this kind of theme to it that they always hit on perfectly, the hippie organic chick thing with her head bobbing like those little plastic dogs you see in the rear window of cars. The world can never scare her, it can only be weird or sad at worst because she is so innocently in love with everything and optimistic. She holds out a peasant blouse and the other uptight friend and Brad Pitt's ex-wife Jennifer Aniston both look at it like it's a fish and the laugh track bursts out of Carla's little TV and Carla joins in.

A fly buzzes her and she waves a hand absently at it, intent on the screen as that Joey comes in with his hair sticking up in front and his mouth open like he's shocked. But behind Carla from his crib, Davy starts to cry again. Of course. And this time his cries rise up and lengthen to long shouted vowels that get louder and louder, one after another.

"Oh, shut up. Please." Carla whispers it, barely audible above the din of the TV laughter and Davy's wailing.

The fly is gone. But she brushes absently at her face again. At nothing.

And then she starts at a sound she thinks she hears, cocking her head as if curious, and then shaking her head at herself because she doesn't hear it, how could she, here, in her own living room, after all?

Cshhh! *It's the sound of ice, clattering into a jumbo soft-drink cup, a sound never meant to be noticed, one of thousands in the minutes of the hours of the days of a week no different from any other in any way at all. Hidden behind the open pantry door of Carby's kitchen, back against the wall, Carla closes her eyes, as if when she opens them again she will be somewhere else completely, hearing different sounds.*

And then she opens her eyes and steps out silently into the bright open space of the kitchen, as if across a tightrope, her hand reaching, as smoke billows from the Carby's Special starting to crisp into blackness on the grill.

The Children ∽

In a greasy pan, strips of bacon curl into blackness, stinking smoke billowing. Scurrying for a pot holder, a step behind everything this morning, Lydia Jaspersen curses: "Damn!"

At their old Formica kitchen table, Jimmy's eyes are wide with panic. He's hunched in his chair, gasping a little as his mother yanks the pan off the stove and bangs it into the sink, slamming the tap on to hiss and billow steam from the sizzling mess. Her moves are jerky, her rhythms strange and unpredictable.

"It's okay, sweetie. Mom forgot and burned up your breakfast, honey. That's all."

Slowly, he calms, because he knows it's her as much as ever, but upset and alone. Her eyes fill with tears until the tears slip from her eyes and she's crying outright, her face contorted and her shoulders shaking as she turns away at the sink.

Jimmy can only watch her silently, numbly. How can he protect her from what he has to do for Anne? How can he keep anyone and everyone from misunderstanding everything? He hates what he's become to others, a reason for anger and argument, a kind of emotional black hole pulling the wrong reactions out of everyone around him— pity, resentment, fear.

He goes to her quietly and touches her arm. And as she snuffles back some tears to chuckle softly and hold him, her chin on the top of his head, he sees out the window those kids again, standing across the street with their bikes between their legs, watching their house silently, like birds on a wire, waiting.

Daylight leaks faintly from between the edges of his shut venetian blinds as Jimmy sits in his solitary room, typing furtively into his computer. His IM is an argument, with a voice in his own head that nags and insinuates and threatens, which is Anne's now, warning him.

He's always teased her and clowned and played the little brother, but also always secretly looked at her when she wasn't looking. But what's wrong with that, really? Because he would never do anything ever about anything like that, but keep pictures of her in his mind, which maybe isn't so great, after all.

She doesn't know how desperately he thinks about her, of course not, but it's enough for him to want to be brave and save her, which means sacrifices to protect her and defend her position at all cost. Underneath everything is what she knows about him now, which he's not going to think about, even though she could tell, any time, anyone, and he has only one undeployed, but tactically effective, deterrent against the dissemination of that information.

His fingers hover over the keyboard, like the pointer over one of those stupid Ouija boards, as if he could sense some message hidden in the arrangement of people and things in their lives to send unencrypted and plain to see across the World Wide Web to her, to free them both.

☙

In her kitchen, Doris hesitates by the sink, a half-washed coffee mug dangling in her hand as she looks out the window to see her daughter again, there in her nightgown and robe in their freezing yard. Days ago Anne's spacey demeanor and evangelist language had pushed Doris into searching her purse until she found it: the business card from that odd, dark little psychologist at the hospital, "Ronald Abler, MFCC." But Anne's interludes in the backyard, spent staring at the pigeons, trouble Doris also, because for a girl who called these birds "gross" and "disgusting" and "rats with wings," her sudden fascination with them defies all explanation.

And still, she insists on returning to school, which relieves Doris as much as it worries her. On the phone, Abler had mentioned the possible outcomes, from "failure to grieve," "aggravation of trauma" from so much "uncontrolled stimuli," to the upside of the spectrum, "healthy reengagement," "resocialization," and a "countering of the constriction tendency." All of which meant, in plain English, that without seeing her, he couldn't say. Thanks very much, since when Doris as much as mentioned the man's name to Anne, she went white and shut her eyes and whipped her head back and forth like a four-year-old in a shopping-mall tantrum. Doris had to hold her and whisper and stroke her hair to quiet her, as if she *was* four again.

Suddenly she misses the sound of another voice so sharply that her breath stops in her lungs: Aaron's, kindly, often goofy, usually conveying not so much information, but somehow helping her focus from an angle that yields decision, thank God, instead of the noisy unstoppable static of equivocation, all the "what ifs" and "buts" and the thousand possible consequences that follow each.

She slams off the tap and dries her hands, to head out to the yard to get Anne out of the cold and hurry her along, if she is going back to school today after all.

❧

All birds have the same eyes of opaque reddish blackness that swallow light, reflecting nothing, though to Anne these pigeons her dad has kept in rusty cages in a corner of their unkempt yard seem vaguely, ominously afraid, always, in their constant restlessness.

Anne shivers in her nightgown and robe and steps closer, between curiosity and awe, because these birds remind her of thoughts that remind her of people and how they, too, are always fearfully ascending or descending some kind of height, closer or further from God, borne heavenward by angels or tormented by devils, winged creatures also.

The last patches of snow crunch in the chill morning air as she steps forward to peer into a cage at one bird, at the small greenish iridescence shimmering at its neck. Its claws scrabble and cling, sharp and ugly, gnarled and gray. They're like aliens, so inhuman, far beyond us and yet a part of her now, because they have witnessed her as another creature just as desperate to fly.

The restaurant is nearly silent but for muffled weeping and the soft drone of passing cars outside on 84.

The end of the gun barrel noses slowly through bright space.

Beneath her table, Jimmy beside her, Anne watches the gunman step away past the bleeding motionless body of the dead guy still in his baseball cap in the middle of the dining area. The gunman's foam-rubber sole leaves a shiny wafflelike print behind, of iced tea, spilled and dripping from the other guy's table.

The gunman steps up to the drink island, and Anne can't see for sure but she hears faint sounds among everyone's held breaths and the soft intermittent sound of traffic outside, like sighing: a straw wrapper torn, a foam cup slid across the drink island countertop, a white paper napkin pulled from a dispenser. Feathery sounds.

The birds' claws grip the wire at the bottom of their cages, like the last purchase in the world, all that keeps them from being flung skyward by the earth's spinning, by whatever force it is that adds more and more distance between each of us and everything there is.

From behind her, softly, her mother's voice turns her slowly back again, saying her name like an unanswerable question, "Anne?"

Later it's like walking in a dream with no sound, as gazes meet hers and slide away with fear and abashed curiosity, as Anne moves along the crowded hall past groups of kids shouting and laughing at their lockers. And so she gives a name to each step she takes, and each step becomes a prayer because the name is always the same, will always be the same, forever and ever: Lord, Lord, Lord, Lord.

Until out of the sea of book packs and T-shirts and quickly averted faces, a small kid with spiky hair and thick glasses approaches her, startling her: "Anne? I'm in the school prayer group? We all think, well, we all believe in what you and your dad stand for and we wondered if you'd come and speak, and maybe pray with us?"

Anne drags her gaze to this earnest little nerd in his striped sportshirt tucked into belted cargo pants. This one's pity means nothing to her, but the world must know about her dad and what he did, so she smiles faintly and hesitates before pitching her voice low in her throat, in a sad weary whisper, "Pray? Well, thank you. Okay. I will. I will do that."

His face lights up. "Really? Okay! That's, you know . . . well, thanks! God bless!" He flees.

Anne hesitates in the doorway of English class; more kids quickly look and look away, even Quentin Klein and Carey Stewart, as if they're frightened, really, and kids entering behind her pause, suddenly silent, as if not to get to close or crowd her as she sits.

Class today is a droning lecture she tries to follow, but she becomes distracted, entranced by the dull glare of the ceiling lights coming off the linoleum and wooden desktops, the rhythm of the teacher's words as he lectures, the droning vowels and creaking of the seats and ticking of the radiator making the room too close and too warm. She shifts in the hard seat and stretches her back and glances at the clock that seems not to have moved, not to be moving, as if this forty-five-minute fourth period will go on forever.

Finally a word snags her attention, and she shifts her gaze back to the teacher, who paces slowly, gesturing: "And so we have Prometheus, the fire-giver, or in broader terms, the giver of knowledge and healing, whom the gods chained to a rock, where giant birds would dive from the sky to tear at his flesh again and again. These may be related to the Eumenides, or Furies, who torment the guilty in quite a few tragedies. . . ." Anne hears a silence here that no one else does, and before she knows she will, she fills it. "A martyr. He was a martyr."

A few nervous giggles. The teacher hesitates. "Yes. Okay. Good, Anne."

The bell rings and the students surge quickly to their feet, murmuring as they bunch up before the doorway to exit, leaving Anne in her seat, pretending to arrange her books in her pack to avoid everyone.

Through the noise and bustle of the lunchroom, Anne carries a lunch tray between crowded tables. Her eyes are wide, unblinking, her step tentative. Everywhere blurred faces turn quickly away, back to Cokes in paper cups, plastic cutlery, bright wrappers, all a frightening detritus, a gauntlet of whispers and laughter and discarded things.

Lori and Sue Carline and their friend Traci sit at one table; Traci has low-rider jeans, Diesel backpack, black eyeliner, more aggressively stylish than the others, with her chopped hair and a quick cutting glance.

Lori surprises Anne. "Anne? Sit with us?"

Anne slows, blinking. "With . . . you?"

Sue looks away from everyone. But Traci beckons, half-laughing. "Sure, come on."

Anne slips shyly in beside Lori.

Beneath the table, in a quick furtive move, Lori slips a wrinkled piece of paper into Anne's hand, a note. Anne blinks down at her lap in confusion.

Across the table, Traci smiles sadly at her. "Anne, I just want you to know, I mean, we all do, how brave we think you are." She turns her gaze to include Lori and Sue. "All of you."

Here is Anne's crossroads, to step forward and claim more than the brief sorrowful regard of these classmates, but their awe and perhaps even their fear, to protect the true memory of her dad. "It was my . . . dad. God . . . gave him the strength to be brave. To save our lives with his faith."

Traci looks away with a blank face, as if counting to ten.

Lori tries to rescue Anne: "She just means if we pray, maybe we'll all get over it, you know, quicker?"

Even Sue tries to help. "Sure. Quicker."

Traci flashes a big fake smile at Anne. "Whatever works."

Laraby ∽

Since Laraby's begun in ER, he makes it a rule to follow up on his few referrals to internal, and so today at shift's end he looks in on heart patient Sam, a wry white-haired newspaper editor from Ann Arbor. Sam reminds him of his own dad, gone almost a month now from angina as well, and as Laraby steps in to check up and trade a little banter he still feels the loss as an unbalancing tug on the demeanor he has carefully assembled to meet this day.

As he checks the monitors, "How're you feeling, Sam? They treating you okay up here?"

From his raised bed, in his raspy droll voice, "Pecker won't stand up, got a tube in my nose, and I'm too dry to spit. You?"

"I think we'll both live."

"Yeah, but I'm lookin' forward to it. You look like you could take it or leave it. Mutual funds go down? Tough match at the club?"

Laraby goes still for a nearly imperceptible beat, before: "Eat your prunes."

They laugh.

In the doctor's locker room later, when the subject of Sam comes up, nothing is funny about the assessment from Dan Howland. "A tough case. He's good to go, but angina's a real lottery—he might hang in for years, and they could bring him back tomorrow."

Laraby hesitates at his locker. "Yeah. Angina. I know, believe me."

"Yeah, you do." He hesitates, too, musing. "Man, right there on the tennis court. I worry about my dad now—"

Laraby interjects, "Hey, Dan? What are they pushing for migraine these days?"

Dan slips a sweater over his head, adjusting it and smoothing his hair. "Molodil. Sublingual. Vasoconstrictor out there."

"Contraindications?"

"Elevated BP, chest tightness."

"Treat with—"

"Statrophine. But then you can end where you started. With the migraine symptoms. Bipolar scenario. The Molodil cures the headache, Statrophine can cause it."

"What I thought. Thanks."

Howland slings the strap of his tote bag over his shoulder and heads for the door. "Hey, see you and Jan tomorrow night. How is she? Say hi for me."

He's gone by the time Laraby replies, "She's . . . great."

Tonight Jan studies her house plans in the yellow cone of light from her desk lamp, softly pecking on a calculator, bending closer with her mechanical pencil and angle to measure and check dimensions and sightlines and clearances.

As he watches her from the sectional, Laraby admires her skilled manipulation of form, these delicate representations of surfaces whose length and width will circumscribe their lives, whose color and texture will become the familiar daily sensations of their world. Around him now in fact are a thousand choices she has made during their three and a half years in this faux-Tudor two-story. He sees suddenly how she has tried to undercut the Anglophile theme of the heavily mullioned windows and the dark mahogany trim and mantel with simpler modern objects of pale color: throw pillows, vases, modern art, sleeker and lower furniture. In the kitchen, their stainless appliances blend with the cabinetry, flush with the cabinet facings and countertop widths. Hardware—the handles and knobs, and pulls we barely notice—gleams dully, clean lines in some sort of brushed matte metal finish, a nod to the industrial and the beauty of utility.

She hums to herself as she leans into her desk, intent, completely unconscious of his stare, of him. She is so focused on her work, so complete in her own world, so fully and finally apart from him, that to Laraby her serene beauty seems distant, remote, even cold.

He watches Jan a little more, until finally she feels the weight of his gaze and looks up, smiling briefly, a reflex.

And then she bends again to her house plans.

Charlie ⁓

Charlie has achieved a sort of rhythm by now, varying the amount and placement of his bets according to a shifting collection of omens that present themselves just before he rolls: the last thing said before the hush falls over the gawking crowd, the last face looked at, the glint of light off the stickman's glasses, whatever song they're piping into the hidden ceiling speakers right then, or even the last line of lyric heard. Colors, too, are important, and he feels encouraged by the preponderance of warm hues, browns and reds and the assorted earth tones between them among the crowd and dim decor reflected in endless mirrors.

Sweaty and dazed, Charlie lays two orange thousand-dollar chips onto the pass line. His stake is now huge, many tens of thousands. The chattering crowd jams up behind him, blocking the aisle as he eyes the stickman, tonight a jowly red-faced guy with a complicated comb-over. Name tag: Vic. Vic the Stick. Of whom Charlie inquires with expansive, if not boundless, good nature: "So, hey, how many brothers and sisters you have, Vic? You come from a large family? Small?"

Vic the Stick looks to the boxman for help, who barely manages not to roll his eyes. "Sir . . . please?"

Charlie grins and puts a hand on his heart, now addressing the crowd at large: "Tempting fate, ladies and gentlemen! Every breath we take, every turn we make, every time we forget to use our turn signal! But still we *believe*!"

Boxman starts to stand. "Sir, please roll the dice or pass them."

Charlie nods and reaches for the dice, but his gaze locks on an obese woman half-turned to face him in the crowd across the table. He smiles at her T-shirt—"Wing It!"—as if it were his personal favorite harbinger, his own sweet sign from on high, in a language only he truly understands. He laughs fondly, shaking his head. And gathers four more orange thousand-dollar chips from the rail to bet on the pass. A gasp goes up as the chatter fades and the crowd of weeknight low-rollers presses in, elbowing and craning their necks.

Vic glances at the pit boss, who glances at the floor manager hovering, who gives a tiny nod.

Charlie curls his fingers over his damp palm to heft the dice, those two smooth cool cubes that giveth and taketh away, as the obese woman in the "shag" hairdo and aviator glasses turns toward him and the instant turns on itself, as she reveals a face misshapen and half plum-colored, scarred by some singular painful misfortune. And fully visible now, her T-shirt actually reads "Blowing It!" Too late, because Charlie has already shut his eyes to let the dice fly in a tumbling arc through the air even while he wishes he could freeze their motion and pluck them out and rewind that millisecond of his life back, so many milliseconds of his life in fact, of so much color and noise and motion and what happened afterward to him and everybody, milliseconds where God if there is one favors you with his gaze, or out of his vast magnificent indifference simply turns away.

A shard of light catches the face of one of the dice midair, glinting white and leaving a fleeting golden square behind Charlie's eyelid, like the fleck of sunlight in Beth's iris when he lay on his back in the summer grass of their little yard, watching her giggle at his Sad Monster Noise, the showy moan he lets out after one of her superhero play-punches to his fat Sad Monster stomach.

Sad Monster, he is a sad monster, to risk Beth and Kathy's future financial security in order to guarantee it. But truest love means hardest choices, or it'd be easy, we'd all be in love all the time, with anybody, swooning and giddy and no piper or price to pay.

What's Kathy's price been? Charlie bets it was passing up the JC degree and maybe a younger and probably better-looking guy with more money and brighter prospects for sure, but maybe not as solid a bet in the long run, and a tougher shot at bucking the divorce stats, the odds of which are supposedly worse than a craps pass-line bet anyway. Or maybe she sometimes thinks she sold cheap, and still wonders what a city career might have been like, wearing the boxy glasses and suits of the women he sees *click clocking* along in their high heels around the Renaissance Center in Detroit, paralegals and insurance company midlevel execs with bleached teeth and streaky hair, their own IRAs and foreign cars and condos.

Charlie's life is Charlie's job, what he's best at, saving people from themselves, and maybe he has saved Kathy from temporary happiness in favor of long-term contentment, a comfortable formulation that feels at once humble and wise and in the best possible interest of all.

As they land with that floppy sound, the dice roll on their edges and over onto one side and then another across a foot or so of green felt, between the stacked six- and twelve-dollar odds and tossed field bets to stop dead even, just in front of the far stickman, who deadpans through a hard drinker's poker face of burst capillaries, "Seven, winner seven."

Charlie's nightshift bellhop looks barely eighteen, a bloom of acne across one cheek, hair spiky and shiny with some sort of product— guys wear as much of it as girls these days. The kid opens the door and flicks on the light, and Charlie steps gingerly inside, carrying a big "Pow ! Atan" shopping bag and a smaller paper bag. Charlie looks around at his comped, second-story Clear Creek Band of Powatan Indians Thunderbird Gaming Casino Motel room, which is unaccountably nautical: a wooden helm, fish netting, and cleats adorn the walls, like an oyster bar. Beneath a bulky wall-hung TV, a daybed with blue corduroy bolster pillows and a faux marble coffee table constitute the "sitting area."

Juggling both bags, Charlie dips a hand into his pocket, coming up with a bill for the bellhop.

The bellhop stares down at it in awe. "This is . . . it's . . . thank you, sir! Thanks!"

"Thank you . . ." Charlie peers at the kid's name tag. "Pete."

"That's . . . not me. He got fired. I just started, my tag isn't ready yet."

Charlie blinks at him, understanding now that the name tag is a piece of uniform signifying nothing, like an epaulet or button, or cuff link. "Well, thanks, not Pete who got fired."

The bellhop hesitates. "Scott. But, sir? Did ya really . . . win all that? I heard one hundred K. Guy in a bike shirt."

Charlie gawks down at his shirt, pretending surprise. "Must be me." He makes a show of checking inside his big shopping bag, and makes his eyes go round with shock. "Holy cats, one hundred large, a CK. Know what it means? Tomorrow, adios, I pack it in, first thing, 'cause that's my step-away point. Daughter's college tuition. Always have a walking point, Scott."

Scott looks frightened. "So, well then, okay, thank you, sir. And I hope you enjoy your stay."

"You, too."

They blink at each other, confused. And then the kid flees, closing the door softly behind him, footsteps fading down the second-story walkway.

Still clutching his shopping bag, Charlie heads through a door, BUOYS AND GULLS, and into the bathroom, where he snaps on the light and stares at the total whiteness of the tiled floor and walls. Shadowless.

Flip, flip. He tries a switch for the Jacuzzi tub. Nothing. Tries the tub tap: nothing.

He urinates into the white toilet bowl, humming absently. Tries the flush, twice: nothing.

He shuffles back out into the bedroom, and sits on the bed, with both bags. He opens the little one and sets out macadamia nuts, Nyquil, and a fifth of Jack.

gryphon ～

The Children ∼

Anne's computer screen gives back a square of white dawnlight from her window, and she has to turn it sideways to read Jimmy's IM from last night, the same question in different words:

Is what happens the real lie, and the truth is what doesn't?

Anne smirks at this message and how Jimmy can purposely pretend to not understand when of course he does, because how could he not? The truth of any person should be their life, not any one single moment that can be separated from all the others for whatever reason people choose, people who don't know and have no good reason to care either way, but who believe they've got to have an opinion. That's an ugly word, that hurts, because it's just as wrong as a fact, which in itself Anne knows can be just as blatantly untrue as any lie told on purpose, and even more unfair because it seems so real to everybody.

Anne types lightly and rapidly back, anger speeding her fingers over the clicky keys as the words she types appear in her little IM window.

No one knows anything but what they think they know. And
that's what's sad and makes me feel so sorry for everyone. . . .

She presses "Return" to send these words through their modem to the
cable of their cable TV system into the giant hidden tangle of wire that
she imagines embodies the Internet like an actual web of contracting and
dilating vessels, breathing like some living thing, to carry along the information that is like food to the living things this living thing connects.

Information: that time her dad picked her up late from fifth-grade
choir and he sounded a little slurry but drove totally okay and made lots
of jokes and was so funny. What does that information mean? Or the
times when she was really little that she wasn't asleep but he thought
she was when he bent over in the dark to kiss her forehead and pull the
covers up to cover her better? Or when he was yelling at her mom
about money and then told her to get out and go to her room, it wasn't
her business, to mind her own business and not be a nosy little word he
spelled out that began with a b? Anne laughs a little now, thinking of
that, because her dad soon enough said whatever, because he must have
figured out girls her age said whatever just as much if not more than he
did. That was a kind of information, too, that she knew better and more
than anyone, like how her dad looked at the world like a kid himself
sometimes, who thought the rules could be pretty silly and could make
fun of it all. Who at lunch at Wendy's or McD's could cross his eyes at
a giant fat lady in a peach outfit like a parade float until Anne spit milk
out of her nose from laughing, which made her cough and laugh even
worse until she was gasping for air with tears streaming and streaming
down like they would never stop, and why should they ever again, since
that day she and her dad stole fries from each other's plates and
laughed just before everything that happened in that place?

Anne flinches suddenly at a vague small motion she senses behind
her, a fleeting shadow in the periphery, but when she turns there's
nothing, of course, but her own dull bedroom, Navajo White walls
and her posters, her shag throw rug and CD tower and blank little
TV, the room as still and silent as one uninhabited.

Is she the only one who sees? The restless fluttering shadows, first in the hours before waking, then all the time? Like those birds, frightened and frightening somehow, with their claws and wings in the yard, or in the wide white sky in wheeling flocks, wanting only to flee, or trying to find their way back home again. Even together they can all be lost, bewildered, turning this way or that in unison, as if trapped and trying to escape. But escape what? What fear makes them so desperate, flashing through the air in a blurred rush of wings, heartbeats racing to burst?

She knows something of that secret, the innocence of that pure animal panic, more than the others ever will, and she holds this knowledge to herself, sheltering it, because it makes her different from everyone, and allows her finally an opportunity for pure unselfish kindness, to feel sorry for them all.

Silently she slips from the bedcovers. In the drawstrings and T she has slept in, she crosses to her window to peer from between the shade and the sill out at their muddy backyard, at the dark motionless shapes of the pigeons in their cages, at the dawn sky, still unflown by other birds.

She hesitates, and turns away from her window, hearing and shutting her eyes against small feathery sounds, faintest flutterings, exhalations.

As the gunman sighs and stands with his jumbo cup at the soft-drink dispensers in the middle of the room, Jimmy shifts beside her, ever so slightly, maybe cramped like she is, with a pain in his throat like hers from the effort of barely breathing for so long, from the effort to fold into themselves and simply somehow not exist.

There's a quick panicky fluttery sound of footsteps.

BLAMM! BLAM! BLAM! Three shots ring out, each one sharp enough to flinch at, stinging ugly sounds.

❦

The pistol is black-handled and heavy-looking in the man's hand but Jimmy can't see his face because he's looking the other way, but he sees the man's medium height, the tender-looking pink scalp of his bald spot, his

Dockers and tan windbreaker like some Kiwanis or Rotary Club glad-hander, as the guy surveys the room looking for who to kill next.

Gun in one hand, Jumbo Thirsty Cup in the other, the gunman shuffles away, past the life-sized Carby's cardboard cowboy, whose shoulder now bears a ragged bullet hole, and past the window that looks out onto 84 and the traffic going by and a few birds flying away out of sight beyond the edge of the sky, above the bare treetops.

Bundled up in binding layers against the cold, hoping for a freshwater perch or trout, Jimmy and his dad fish from lawn chairs set in the muddy bank of Tompkins Park. Clouds of their breath rise in the raw Michigan air, a few geese cry out as they pass overhead and disappear beyond the tree line, but otherwise this early morning has brought a stillness as of a deeper winter still to come, all signs of life frozen and mute, encased in ice for an ice age.

His dad nods toward the rusty tackle box beside Jimmy. "Hand that tackle box over, Jimbo?"

Jimmy hands over the box, and his dad looks at him a second too long, which he has been doing too many times, staring like judgment day. Is that why he took him out here, to stare at him like he's some kind of freak? His dad is a prick, is what. Who knows why, but it started before his brother, Michael, got hit in Iraq. It started too long ago to even remember how or why. The funny thing is that deep down his dad really feels sorry for himself, which is exactly what he hates about everybody else, and so he can't just cry about whatever it is (Michael, his job, whatever) and get on with his life, which maybe could include a laugh now and then. But here they are, as if his dad suddenly today is going to morph into someone willing to understand someone else's feelings and try to let them know just that. A sad joke.

As his dad bends to tie his lure, Jimmy almost prays for a fish, a flipping tiny black perch with slimy scales, because that would bring their world back into balance, where he and his dad could pass a few hours and just catch a fish, that's all, just so you couldn't say the time was totally wasted.

But his dad is too nervous to let the silence stand. "You remember I used to take you boys out here early, don't you? Not one to get out of bed before the trout, not you. Your brother maybe. But you? Had to shake the bed, scare you half to death."

He stops short at this last word, and Jimmy knows he's frightened that he has actually said this word and brought up the big taboo subject. But stopping here creates another moment of silence that's too long for his dad, and so he asks, "You remember?"

Jimmy looks at his dad, but he's already ducked his head, making a show of carefully working his reel to pull in slack, as if it will somehow improve his chances.

***

Outside the county building, a few concrete benches surround a kiosk festooned with flyers, forming a tiny park where county workers gather for a last smoke before clocking in or returning from break. Abler spots Doris Hagen approaching, as promised, and he sets down his pad and folder to stand quickly and shake her hand with a brief dry grip.

Sharing his bench, Doris seems to look everywhere but at him as he thanks her for coming and encourages her to start, anywhere, with the kind of girl her daughter has been and has become in the wake of this event.

Mothers resist, almost always, with a firm proprietary perspective on their children that doesn't often or easily admit to missing anything, since daytime TV is nowadays filled with lurid tales of oblivious moms and their kids suffering from various addictions and/or abuse, about to commit suicide or murder or both, and all the earliest warning signs thereof. But Doris surprises him and he nods and jots on his pad, as her frankly worrying narrative circles closer and closer to what he needs, without much prodding.

In her lap, Doris's hands rub at one another as she murmurs, "Never really a popular one, always writing her poems and stories. Her dad was always her best friend, except maybe for Jimmy. Head over heels for her, they rode the same bus since second grade. So now who is there? Of course I'm concerned about her not sleeping, barely eating, but . . ."

Abler hears her voice trail off and because there must be more, there always is, now he gently prompts her, "Anything else?"

"She talks like a born-again, nonstop. When I tried to tell her what the police said, that it was most likely a random, senseless thing, she said 'No, it's God's will.' She's suddenly all faith and forgiveness."

Abler nods, jotting again. "It's natural to want a reason. We see an increase in that behavior sometimes, in cases like these, in adolescents raised to be devout."

Doris shakes her head. "Anne? Never finished Sunday school. Hasn't been to church twice in years."

Abler goes still, and then slowly lifts his eyes from his notepad.

Leaving the University of Michigan's Rackham Building, Abler gets stuck holding the door for a gaggle of undergrad girls entering, giggling and flushed with the cold. Abler shrugs helplessly at psychology department chairman Ned Hayward, his thesis adviser, whom he has come to see without notice late this morning, and who has exited the building a step ahead and now waits, faintly amused, in his pedantic scraggly cardigan and beard.

Abler steps outside and lets go of the door as the last of these girls hurries off to their Psych 101 undergrad survey lecture, or freshman-level behaviorism lab, or core studies seminar.

Hayward claps him on the shoulder, laughing softly, and as they start down the broad steps onto the quad, he frames his reply to the questions Abler has come to ask: "Glossolalia—a private language or obsessive rhetoric. If it's religious, even more precedent—Joan of Arc syndrome, believing you've been chosen by God."

"All a reaction to emotional trauma?" Abler knows the answer to this, but wants to hear his own voice ask, as if to gauge his incredulity at the truth.

Hayward shrugs. "No atheists in foxholes. But from what you

describe, it could be a denial or distancing mechanism. Symptom of extreme disassociation. Or she could just be hiding something about the incident. Or all of the above."

Abler slows, the possibilities shifting and presenting themselves as effects preceded by causes, an unbreakable chain leading back to an event he simply knows too little about, but which for each participant may remain moments to deny and flee, and yet relive again and again, until these opposing urges tear apart their lives. And there is no way to work backward and divine the truth, certainly not from conversations with Anne's mother, helpful as she means to be, or from the steadfast silence from Jimmy and his parents.

As they walk, Abler glances across at the law quad buildings, with their Gothic revival ogivals and inscriptions and dim green gargoyles, mythic guardians of secrets. Hayward stops here, thoughtful. "The other subject, her friend, struck mute? Not uncommon, obviously harder to interpret. But there could be a fear of some imagined consequence of speaking."

Abler tries to see it, fear of reprisal, for revealing a secret? Or is Jimmy's fear about making any sound at all, an endless reenactment of the fear of being discovered in their hiding place?

But Hayward is chuckling, as if he's just seen an angle. "And by the way: no. Your fieldwork does not buy you any slack on your thesis."

Abler gives a wry smile. "As if I ever dared to hope."

Charlie ∽

As Kathy Archenault climbs from her cheap SUV with groceries, sallow-faced Detective Cavalis approaches. She's startled at first, and then notices his black plainclothes car at the curb just across the street.

Cavalis must see her tense, wary look, because he quickly holds up his palms, shaking his head. "We still don't know your husband's whereabouts, Mrs. Archenault. I'm sorry."

The moment brings relief to Kathy first, and then a return to the baseline of barely controllable fear she has been living with for days. She turns away, to reach into the car for a bag of groceries.

Cavalis plunges ahead, probably no help for it: "Ma'am, if you don't mind? Just a few questions we need to clear up if we can. To your knowledge, did he know any of the other victims at the scene? Mr. Hagen, or Mr. Carline?"

Kathy shuts her car door, not softly. "I've already told you, Detective. No, he didn't know any of the others."

"So you wouldn't be aware of any bad feelings there, or business gone wrong?" He points to her groceries. "Can I give a hand with that?"

She almost flinches away. "No, thank you. My husband owns a driving school. A home office, one car. So that would be no—I'm not aware of any bad feelings or business deals."

Cavalis works his lips, like he has a bad taste in his mouth. "Reason I'm asking, we show a pretty big withdrawal from your joint savings."

Kathy goes still. "Withdrawal?" Charlie never liked the decisions that came with money, always afraid to do the wrong thing with it, that he'd never have it again.

Cavalis looks away and nods. "I'm sorry. Eight thousand dollars. We trace account activity on all missings. But we have to go through the branch manager, so usually you'd see the activity before we do. You didn't know about it?"

"God, no. I haven't even looked. Eight—" More than enough to miss, it's a dangerously large proportion of their savings, of a covenant between them all, for the safety and security of the years they know will come, they hope will come. She shakes her head.

"I'm sorry, yes. Unfortunately, the withdrawal's from the local branch, so not much help in terms of where he's headed. Are you sure you don't know of any reason for him to take off with such a large sum of cash? Do you have any reason to suspect he was having an affair?"

She studies him, deadpan. "I have a babysitter inside I have to pay."

He looks at her, unhappy, and hands her his card. "Mrs. Archenault, I know this is hard. I know you want word, any word, on his whereabouts and his condition, and so we want to be sure that we're exchanging every bit of information we have with you and vice versa."

Kathy narrows her exhausted eyes at him. Dryly: "Thanks for saying so, Detective."

She turns away and walks up her driveway.

"Sure," Cavalis says, to nobody.

In the cheap new sweats he purchased last night in the casino's Odds 'n Ends shop, Charlie emerges from his room, blinking against the bright morning glare and the din of trucks and cars roaring past behind the chain-link fence, headed so quickly elsewhere they might be fleeing. He hurries down the concrete steps, heavy from the fitful sleep he forced on himself with Scotch and gift-shop cold medicine in the early hours near dawn. No matter, to Charlie his time is as appointed as any nine-to-five office job, and he is way late to clock in and begin this day's single most vital task: the maintenance and growth of his gambling winnings. This is his calling, the fulfillment of the destiny dictated by the new fact that he is simply, ultimately, luckier than not.

He crosses the casino parking lot and pulls open one of the heavy glass front doors, stepping into what at first seems a hushed muffled place. Almost deserted on this weekday morning, stinking of cigarettes and petty defeats, the big gaming floor with its gaudy carpet and neon beacons stretches away into a dimness of mirrors. Charlie cannot even find himself in the complicated reflection far across the room that gives back banks of slots and stools and blackjack tables, a blurred jumble of angles.

Employees trade glances at his approach and behind his back, but Charlie is fine being a curiosity, and if he could lay on hands and bless these poor stiffs with some of his own luck, he would. Because, hey. He shoots out a finger, does a little spin and continues on his way down an empty aisle of slots.

A few straggling midweek tourists nudge each other and point as he shuffles by into the Odds 'n' Ends shop, where last night's bellhop is today's clerk. The kid smiles at Charlie as if they were fond old acquaintances, and Charlie grins, snaps his fingers and points, unable to remember the kid's name, and his eyes too shot with blood and blurred to see it on his tag.

"Hey, who it is, Captain! Good, I need some presents to go back to family with. You get commissions?"

The kid blinks as Charlie steps to a display table and grabs a pastel pile of "Pow ! Atan" sweatshirts and sweatpants. Charlie hovers a hand near his knees, "Beth is three, a real pistol, about yea high. And her mother is about your height but not so big in the shoulders and—"

"Well, small, medium, or large. That's what we got, sir."

"Straight-shooter, Captain. I like it. Call me Charlie."

"Charlie."

"Hey, Charlie CK, could say. Because that's where I walk. Gas to get home I already have, which leaves me . . ." He checks a scrawled crumpled bit of paper. "Five hundred and sixty-eight dollars and twelve cents in my pocket, to spend right here. So however many of whatever you got it'll buy for my girls, I'll take, and that's it. What I got in the bag I go with, not a cent less. So, can we figure it out?"

Charlie's smile is a bit dazed, but he sees now the kid's tag says Pete and he remembers Pete was fired, Pete is pounding the pavement and probably without luck if he is looking for bellhop work locally, because Powatan is about it.

After ten minutes of frowning and scratching and fretting over a Powatan stationery pad, "Pow ! Atan" sweat ensembles, mittens, socks, and ashtrays are assembled on the counter and the cash register display reads: 567.12.

Charlie exults. "Bingo, and a buck to spare!"

The kid carries the eight or so big "Pow ! Atan" shopping bags for Charlie, who clutches his own as they head for the big glass doors out to the lot. Murmurs and stares trail him.

Charlie slows at a winged "Batman" slot machine, last one before the exit. He stops, takes another step, stops again. He sets his bag down, reaches into his pocket, and pulls out his last loose dollar.

"What the hell. In for a dime, as they say."

As he smoothes the bill on the edge of the machine, the kid's smile fades. "Sir? Uh . . . Charlie? Hey, maybe you—"

"I'll split the win with, whattaya say? Always leave on an up note."

The world slows to a crawl, filled with the pale blurred shapes of faces and dimly mirrored lights as Charlie feeds in the dollar and pulls the handle. *Clickety click clickety, snap, snap, snap.* Silence.

Charlie chuckles at himself. He picks up his bag to move on, but sets it down again, because it's annoying, really, to leave to see his winning streak sullied and diminished, like chrome with a spot on it. He shakes his head and reaches into his pockets. Nada.

So he reaches toward his bag of winnings. His hand stops in midair, tingly and twitchy, a good sign no doubt, and so he shoves it on into the bag and watches it pull out a crisp C note.

Carla ~

A twitch worries the tender skin beneath her eye as Carla stares down at a letter and accompanying check. Her eyes and mind refuse to take it in all at once, and so she comprehends this vast import in small rushed fragments. "The management of Carby's Restaurants regrets . . . ," "closed until further notice," "by cashing this check you agree to hold harmless and indemnify . . ."

Carla stares down at the check, awed. "Pay to the Order of Carla Davenport—$ 2,000.00."

In Carla's life this amount signifies an end to all worry in the intermediate term, whole months she envisions as luxurious endless hours of idle television, magazines, shopping for a lipstick or nail polish or even a skirt or shoes, without the vague twitchy sensation of bad news and ugly payback waiting around every corner, which lately she has had a hard time shaking.

And with this sum, maybe she enters into another world, not entirely or forever, of course, but maybe just far and for long enough to appear to belong there, in the better restaurant in a cute new skirt and blouse, where who knows whom she might possibly encounter, who might just happen to be in fact oddly enough just thinking about her, and with whom she might possibly find a way to pass a pleasant hour or two, strolling by fountains or the windows of exclusive shops, laughing softly at subtle remarks.

Carla has brought Davy to this playground once before, to take in the shouts and laughter of other children, but more to watch and listen to their mothers as they trade advice and sympathy, rocking their prams with a practiced hand or shielding their eyes against the glare to check on a child's progress up the slide's ladder, or the height of their swing, or the volume of a taunt or tearful cry.

Carla had winced sympathetically at a boy's skinned elbow, but his mother didn't seem to notice, and when she commented on a little girl's sweater or the weather, the faint distant smile she got back reminded her that she was a few blocks into a better neighborhood than her own, and that her acid-washed jeans and Target snorkel parka gave her away.

This morning Carla has come too early, and the little hillside park with its swings and sandbox and benches is empty and silent, eerie. The swings hang motionless in the still cold air, the jungle gym divides the world beyond into empty boxes of sky.

She sits on a bench, holding Davy. He cries weakly, a frail exhausted sound. He wears only a diaper and is wrapped in a blanket which hasn't really fallen away, maybe it's wrapped a little loose, but other mothers have been here with other children overdressed, ridiculous, stuffed into expensive, bulky fake ski clothes they can't really even play in. And they've cried and been shushed, because sometimes you just have to, or be run ragged in the end and be no good to anyone anyway.

Carla slowly turns her head this way and that, looking for anyone nearby or approaching who might possibly see her and presume to have an opinion about anything, especially about what they know nothing about, because what have they seen and how do they know how anything really feels, about how it hurts to just want someone to smile at you or say something that means they *see* you, that in that single moment they might actually truly be thinking about you.

Thinking of you. They're words in a song, or in a drugstore Hallmark card, aren't they? But then old chestnuts are just that for good reason, the solid seed of truth they contain, and there is for sure none more solid ever in this world than the happiness of knowing we are thought about.

Back in her tiny second-story courtyard studio, Carla holds on to squirming runny-nosed Davy as she listens to Abler finish his pointless message on her phone machine, "to call with any questions or anything at all. That you feel you want to share. Thank you."

She smirks, shaking her head, picturing the dark wiry little man with his big glasses and kinky hair. She presses "delete." And *beeep!* Another message begins, her babysitter Jenn clearing her throat nervously and, "Carly? Just wondering how you are, you know, and Davy, and . . . if we could maybe meet to settle up—"

Carla frowns and quickly presses "delete" again, and carries Davy to his crib, stepping accidentally on a little Styrofoam Burger King box that has slipped from her overflowing trash can, giving it an angry little sideways kick out of the way as she sets him down. He fusses tiredly, without the usual vigor he brings to his complaints. A catch of mucus clicks in his throat and his little hands open and close, and Carla smiles absently down at him, and then turns away to search for her television remote control.

Laraby ~

Like ghosts, tall and white in their lab coats, the memory of his father and his father's associates in this cafeteria returns to Laraby on his break, with his coffee and creamer and Yoplait at the corner booth. The room has not changed: lit by buzzing fluorescents, polished linoleum giving back vague blurs of the world in squares of watery color and whiteness; faintest music seeps from tiny speakers in the beige dropped ceiling, amid the clatter and murmur of visiting families and staff. There were faint fond smiles, then, kind looks from these men and the passing faces of nurses floating by as Dad had hoisted him up to hold him sitting on the edge of their table, a little frightened but finally seeing and laughing the way they laughed, to be like them all, which made them laugh harder.

Now laughter turns him to see Howland and a nurse just sitting at a far table with coffees, and even from here Laraby can see she's one of the slimmer attractive ones for sure, an Ellen or Elaine, flushed and a little flustered, and that this flirtation will be hard currency when self-serving gossip is swapped at lunch or in the ladies' room. Howland slouches, insouciant, almost grandly relaxed, in the certainty of her unquestioning regard.

Laraby wonders if this coffee is a prelude to an assignation, a sweaty hour in the Quality Inn out near the fast-food parlors on the edge of town, or just breathless fumbling in a utility closet—do single doctors really do that, or is it just a broad television conceit? Elaine or Ellen is practically blushing and Laraby is suddenly unaccountably affronted by it all, by Howland and his murmured false stories of self-deprecation, trotted out again and again to carefully counter any impression of vanity, because he is a vain, shallow, showy creep, really. Is he ever not working an angle for sex or money, to get laid or for career advancement?

Laraby stands with his tray and steps to the trash to tilt and let it all slide in and clatter the tray onto the stack, and the smile he gives Howland as he passes on his way out is thin and rushed and preoccupied, no hint of judgment, because why give him the satisfaction of misperceiving for even a moment that anybody's anything remotely like jealous?

The dispensary is a white shadowless room, shelves of pharmaceutical medicines in wholesale bulk bottles and boxes and in free sample form, clear plastic blister packs that don't stack so easily, probably on purpose, so they get dispensed in a hurry, over and over again, and the name finally sticks. It's almost like slotting in a supermarket, or banner space on a Web page these days, where every inch of real estate is about driving the impression of a brand into someone's brain. Xerox, Coke, Tampax, Metamucil, Life Savers, so many have entered the vernacular as pretty much nonproper nouns, category owned, end of story, because now the brand name *is* the thing itself, and vice versa.

The pharma reps who bring these samples are funny, garishly attractive women, heels clicking down the linoleum ahead of their little rolling carry-on bags, with high school names like Courtney and Heather, and plenty of jokey innuendo. Unimaginable, though it seems as if a nod toward the nearest utility closet would be all it took, or a walk back to their little Mercury or Toyota out at the far end of the lot.

Laraby pauses by a shelf, scanning until he sees some Statrophine, the brand of vasodilator chosen by "leading physicians," and in fact spots a few vials of injectable doses, for quick administration to an IV line, or straight in, for acute angina or any infarction episode due to vascular constriction. His hand flashes out and grabs two and jams them down into his lab coat pocket.

He hums to himself and moves on down the line, almost chuckling because this is ridiculous, who cares, it's no controlled substance and no one would ever think twice about a few doses in a doctor's medkit. And especially his, never, since his dad went so quick with acute angina, down and gone in ten minutes before anyone had one of these handy, which might well have done the trick.

Well, headache is contraindicated, so he'll grab some Molodil, too. Sublingual, like Howland said, and quick into the other pocket to slip into his bag later on, in the locker room. Laraby hesitates for a small beat by the door, and then steps out again, into the hall across from ICU, where things are quiet enough at the moment and the day nurse idly turns the pages of a magazine, yakking into the phone, "He *what*? No way, shut up. Get outta town!"

flies ～

The Children ~

Standing on the low hill of pines behind the high school playing field Anne's tired of waiting in the cold. Cigarette butts litter the last snow, and probably beneath that some condoms and beer bottles and trash from whatever else everyone gets up to out here, not that Anne would know firsthand, since this turf is invitation-only, or at least requires membership in one clique or another, stoners, jocks, JDs, or sluts, whichever.

She clutches the note from Lori, which she has unfolded to read and reread until it has become creased in a thousand directions and as soft to the touch as some ancient document. Anger has risen from within her, little by little, and she feels a new and calm certainty of her sudden power over these girls she has grown up envying and admiring and finally belittling to keep the last of her own battered dignity intact.

Among the trees, sparrows peck at the dirty patches of snow. Two fly at each other, bickering, and Anne stares at them, entranced. One bird flies up, jeering, startling her, and she steps blindly back as a voice sounds behind her and it's Lori standing there, practically wringing her hands, for God's sake, almost whispering, "I wasn't sure you'd come."

The birds fly off. Anne watches them a second more as they flit away above the tree line, and then she faces Lori, lifting the crumpled note, her face stony: "We were never friends. You and Sue and Traci wouldn't have it. But now who's there for you to talk to? That understands anything?"

Lori begins to cry. "I know. I'm sorry. You *are* my friend. And Sue, and Traci's. But . . . does your mom hate you, too? Always in her bedroom? With the door closed?"

Anne grimaces and tucks back a stray pale strand of hair. "Mine? Uh uh. She wants to understand, but she can't."

Lori wipes snot away with her sleeve, sniffling. "That man called us. Abler? From the hospital?"

Anne gazes straight into Lori's shifty frightened eyes. "You're different now, Lori. We all are. He wants us all to be like we were before. But we can never be."

"Don't you want to be?" Lori's voice is small, broken.

Anne shakes her head. She sorts through possible expressions, from a teary-eyed slack look of sadness to a blurted sob of sympathy. All wrong, because in this moment Lori's submission is all Anne's to guarantee, easy, a deal to be sealed. So Anne raises an eyebrow and gives Lori a faint distant sort of smile: "What God wants is important, not what you or I want."

Lori blinks at her, wilting. "I know that. I do."

Anne narrows her eyes appraisingly at the other girl for a long moment before, "Okay."

Lori ducks her head. "Are you gonna talk to him? Or Jimmy? I mean, for you guys, you were—"

Anne actually laughs. "Jimmy will never talk. To him. And me either. We can't be like we were before. Ever. And there's nothing that man or anyone can do about anything now."

Lori's mouth is a dark slot of wonderment and fear, her eyes wide as she swallows and nods, because all their eyes will be, to look at Anne and imagine even a fraction of what she has known. Their lives are shallow, she's got actual human experience now, which is emotional and important and dramatic, like in books or movies, but it's her real life.

Most of the dozen or so kids in the Hunt Landing High School Prayer Group are never going to be popular, but a few try for style with an oversized T, an extra earring, a modified rock or hip-hop haircut. They stare entranced as Anne smiles faintly, careful to keep her voice strangely and beautifully free of what she lately hears as the rushed shrillness of other girls her age. Measured and slow, her words barely carry the airy space of this borrowed science lab and lecture room. "Luck is not why I'm alive. It was God who made my dad brave. He provided people with homes. For their families. Because that's what faith is. And having it says what other people think doesn't matter. And praying with our eyes closed means we are with God in that moment. So . . . will you do that with me now? For my dad?"

At their desks, with shy tearful nods, they close their eyes and fold their hands, bow their heads and pray. The small creaking of chairs, the faint breaths of the group, the distant hum and drone of the interstate—these sounds measure the interminable moments like gradients on a ruler.

What is there to be truly felt, more than imagined? Other than agreeing to stillness, how can anyone acknowledge a belief in what is infinitely larger than ourselves and our lives and our petty longings? Anne wonders at so much vastness, so much as to be incomprehensible, so much so that the voice of this vastness may as well be incomprehensible, which is a new joy to believe, that by speaking in tongues and riddles to honor her father she can for the first time in her life command a kind of respect.

Anne opens her eyes ever so slightly, to see a small red-faced girl seated toward the back of the room, watching her. The girl quickly bows her head, closing her eyes again.

At prayer's end, waiting for her mother outside, Anne is surrounded by these classmates even more unpopular than she, their eyes round and glistening in earnest imitation of hope and pity, as if any one of them could know the slightest about either.

Beside her the same kid who invited her is sputtering, ". . . felt the force of you with us! It's such a different energy! Next Wednesday night maybe we could—"

But Anne is already looking over the kid's shoulder, at Ron Abler standing there in the cold, waiting like an undertaker.

Anne barely glances at the chatty little geek beside her. "I'll be there. Yes. Okay?"

The kid nods gratefully, eyes shining. He runs to his mom's car and climbs in, gesturing excitedly. He and his mom look at Anne with a kind of bland astonishment, as if at a television personality who has stopped to acknowledge a kind word or to sign an autograph.

Abler approaches with his sad professional sympathizer's smile. "Anne? I hadn't heard from you, and I wondered how you—"

She cuts him off. "I'm fine." She gives him a bright-eyed smile of her own, quick and perky, as plainly discouraging as turning her back.

Abler has seen this hard smile and heard the chirpy tight tone before, all from the rigor of a body's musculature fighting itself, trying to maintain control, always, against terror or bottomless grief or both.

He pauses to regroup, hands in his pockets, shoulders hunched. "Because . . . when we go through something like what you did, Anne, the mind wants to forget it. But it's funny—we can't until we remember it. And so some of the feelings never go away, some of them can make you do things you wouldn't usually—"

"Remember it? The truth, all of it, I do." She fixes him with the clear straightforward gaze of the self-possessed, or the true fanatic or insane. "Because who but God can save us from lies? Who but his angels on earth can keep us from false witness? To testify—"

He shakes his head. "Anne, I'm only trying to—"

"Then pray with me."

Abler looks her in the eye now. She meets his look evenly, a challenge again, to disbelieve her even for a moment.

"No, Anne. I can't help you that way." He shakes his head sadly.

Anne gives him another big fake smile, and shrugs. "Oh well. Thanks for worrying about me! But don't."

She turns her narrow back on him and walks rapidly down to the curb, where her mom is just pulling up in their SUV, exhaust muttering and billowing in the cold.

Through the windshield, Abler and Doris lock eyes. He gives a barely perceptible shake of his head.

Jimmy looks silently out at Hunt Landing High as they drive past, and Lydia sees his fear and longing at the scattered students with their bulky book bags and parkas, bunched in groups as they wait to be picked up by their parents or by carpools for this week's prayer group.

She means this outing to provide another opportunity for Jimmy to finally speak, under the guise of an inconsequential business-as-usual trip to the grocery market. Her best hope is slim to none, since in every encounter with him, in the hall outside the bathroom, or in the kitchen after Bob has gone to work, he has answered her gentle questions with averted eyes and shrugs.

She misses his mouthy banter, sometimes just plain silly, sometimes so funny as to seem inspired, and often so nonstop that she watched a talk show one afternoon about attention deficit disorder and wondered if the diagnosis didn't almost fit, if Jimmy wouldn't one day wake up as one of these scattered and hyperactive kids, a candidate for Ritalin or worse, since these things could likely as not be progressive. Some ended up in football helmets, racing around at the end of tethers like leashes to prevent them from injuring themselves or even others. She imagined herself as one of those brave moms the neighbors pitied and then she had laughed at herself and turned the show off, finally, shaking her head at the alarmist shrill stuff women needed to scare themselves with all day long, some tiny excitement for the stay-at-home soccer moms, between the laundry and dishes. And the having-it-all pressure and full-up date-book schedules of today's on-the-go career women.

Lydia pilots their dual-cab truck into a parking space outside the Kroger's, looking carefully around, wary of chance encounters with inquisitive neighbors or classmates and their families.

Inside, Jimmy follows her as she rolls a cart along. Lydia glances his way and his tentative darting looks weaken her determination, her agenda fading as she fills the silences with easy reassuring chatter, checking off items. "Here's that cereal you like. How about tonight for dinner, honey? I bet I know what you'd like. . . . Wait, I need one of these . . ." She reaches for a box of salt, flashes a smile at him, and turns back to pushing her cart along, already distracted by colorful plastic boxes of pasta and little tubs of red sauce. "These look new. Should we try some?"

But Jimmy is looking around wide-eyed at the bright cans and packages stacked head high, and then up in a panic at Muzak suddenly surging from hidden ceiling speakers just above them, a U2 song with soaring lush strings instead of singing. The cart's wheels squeak and skid, and suddenly behind them—*cooosh!*—a jar of pickles hits the floor, a toddler begins to squall, and a voice crackles over the intercom, squealing with feedback in code, "Price check, price check. Cleanup four."

Jimmy backs up a step against a shelf, looking around out of the corners of his wide eyes, as if he has discovered himself on a tightrope over a canyon, or at the edge of an elevator shaft, unable to take a step or a breath.

For the thousandth time she asks, "Honey? You okay?" But he shrinks from the hand she lifts toward him.

At the end of the aisle, shoppers stare openly, faces slack and stunned, and Lydia suddenly sees what Jimmy must: the cans behind them stacked high enough to clatter down without warning, the glass bottles ready to burst into needlelike shards, the world itself ready to open like a curtain to reveal a next moment no one should ever have to live through.

They stand this way for a moment, Lydia with her hand extended into space toward him, and Jimmy frozen there, blinking, until finally he allows his lungs to fill again and he nods.

Lydia turns to glare at the stupid women with their carts crowded in and staring at them like dumb cows from the end of their aisle. They turn their carts away, but not without one glaring back, because she has as much a right to be there as anyone, and proud of it, apparently.

Lydia smiles at Jimmy, no longer tearful herself, and she takes his arm and they walk together from the store, leaving their half-filled cart behind.

Charlie ∾

A laugh somewhere is choked off, and the crowd gasps as they take away half of Charlie's life savings and the money he has so diligently multiplied that stake into becoming, what a few hours ago was spare change over a hundred thousand dollars. They rapidly stack and restack the chips into even amounts, locking the little grooves in their edges *clickety, clickety,* and sliding the neat piles up against the others, grouped by denomination color before the seated boxman with his shiny expressionless face.

The hours of Muzak and mirrored light have grown indistinguishable, a blur of unfamiliar faces that startle and become as quickly forgotten as they fade into others: the elderly gent with his ascot and baby blue sport coat who chain-smokes like a recovering addict, the diminutive bald man with the handlebar mustache, muttering incoherently, his eyes darting furtively around the room, as if for pursuers. Charlie loves them all equally, he is of them and vice versa, each struggling to reach a moment when mysterious forces merge, like some huge but invisible alteration in the chain of causality, or the fabric of space/time. He laughs out loud, because baby needs a new pair of shoes, pretty much, in other words.

Charlie tosses up his last red five-dollar chip, and slaps it on the pass. Swaying on his feet, in a nether world far beyond drunkenness and exhaustion and any idea of reason, Charlie places a hand on his heart as he regards them all with a wry pseudogravity he's certain will convey good humor and classy bonhomie: "Gentlemen, faith. If you will, or would. We're all lucky a little while, now and then. Not if but when . . ."

"Sir . . ." the stickman says yet again, in that same ever-so-slightly warning tone, and Charlie this time locks eyes on his as he lets the bones fly, not even breaking the stare as they flop down and the man glances to see and then meets Charlie's gaze again to declare, "Three craps three. Line away."

Charlie gives a sick goofy grin and spins away from the table into the crowd, blundering through the sea of stunned murmuring faces and out of the casino, to stand gulping for air in the cold, half-empty parking lot as traffic flees along the interstate, as if from some giant catastrophe.

Darkness spreads across the cloud-hung sky, like a shapeless stain. Across the freeway, the lights of the scattered low buildings of Powatan fail to beckon, purplish and white smudges illuminating patches of inky parking lot, empty windblown street, shabby storefronts. What is this place, what is anyplace? Where is the hand that guided him to step left instead of right? Can it not be the same one that brought him here, south instead of north, to one game of chance instead of another?

His wife and daughter's faces come to him now, asleep, oddly enough, both with their small upturned noses and half-parted lips and fine thin eyebrows, breathing, oblivious, each in dim light floating sideways on a crushed pillow, with a fistful of blanket clutched under their chins. Hot tears sting his eyes, suddenly, and a thick sob lodges in his throat, at how no one will ever truly understand the depth of risk he has undertaken on their behalf, and the consequent vilification, as immoral and irresponsible, as sheer utter lunatic, which he inevitably will suffer from all corners.

But hey, who cares, because how can it not be worth it? Risk is risk because without it there's no reward, no pain no gain, spoils to the brave, devil take the hindmost, nothing ventured, etcetera. Man, there is more square inch of homily to cover the subject than mutant corn in Iowa, asbestos in Detroit high schools, alcohol- and drug abuse–related traffic deaths. We're all whistling past the graveyard, but secretly dying to get in.

He giggles a little, a short girlish peal of mirth that turns the heads of a few frat guys exiting.

"Party on, bro!" one of them mutters, and the others smirk and laugh.

Carla ～

On the talk shows the women seem like some sort of well-groomed suburban cult, awed and somber and glistening-eyed about the evils that threaten them all: thinning hair, cellulite, porn-addicted husbands, dust mites, and mold spores. A blaring ad for that psychologist's show demands to know "Can this family be saved?" One woman seems smug and almost happy about the spread of teen drug abuse and promiscuity, as if at a brand-new scientific discovery or advance. On the CNN all-news channel, men in nice suits are yelling at each other, pale heads with expensive haircuts shaking back and forth in woeful dismay about whether or not to "take out" another foreign dictator, which as a phrase to Carla always meant going to the movies or the mall with some guy who asked her, funny how that one got changed around. On a soap, a beautiful woman in a dark size-two pants suit and heels cries and gets hugged by a broad-shouldered young guy with amazing teeth and hair, like a magazine model, no cellulite or porn addiction there, probably, but of course there must be other problems, because otherwise what is there to watch? Somewhere lies eat away at the relationship, secret uncontrollable urges slowly surface, or suddenly erupt and tear apart or spin out of control. It's all violence, the words of it all: the prices slashed, the binge-eating cycles shattered, the barriers to great sex smashed, carbs burned, germs killed.

Carla hears a sound, or maybe only thinks she does, the radiator sighing or Davy softly coughing or a neighbor's door closing, but now that commercial comes on she loves with the talking kitchen appliances, and she kicks off her shoes and pulls her feet up and makes herself small on the sofa, turning it up to watch.

In summer, she keeps her front door open to let some air in, and she's glad to have a screen door to keep the flies out, but to suddenly have this one buzzing around now from nowhere in the winter, hovering at her ear when she's watching TV, or worse, when she's asleep, it just wears on her last shred of patience. Always at the edges of her vision, it's a faint buzzing that tickles with its faintest touch and makes her shiver. It's disgusting, dirty, and as she sits on her unmade futon reading *TV Guide,* she tries to ignore it like the sounds from outside that tug at the edges of her attention—the same car engine revving, a faraway dog yapping, or like anything remembered that you don't really want to, but that you can't forget either.

She brushes absently at her face, peering down at the magazine, resolving to focus. But she has read the same sentence it feels like a hundred times and she can't remember any of it when she finally sighs and looks up to see if she can see the goddamned thing and squash it with her magazine or her hand into a twitching dying little smudge.

A dot of motion flickers just beyond what she can see and she whips her head to see nothing there, and then it flits in a dark blur against the other side of her face and she stands, in fury kicking aside a clump of strewn underwear and her Carby's uniform late for the Laundromat, moving into the middle of the room by Davy's bassinet to stand there turning slowly in place, scanning the room with narrowed eyes for the filthy infecting winged thing.

A Carby's Cowboy Special burns to a stinking crisp on the grill.

There's shafts of sunlight cutting through the smoke, from the two bullet holes in the back door, like somebody drilled them and made a bad job of it, splinters protruding every which way, you could jab a finger easy.

A third bullet has ripped through the shoulder of the life-sized cardboard Carby's Cowboy, so fast it didn't even knock it down.

In the kitchen, behind the pantry door, Carla shakes her head, silent tears streaming as she stares at the cheap little piece of shit cell phone she now holds face-up beside her leg.

She hears the soft gurgle of someone sipping a soft drink, it must be him but she doesn't want to look, who wants to see him sipping a drink anyway, who wants to remember a thing like that, and suddenly a tinny U2's "Beautiful Day" blares, that Irish Bono's song with the chugging beat of busy drums, like a radio snapped on right at the part where they repeat the title and the rest of the band sings echoey backup.

Carla jerks her head up, staring out at the dining area to see what there will be to see.

Just as suddenly as it began, U2 stops. And in the seconds before it starts up again Carla sees the man with the gun at a table with his drink, tilting his head back to shake his head at the ceiling and sigh with world-weariness.

And now the fly lands on her cheek and begins to crawl, the lightest touch of its legs nearing her eye, which she cannot blink or brush away because she cannot breathe.

She sees it now, a tiny dark triangle moving delicately across a diaper on the floor that has spilled from the full trash can, and then it takes off and lands again, on the perfect smooth whiteness of Davy's cheek, inching toward his runny nose as he lies there sleeping.

Carla crosses to her open Pullman kitchen and jerks open a cabinet, yanking out and tossing aside one can and bottle after another of Comet and Drano and PineSol until she finds it—a tall yellow-and-black can of roach spray, Raid. She yanks it from the shelf, gritting her teeth in fury to twist off the yellow plastic cap and shake the empty can again and again in disbelief and slam her thumb on the stupid nozzle that won't spray even a droplet, and to fling it, finally, clattering to the dirty linoleum where it rolls and stops against a dirty paper plate, as she tries to breathe again.

Laraby ~

The Larabys' new house is on a hillside, nestled among sparse deciduous woods, meant when finished to present a tall facade of posts and beams and glass luxuriously and warmly lit from within.

On this rare evening off, Laraby and Jan have driven here in her Volvo wagon and parked just beyond the chain-link security fence, to share potato chips and coffee from a thermos and admire their future home. The car heater hums quietly and they stare at the half-built house they plan to fill with family and inhabit for the rest of their lives.

Laraby imagines it finished as it might be, in this first purplish descent of evening. He imagines it surrounded by the lush boughs of summer, affording vistas of birdflight and shades of sunlit verdure. He imagines the house in spring rain, the lulling *drip drip* from the eaves and the gurgle of runoff from the gutters, the rivulets along the full maple-sashed picture windows of the great room and the crackling of a good hardwood fire as Jan teaches his bright inquisitive children Scrabble or Parcheesi or Go Fish, laughing and clapping her hands.

He imagines it engulfed by apocalypse, the wrath of a vengeful deity.

He imagines it in flames.

He imagines it as charred embers still exuding the noxious stink of loss, like the breath of the bereaved.

Right now it is a foundation and partially framed structure surrounded by piles of composition roofing rolls, moisture barrier tar paper, stacked lumber and copper pipes. Sorted detritus, neat debris.

Jan touches his hand. "Do you think it has . . . a personality?"

Laraby remembers to smile. "How could it not?"

She smiles back, and starts their game. "Come on, what kind does it have? What kind of people would live in a place like that, anyway?"

Laraby stares out at it again, silent, thinking.

She leans back, sighing happily. "I'd have to say . . . commanding, willful, yet kind, and with a really great sense of humor."

He doesn't laugh. "Hopeful."

"Hopeful? Okay. Hopeful is good." She studies him curiously as he stares out at the building.

Finally he turns his gaze to her. But she has already turned hers away, back out the windshield to the wood and galvanized nails and gypsum and concrete.

He asks carefully, watching her, "How're the headaches?"

She doesn't turn. "Good. What about a bigger header beam across, and lose the post? Just glass, out to the balcony, to really bring in the sky?"

His eyes, his mind, his heart, all will her to turn her face to his and smile and take his hand, but she stares out, lost to him, as if across miles to some distant shore his vision has grown too dim to see.

Is there any way back to her now, words to murmur, but how, because why didn't he sooner? So the unspoken becomes the secret, and the secret the empty space between them, slowly and irrevocably widening, as they drift in their ether of absence and longing.

In the hall just outside the ER admittance area tonight, senior Hunt Landing Memorial LLC partners and staff surgeons Gretchensky and Carlson have invited staff and spouses to an informal commemorative event, to cut the ribbon around the new cardiac monitor/defib unit they have purchased per a bequest from the residuary estate of Laraby's dad, attending ER surgeon and senior partner Mark Laraby.

In his usual cashmere sport jacket and knit polo shirt, Travis Carlson addresses the small crowd in easy self-assured tones: "Great doctors like Mark Laraby, who left a legacy of skilled, caring medicine, and also enough for some pretty pricey new cardiac gear."

Fond laughter comes from Howland and Laraby and Jan, and the few nurses holding plastic cups, drinking cheap champagne.

Carlson winks and lifts his hand to point at Laraby, continuing, "Not to mention Laraby the younger, whom we are well pleased to have join us here in emergency."

Everyone joins in polite applause. Laraby blinks rapidly, attempting a smile. Jan clings to his arm, beaming.

As the party shifts into little groups of murmuring staff, Howland immediately flirts with Jan. "So if designing your own home is anything like me taking my own medicine, you're a brave girl."

Unaccustomed as she is to disliking anyone, Jan rises to the occasion. "Not so brave. I know I'll live to tell."

Howland blinks. "Ouch."

They all laugh, except Laraby, who shifts uncomfortably, tonight unable to inhabit these moments of inconsequential friction and playful innuendo with any balance or ease. In the bright space between himself and these chuckling strangers with their prickly wits and agendas, Laraby knows whatever he offers up will die, too earnest by half or just as silly. The right tone to strike is beyond him, and he chuckles and slips away down the hall, without a word. None of them, not even Jan, looks twice.

He passes a gaggle of nurses chatting in confidential tones, hearing, "Knew when to hold 'em, knew when to fold 'em—"

One spots Laraby approaching and coughs, and they fall silent. The comment hangs, obviously overheard: reminiscence, comparison, judgment. Laraby gives a quick weak smile and moves past toward the men's room from which Carlson emerges.

Carlson skids to a stop, crepe soles squeaking on the buffed linoleum. "Bruce, looks like the HMO people'll sign off on those trauma cases. No question, no worry."

Laraby can't stop blinking. "Worry? Should I have been?"

"Absolutely, no. These were just higher profile, 'specially for week one in ER. But you should not, repeat, not, have one doubt, buddy boy. 'Nuff said?"

Laraby believes none of it, but he would pay money to learn this man's unthinking hurried poise and reassuring smile. He stares at Carlson a beat before he even remembers to answer, "Thanks, Travis."

"Your dad'd be proud."

Carlson swats Laraby's shoulder and ambles off down the hall. Laraby stands there, numb, staring off as if contemplating a riddle, holding his empty plastic cup like a panhandler.

sphinxes ⤳

The Children ∽

Soundless among the small sounds of night's last hour, Jimmy steps in his bare feet across the dark bedroom that was his brother Michael's. He knows the lay of the land by heart, and reaches out for the dim gleam of the old closet doorknob and pulls the door open, easy, easy, listening for the squeak of the hinge, or the cough or approaching footfall from out in the hall.

He waited and now has successfully and covertly infiltrated his dead brother's bedroom, which has long since been secured as is, to gently reach among Michael's remaining clothes to touch the dry-cleaner plastic covering an olive green dress uniform.

Jimmy holds his breath as he slides the hanger closer, and lifts it from the bar. He pulls the uniform out into the bedroom and carries it to the bed, where the half-open curtains admit shadowy streetlight from the small casement window. He gently lifts the plastic up and over and off, silently and slowly so as not to tear, his fingers finding the buttons as dull glints.

He's told himself he wouldn't, that it would be truly dumb, but he slips an arm into one sleeve and then the other of the big dress jacket, the scratchy heaviness hanging down over his hands, and then suddenly he's choking back spasms rising in his throat as he remembers their name-calling wars, for some forgotten reason strictly limited to two syllables, preferably "rude, lewd, and with attitude": "dipstick" trouncing "toadstool," "buttstain" beating "membrane," "fartbreath" easily defeating "skidmark." Thick gurgling noises are climbing his windpipe and tears sting his eyes, when he hears the tiniest *ggriinnnt* of a carpenter's nail snugging deeper into old wood, floorboard into joist, as his father steps softly this way down the hall.

Heart pounding, Jimmy rushes soundlessly with the plastic-covered pants still on the hanger into Michael's closet, pulling the door nearly closed behind him but not quite, afraid the latch will catch with a click loud enough to reveal his position.

Through the inch or so of open closet doorway, Jimmy sees the bedroom door swing slowly wide to reveal the vague darker shape of his father standing there, as motionless as Jimmy. But then his father enters and crosses to the bed, and the springs squeak as he sits on the edge, and then reaches over to unlatch the casement window there and crank it open just a little, with soft clicking sounds as the sticky jamb and sill grudgingly part. And then there is the *fssshhht* and sudden small light of a struck match, illuminating his father's sagging face as he cups the flame, as if against a wind, to light his cigarette.

The bedsprings squeak again ever so slightly, and Jimmy sees the tiny glow of his dad's lit Winston rise and hesitate, glowing brighter as his dad inhales, and then dim and move to the open window and bounce slightly in the air as his father tamps off the ash and exhales with a soft hiss.

Jimmy lets his own breath out, carefully, and waits and then inhales again slowly, also, in the endless moments that follow until his dad finally stands and leaves, and the long moments after that, until the house is restored again to stillness.

⁊⸱

Beneath the Hagen table, wedged behind Jimmy, Anne notices the hairs on the back of his neck, tiny and dark against the tiny bumps and pores of his

skin, which gives back light from the window, which if she's careful enough
she may be able to turn just enough to look out of, because why would she
want to watch the gunman scuff away toward another table, leaving that
print of spilled iced tea behind, why would anyone want to see him grab a
napkin from the dispenser there and carefully wipe the tabletop down, and
then sit and jam his straw into his full jumbo cup of mixed sodas, and sip?
Why would anyone want to watch any of it, when a few inches away
there's a world outside, of people in cars going other places entirely?

This morning as Anne stands at her open locker, gone still and staring
at nothing as if through a window only she can see, from the confusion of shouting laughing kids crowding the hall, geeky Prayer Boy is
suddenly in her face, with the white gunk at the corner of his chapped
lips and his bad desperate breath as he babbles on, ". . . and some of
the younger kids from the junior high group want to join, and some
kids from North Lake and some parents, too! And the more we have,
the more we can pray for! It's just so great—it's all just so—"

But he stops as she turns toward him, seeing the hard glint of mal-
ice in her eyes, so devoid of Christian charity and forgiveness. She
may as well grab the neck of his giant dumb LifeHouse concert
T-shirt and hiss into his zitty pink face, but instead she smiles as cold
as dry ice, "I pray to honor my father, and the bravery that God gave
to him. Understood?"

He backs up a step as if slapped. "Okay. We know that. We do,
too, so much." He squirms under her flat pitiless gaze, his head jerking and nodding, his eyes wide with panic. "So . . . okay. We'll see ya
Wednesday night? And thanks again. See ya!"

He flees.

At the end of the crowded hallway Anne sees a flash of brown
ponytail between the heads of a crowd of seniors and then not, and
then sure enough it's Lori Carline with Howard bent forward talking
softly to her as she lets out an embarrassed laugh and in fact turns furiously red and backs away with a weird frightened and glad smile.
Unbelievable. Howard is there already, flirting. It's like the girl's dead

dad club, is he going to comfort her now, be the shoulder to cry on, for God's sake, tell her the world will never understand, while he tries to feel her up, no doubt?

Lori moves off in rushed steps with her books pressed against her chest and her eyes wide and joins a group of anxious juniors, quad squad wannabes who hang on her now more than ever, and she makes a quick comment with a roll of her eyes and they all giggle like idiots and head inside for Spanish II.

Anne looks the other way and sees Howard's bird-skinny shoulders moving away and his eyes, which for a second look like someone else's, flicker back and past her as he turns away and moves off, joining a group of his jock A-hole friends, who look ready to burst into laughter, making snorty noises and acting off balance while they try not to. And then they do anyway, of course, show-off phonies loving the quizzical smiles of the juniors who want to join in, want to know what's the inside joke going around now, some paragon of sarcastic wit, some keen observation of someone or something pathetic or lame or beyond gross, or "just wrong," which kids are saying all the time now, and why not just own it, so thumbs up or down, yes or no already, every day on earth is judgment day, and there's something funny and cool and even real about not pretending otherwise.

Charlie ∼

The world contains many messages for those sensitive enough to receive them. From abstract ideas like words on signs and on television and from faces whose features form expressions, or impressions of expressions, to mere haphazard arrangements of light and sound stimuli that suggest bits of meaning, shuttling like sparks along the neurons and dendrites of the brain to induce laughter or tears, pain or fear.

Why fear? Because red plastic cubes land on a green felt surface to expose white dots in one configuration instead of another? Why buy into the assumption, widely accepted or otherwise, that one configuration will in fact result in a certain action by the man with the long curved stick and the bow tie and name tag and big dark pores and sideburns turning white? Whereas another configuration will presumably not? Just because the dice have failed to land showing seven white dots, or eleven, when Charlie has wagered thousands of dollars that they would, does that mean the next time these events occur, the man will take Charlie's money away again?

Charlie's own weight seems to bend him a little sideways somehow, since one foot has begun to throb hotly and there's a stab of sciatica and funny-bone tingling down his leg, from standing how many hours, probably, but who knows or cares, because anyway time is on his side, yes it is.

At the end of a row of "Tomb-Raider" dime slots, a blue haze of side-lit cigarette smoke envelops a Madonna and child, sad pietà of the maximum payoff odds aisle. Up all night, past drunk, Charlie sways in place, staring at the two. He shakes his head, pitying; in a moment Security will roust this chain-smoking homeless woman and her baby, since minors aren't permitted on the gambling floor. Kids don't come with a manual, which is too bad, and this one will probably grow up haunting the edges of the same gas stations and malls as its mother, not knowing any better. No hurry, because for now the baby sleeps on, the way kids can, beyond the flash and din and cigarette stink, limp in her mother's arms while she drags on a Kool and feeds a slot.

He fishes in a pocket and looks down at his palm: a paper clip, some lint, and a quarter: the eagle motif, wings outspread. He lets out a strange manic giggle, shaking his head in fond wonderment.

But when he looks up a security guard is already herding the mother and child toward the front doors and the bitter day outside, to wander down to the rest area nearer the interstate and whatever better fortune may await them there.

Charlie steps up to the ATM, a surer thing than any of these fancy new video-slots, but when he swipes his card and enters his PIN, he has to backspace and correct and then cancel and start all over to have the stupid metal box flash him the same terse refusal, "unable to complete transaction." It's a riddle, the meaning of every sign and portent, the spelling of his own password, his clumsy hunt-and-peck on the flat flush keys, the hidden messages in the magnetic stripe of card, whatever, wrong answer. He tamps down his fury, because hey, what about all the times these things work great and we never give them a second thought, right? So he chuckles out loud, which a few people stare at as he stabs a button, grabs his card back, and heads over to the cashier cages. He steps up to one cashier, a no-nonsense-looking fat woman with her glasses on a chain and her hair in a bright yellow swoop and a pale blue Powatan casino name tag stuck to her sequined T. "Pat."

Charlie does a little drumroll with his index fingers on the faux marble counter in front of her window. "Greetings, Pat. If I may call you that." Suddenly he cannot stop rhyming. "Got no checks on me. Unfortunately. But my savings account? Is there another way we can get money out? All that's in it? Way more than that pesky old ATM limit?"

Carla ～

Carla crushes her paper Macy's bag against one hip and squeezes Davy against the other as she hauls his stroller bouncing up the peeling concrete exterior steps to her apartment. Inside, she sets the stroller aside and Davy down in his bassinet while he frets and coughs listlessly, but she needs to get her brand-new dark blue cocktail minidress out of the bag and mashed tissue paper and smooth it before it wrinkles, and make sure again that the snobby clerk remembered her free gift with the bottle of fragrance by JLo she also bought, all with one check, signed and ripped out of her red leatherette check-book with a tiny flourish.

The clerk had been a bitch, for sure, and those two older rich bitches also, who bent over Davy's stroller and were all smug funny about how someone's got the sniffles and sure needs a changing, and the clerk impatient for her to make up her mind on the fragrance, Beyoncé or JLo or Obsession; she had misted each on her wrist and sniffed at it and wiped it away with the Kleenex like everybody else, but maybe Davy's crying was getting on the clerk's nerves, how could it not, but welcome to the real world where, helloo-oo, guess what? Kids cry and shit happens, and sometimes more than not, turns out. Even so, in her purse Carla's got a strip of black-and-white pictures of her and Davy from the photo booth by the sunglasses hut of both of them happy. This one has her lifting his hand to wave "hi" to the camera, and his eyes big and surprised at the flashes across from their little bench, and her laughing, which maybe was laying it on, but who doesn't have their picture face? Then he didn't want to and started to cry but at least she has the first few, which she'll put in her drawer or maybe even her wallet, or on the refrigerator door under a magnet, where she can always smile to see it.

Carla grabs the dress from the bag and unfurls it, kicking away a magazine and some laundry to stand before her closet sliding door mirror on tiptoes, as if she were wearing heels, as she holds the little dress against herself and poses with a raised eyebrow and a sideways little smile, a smart sexy look that says hip and feminine and confident control over situations. She likes the plain elegance of this dress, the "understatement," because the perfect look is always one less accessory or bracelet or necklace or ring than you have on. This neckline suggests, but not much and that's it, perfect, which says plenty about her in terms of taste, a subtle but really important message to get across, and one that won't be lost on someone perceptive.

She's glad she went with the six; it stretches taut at the bust and hips when she turns but is otherwise completely classy, though maybe a little short, but okay. Shoes she doesn't want to think about now, though she has a pair of brown sling-back heels that don't bear up under a really close look but that will probably go okay. Flats are out; she needs the sly forward tilt at the hips and the inward curve at the small of her back that heels give her, with the look of extra length of thigh to smooth the hem over after she sits in the chair he pulls out for her, before sitting in his own across their discreet table for two.

She lays the dress down, smoothing it across her futon, and then she flashes one more look in her mirror and takes a breath and grabs her cordless phone, speed-dialing. She waits, and then speaks brightly, confidently. "Hi, the emergency department, please? Hello? Dr. Laraby, please? Okay. Sure. I'll hold. Ummm. . . . Carla Davenport. Thanks much."

She waits again, as U2's "Beautiful Day" blares from the handset into her ear, thin snapping drums and jangly electric guitar, with lots of voices singing echoey backup behind that Irish guy Bono who wants to save the world, and why not, it's worth the effort after all, or why sing about anything in the first place?

"Carla?" Laraby's voice bursts through, sudden and loud.

She starts, as if she has been there for hours and fallen asleep and he has awakened her. "Hi. How are ya?"

Laraby's voice is distant and rushed. "Davy okay? Something wrong?"

"Oh, no. No. He's . . . I mean, I guess not. He's . . . asleep now, fine. So, oh, well." Carla squirms in the next beat of silence, gripping the phone. "I guess I called just to . . . say thanks again, Dr. Laraby! And maybe even—"

"You're very welcome, Carla. And don't forget to call a clinic from that list, get yourself a pediatrician. You take care now."

"Sure, I will. Call one of those clinics, too, and so, thanks again!"

But he has already hung up, and she stands there listening to the flat buzz of the dial tone, as she closes her eyes at the depth of her own foolishness and her own unending humiliation.

Laraby ∿

The flat electronic buzz blaring from the vitals monitor in Sam's room signifies absence also, of the systole and diastole contractions of a human heartbeat, and of a life continuing. Laraby moves rapidly in a sort of controlled panic, eyeing the flatline EEG and prepping the defib paddles as Sam's cyanosis deepens with the oxygen deprivation of severe cardiac arrest.

"Clear?" The floor nurse up here isn't new, but she has a slack-faced beat of slowness like fear before she nods and yanks her hands up, like someone at gunpoint.

The defibrillation unit whirrs and crackles and Laraby hits Sam hard with the paddles, gritting his teeth as Sam jerks upward like a fish beneath him and falls back again. To Laraby these are the longest moments on earth, waiting and simultaneously sorting through an expanding decision tree of possible outcomes and attendant contingencies, burned into his brain by the sheer rote of medical school study, and the grueling days of clinical practice during internship and residency.

Sam has become a familiar pale gray, faintly bluish.

They stare at the vitals monitor, waiting, but it's all flatlined: nothing. Laraby glances at the clock. "Time?"

"Five and half minutes. Going on *six*." She adds the small emphasis, but keeps her face impassive.

Laraby's eyes flicker from the monitor to Sam's dim face to the clock and back. The nurse seems to wince almost imperceptibly, as they wait staring at the monitor, not breathing.

Bip! A systole, a heart contraction, half a beat.

Bip! Bip! Two rhythmic waveforms appear on the EEG line. Blood gases begin a jerky climb higher.

Bip! Bip! Bip! Laraby exhales, letting his fear dissipate like the breath he has held too long in his own aching chest.

The nurse looks stunned. "You did it. You got him back, Dr. Laraby."

Laraby leans over to lift one of Sam's eyelids. The pupil remains dilated, a round black portal into the emptiness Laraby has tried to stop so many from entering. Laraby sighs. "Not the better half."

Sam's unseeing eye reflects nothing, only the white glare of ceiling light.

Hallways lead Laraby, blindly. He has lost track of his next move, next patient, time of day and the day itself, seemingly wandering into rooms where he seems expected to say some expected thing, which somehow seems to require no real consideration or studious physical examination, only an impression of those things, to arrive at or adjust a diagnosis or course of treatment, which for the moment seems to suffice.

What more is there than seeming, and the moment, than getting through the now into the next, which barely in the end connect? Chance looms in a heartbeat, for which nothing in the past was prelude. Randomness threatens all, from the realm of the molecular to the vast meeting of isobars, above mountain ranges and seas and continents, to the supernova burst of a star a trillion years ago, just reaching us, a glimmer in a darkness no one sees, among other glimmers, in other darknesses.

Where is there power to affect, ours to wield? Where is there honor and respect? With his heart and his hands Laraby has striven against the inhuman causeless universe in which we are now and are always becoming nothing, ceaselessly, like those fading stars. Why? For what? To suffer this weariness, this profound exhaustion that fear brings, the clutch and catch of the diaphragm with every breath dying to live, the grip of tendon on aching bone, the throb of light in our eyes?

It is all to be truly loved, by one creature, with the face of a woman, and the lean graceful body of a lioness. With the wings of a bird she would be his Sphinx, posing a question, always, which he must answer, or be thrown from the heights to plunge to his death, dashed against the unyielding stone of this earth.

locusts ～

The Children ～

Twisting in his folding chair, Abler turns to shield his phone from his chattering HR neighbors, unhappy to leave his uncertain hopeful voice on an answering machine, "to talk about what you've been through, or even any of the others, please don't hesitate . . ."

Abler's "cubicle" is really a small melamine desk shoved against a shared partition in the Case County Building's basement HR Department, a temporary workspace assigned to what the county considers a state employee, and vice versa. The county and state "matching fund" finance of the Michigan Post-Traumatic Stress Disorder Counseling Program blurs jurisdiction and doubles the bureaucratic wrangling over pay (a part-time sliding scale percentage of entry-level civil service salary), supply requisition (pencils, pens, paper clips, stapler, and legal pads), and reimbursement of employee expenses (cell phone charges, gas) and whether his county windshield sticker and ID and MFCC should guarantee access to trauma scenes and medical treatment facilities involved in the aftermath. Abler has sat through the debate in the county boardroom, with lawyers and supervisors and committee members weighing in endlessly with self-important ass-covering caveats "vis-à-vis" the liability insurance and lawsuit hypotheticals. In his four months in this part-time county program, red tape has defined the job, sad to say nearly as much as the multiple vehicle pileup in the fog that killed six and injured nine others, or the lightning strike at a church picnic that left a middle-aged father of two alcoholic and ago-raphobic.

Abler understands the waffling; he knows enough from his stud-ies to realize his field meets the same resistance its exact subject meets; the emotional pain of others will always be a chore to fathom, because to understand it one must empathize with it, which is to say feel it as well, a prospect which for most is always at least unpleasant and preferably avoided. Despite all the "we feel your pain" hand-wringing after the latest natural or otherwise disaster, the very idea of a money-costing program devoted to exactly that re-mains deeply unpopular at every administrative level, particularly in these days of runaway deficits and the bipartisan hue and cry for fis-cal accountability.

Abler pauses at the prospect of his next call, and sighs, leaning back, rubbing his temples. And then he slips into the coat he has hung over the back of his chair and leaves.

At the Jaspersen house, Bob Jaspersen is out front with suds, hose, sponge and bucket, washing his big dual-cab truck. His eyes flicker up, once, as Abler pulls up to the curb in his banged-up old Yugo.

Hose running on the ground beside him, Jaspersen bends to soap a chrome bumper as Abler climbs out and approaches.

"Mr. Jaspersen?" Abler stops short, respectful of whatever sense of territoriality Jaspersen may feel about his driveway and Abler's unin-vited presence.

Jaspersen just keeps on soaping, ignoring him.

Abler tries again. "How's Jimmy? Do you mind if I speak with him?"

"We had that conversation, if memory serves." Bob Jaspersen dunks sponge in bucket, splattering suds.

Abler's not so easy to deter. "Yes, I do remember, but I'm not sure you understood—"

"Maybe *you* didn't. We can't have medical records now. I told you. And like you said, he could talk any time. What's there for him to say, anyway? For anyone?"

Abler blinks at him a beat. "Everything. He could help Anne with what she's going through. They were friends. And there's no medical record that needs to go to your insurance, like I said—"

"Until someone makes a mistake." Jaspersen has picked up the hose and half-turned toward Abler. "Then we can all blame somebody else, and my family'll have no insurance. My wife tell you to come here?"

The hose spatters the drive near Abler's feet, wetting his shoes. He doesn't step back.

"No. I'm concerned about Jimmy, that's all."

Jaspersen glares at Abler. "Anybody in this goddamned world concerned about my other, Michael? W.I.A., Khafji, Iraq, dead a half year later in the Detroit VA? What about him? He's not talking a blue streak either now, is he?"

Abler stands there speechless for a long beat, as the likely heartbreaking dynamics of this family present themselves with sudden clarity. What he offers is more than a guess. "I'm sure Jimmy misses him, too. Just like you."

Jaspersen draws a sharp breath and his eyes water, like he's been slapped, but his face hardens again, instantly. He hoists his bucket and hose and walks back to the house, where he twists off the spigot. And then he continues with his bucket into his cluttered dim garage, and turns and looks impassively at Abler. He presses a button on the wall, and the garage door shudders and groans as it lowers itself, closing between the two men.

❦

Jimmy knows his silence is a path that no matter how it winds will end best in somebody official's office, sooner or later, that guy from the hospital's, or some new guy's, or worst, with him cornered in a stand-off with himself as hostage, cop-drama style, with patrol cars pulled up this way and that and grim officers cowering behind the opened doors with megaphones and pistols, and SWAT sharpshooters taking up position on nearby rooftops and waving away the news helicopters circling like big angry bees.

When it's all over, of course, neighbors will shake their heads and speculate, and express shock and sadness. Classmates will recall. But Jimmy only wants to know, what will Anne do, will she be glad, finally, when he's shut up for good?

Jimmy suffers these endless hours with his bedroom's fake-wood venetian blinds drawn, lights dimmed, lying on his bed with his fore-arm over his eyes, rising only to smile weakly and nod thanks to his mom when she knocks softly and carries in trays of tomato soup and grilled cheese sandwiches. He shakes his head at the same questions, over and over. "Do you want to watch a little TV?" "Would you like me to pick you up a movie at Blockbuster?" "Can I get you some-thing else to eat, honey?" "Have you had any e-mails from your friends?" These are all easy, harmless, the same, like another line in another scene of another episode of a repeat TV show whose sound he can turn off without missing a thing.

Meanwhile, he knows his command decisions will eventually place him in a position when and where important adults will hold confer-ences, shrinks and teachers and cops, and tears will definitely be cried. But not now, not soon, not so long as he can still shake his head and moan and open himself up just enough to let his realest fear shine out from his wide rolling eyes at the question his mother will not likely ever ask again, "Do you want to go and talk to that man from the hospital?"

From the yard comes soft idle whistling and muffled footsteps. Jimmy sits up to pry a slot between two blinds and peer out to watch his dad cross a weedy patch of yard to the shed, where he opens a rusty hanging padlock with a key, which he returns to his jeans pocket. Whistling tunelessly, his dad opens the shed and pulls out a folding chair, and a long thin object wrapped in a blanket. He tenderly unwraps it: his long-bolt hunting rifle.

Jimmy holds his breath as his dad unfolds the chair, lights his cigarette and sits, holding the rifle in one hand, pulling a rag from his jacket pocket with the other. Tenderly, his dad cradles the weapon in his lap, cleaning it while he smokes, pausing now and again to tamp his ashes onto the muddy ground.

✍

Out of the busy noise and color of the crowded Hunt Landing High School hallway, Howard surprises Anne, with his bony hawklike face, pushing in next to her, raising an eyebrow. "You okay?"

With her heartbeat pounding and her ears suddenly hot, she nods, not gratefully but longingly and afraid because the color of his eyes is so green and the hair that hangs over his forehead so straight and sand-colored and perfect where it falls.

He leans in closer, smelling of cigarettes and Altoids. "Me and Billy made first string. There's a party at Mitch's. This time I might ask you. I really might. If you wanna go."

She almost shakes her head at him, to say no, which is what she almost really means, anyway, but she feels eyes looking at her, wondering faces turned toward her, can almost hear the voices that have barely just begun to talk, about her.

Howard smirks and disappears into the crowd.

Laraby ∿

Driving home at shift's end, Laraby doesn't want to remember Sam's confused face the last time he was conscious, the monitor alarm blaring, and then the blood gas signal joining in, harmonizing at a perfect third higher, Laraby has noticed, apropos of nothing, which is exactly what all these instruments eventually report sooner or later anyway, in the end.

He takes an extra turn around the neighborhood, admiring the Tudor and Normandy facades of the big solid houses of this older established Hunt Landing tract. Houses of good stone, he thinks, though mortgaged probably up the ying-yang as they say, because anyone not living under a rock knows interest rates are so low, it's like borrowing money for nothing. If you can't beat the six and a half percent that money costs with ROI then we're all going to hell in a handbasket anyway, so may as well do it with your mattress lumpy with cash. Even the estate planners are pushing borrowed dollars now, not that you can take any with, but the equation works for your survivors if you die, or rather, when.

He passes a neighbor standing hunched against the cold, coaxing the family dog with clucks and murmurs. Sad to see dog owners now, with their little plastic bags and scoops and sheepish smiles. It's all about cleanliness and safety these days. Kids riding tricycles are chin-strapped into Styrofoam helmets; people at work in surgical masks because they "feel a tickle." Will anyone live longer because of any of it? Not if he can help it, apparently.

Laraby turns into his driveway and shuts the engine off, letting the moments of quiet wash over him; the cold creeps in quickly, clouding his breath, making the engine block faintly *tick tick* again as its precision machine–tooled alloys contract, or as an aerodynamic body panel shrinks infinitesimally against a tiny rivet or weld.

Evening begins while he sits here, immobile, his seat reclined so he can stare out the windshield at the eaves over his garage and the darkening sky beyond, broken by the darker shapeless tops of trees. He deconstructs the silence and realizes that within it he barely hears faint squirrel chatter, the hush of his own exhalations, the drone of a small airplane, the muffled murmuring of a neighbor's television, sounds of ordinary extraordinary life, existing in a moment which is but one in a multitude of others that will always contain other sounds, of other lives, not his own. Significance slips away in these formulations, and by way of restoring it, as one must, Laraby wants so badly and earnestly to believe in the import of human effort. But how can he when his best efforts create or prevent nothing? Why not remain immobile in his car; why move when every move perpetuates his fraudulent receipt of the world's regard?

A decision begins, a glimmer of intention in a carefully unacknowledged area of thought, which lifts his hand to pull the keys from the ignition and opens his door with the other and takes him up the spot-lit walkway, slowly but resolutely home.

Laraby smiles vaguely at Jan's exuberance for the months ahead, their half-constructed house and her near-finalized plans for it. For her, these blueprints describe an actual path around dead ends and looming hazards to a beautiful and untroubled outcome, but as they hover over her drafting table, Laraby feels lost, unable to discern the point of all the pale blue lines and arrows, dimensions and specs.

Jan points. "So, maybe a wainscoting effect here?"

Laraby blinks. "Wainscoting?"

Jan laughs gently, without lifting her eyes from the blueprints. "Good thing you heal the sick."

Laraby stares at her now, a look of fear and longing and of a maudlin urge to always remember her this way, beautiful and happy in the dim light, gazing so purposefully at their future. He takes in the moment, significant in its sheer unremarkable ordinariness; they are simply here, husband and wife in their suburban home, already so accustomed as to often attend to each other out of habit, a smile or touch or word become automatic. Laraby understands that taking each other's love for granted can signify the safest haven of all, a simple certainty missing from and aspired to by many marriages, and he imagines his knowledge of her love should be like a secret he has learned and memorized, from a whisper intended only and forever for himself alone.

She feels his gaze, as always, and sends him her quick smile.

Laraby has resolved to ask again, "Any headaches? Since the last?"

She shakes her head and says girlishly, "Uh-uh." And focuses again on her plans.

In jeans and bulky cardigan over a T-shirt, again Laraby slips quietly into his study to lift his bag into his lap, again fondly touching the winged staff of Hermès insignia he loves, that brings his father and his own childhood back, wondering at the mythic grace and skill and kindness of a man blessed with unique abilities to give and save life. His mother's eyes, the eyes of so many women, had followed his father across so many rooms, with dark pupils wide as if to swallow more of his light, with small fond smiles ready to brighten should he turn with the slightest word or glance.

Laraby unzips the bag and pulls out two sample packets bound by a rubber band. He separates them and stares down at both packages, knowing their effects and contraindications by heart. One is Molodil, for treatment of migraine, but which may cause vascular constriction. The other is Statrophine, of course, for treatment of vascular constriction, but which inversely may cause migraine. A packet in each hand, he holds them up, feeling their weight, like he's holding power.

Exiting, Laraby hesitates with the heavy glass door against one hand and his "Joe-to-Go" in the other to glance back, and then the glass throws a square of reflection, a flash of tan, walls and booths and whitish light from the big windows inside as he lets go and moves on and away into the day he brought mercy or solace to no one.

He pulls out the small liquid sample, a plastic vial of Statrophine, to verify once more the contraindications in fine print, right there on the little cardboard box, "may cause migraine."

Laraby unwraps a syringe and punctures the sterile seal on the Statro with the needle tip. In the light of his desk lamp, he draws the fluid into the chamber, viscous and gleaming.

Carla ⁓

Carla's studio apartment has become a little cluttered, she knows, with a few waiting chores—unemptied trash, backed-up laundry, strewn *People* and *Us* magazines, and a few glasses and dishes scattered here and there that she knows she will get to, of course, when she finds the energy to climb out of her unmade futon and face the mind-numbing uselessness of all this unending housekeeping busywork that will only have to be done all over again in a day or two.

She thinks of maybe calling Jenn, but still can't believe that Jenn called her looking for money after what happened, so she reaches for the remote control but then sets it back down, and then yanks it up and flings it across the room to clatter against the wall by Davy's bassinet and fall with a thud onto the old worn pea-green carpeting that could use a vacuuming, too, while she's not at it.

She tilts her head back to see the water stain like a dim comma on the ceiling, which may have spread slowly over the weeks, she can't be sure, through the pebbly cottage-cheese spray-on stuff, probably full of asbestos reawakened by the dampness, or maybe even mold, it's everywhere now, and dangerous and capable of causing serious long-term illness.

Voices reach her from outside now, fading, a girl's laugh like a short flat melody, cut off by a slamming door. The wall heater clicks on, sighing. A drop of water trembles from the end of the kitchen tap and lets go, falling into a pot of water greasy with orange scum from last night's Buon Giorno marinara sauce. There's a sudden faint buzzing from somewhere, an oddly electrical sound, or from an insect, which just as quickly disappears into other small sounds, refrigerator hum, the whine of trucks off the far interstate, her own fingers scratching idly at the wrinkled thighs of her sweatpants.

She drops her forearm over her eyes against the light from the lamp she's too tired to reach over and turn off, and sighs a big theatrical sigh as she sneaks a hand beneath the sheets to trail her fingers across her belly and lower still to the edge of the short curled hairs between her legs. What would his first touch be like, a gentle question probably, since a doctor and someone kind would know enough to sort of ask and listen for an answer, not like most.

As she closes her eyes and begins the perfect practiced touch of her middle finger rubbing in a tiny circle, patches of color bloom behind her shut lids, shapeless shifting pastels that refuse to resolve into anything to aid her motion, which she quickens out of desperation to finish before she can think that it may be useless and it becomes just that. And of course too soon she feels the faint sting of rawness there, and a race between pleasure and pain begins that neither wins because she quits with a sound between a laugh and a sob, and rolls over on her stomach and pulls her knees up under her, burying her face in her musty pillow.

She holds this pose until a thought occurs and fades and returns, as less a thought than the memory of an idea, that has her rolling onto her back and wincing up at the ceiling, and then rolling to reach into a night table drawer for her old fringed rawhide purse, long unused. She yanks it out and overturns it, spilling it all onto the sheet beside her. The detritus of her past life scatters out, change, a "triple A" battery, an envelope of rubber bands, a paper clip, a rolled matchbook cover, a hair scrunchy. A blue foil square, with a condom inside.

Charlie ❦

To Charlie, the gray five-thousand-dollar chip has until now existed only in James Bond movies, where Pierce Brosnan dares some urbane tuxedoed European nemesis at baccarat. Tonight twenty of these chips and change constitute the remainder of his and Kathy's life savings, withdrawn by electronic wire transfer, now nestled in the smooth wooden groove of a Powatan Thunderbird Gaming Casino craps table rail.

New shooter, new stake, new luck; everything is new again, the come-out roll of come-out rolls about to reshuffle the potential of all possibilities his way again. Why not, isn't this how it really happens, after all? Luck touches us in waves, a rhythm we need only learn to ride, dancer to the dance, singer to the gorgeous song sung by a universe of parallel worlds, all stretching off in a row like the infinite reflections in a hall of mirrors, arranged by probability.

In his new but ill-fitting rapper-"designed" jogging suit, hair awry, Charlie lays four of these precious pink chips on the pass line. The crowd swarming around him now is smaller; a few low-rollers in for a midweek night of slots or a dozen hands of dollar blackjack, trios of laughing middle-aged gals detoured from their insurance or escrow offices, and a few new out-of-staters just discovering this big loud man with his winks and showy laughter and thousands. The consensus of rumor has him pegged as the beneficiary of some enormous life-changing good luck, a sudden lottery winner or heir, but the bunch that has followed him from cashier's cage to craps table seems free of jealousy and untouched by schadenfreude, adopting him as a sort of wacky mascot, a symbol of good fortune and the undying hope that any of us may at any moment be touched by it.

Oscar the Stickman is back on shift, and everybody's friend Charlie winks and opines, "Vic's day off, huh?"

Oscar looks away; barely moving his mouth, he intones like a ventriloquist, "New shooter, new shooter. Coming . . . out!"

Charlie reaches down to the felt to touch the red, polished, razor-edged regulation three-quarter-inch dice Oscar has shoved his way with his stick, 3 and 4 showing. Charlie shuts his eyes for the briefest of seconds as he gathers them up in his fingers, loving their cool solid heft, and the dull clicking sound they make when he snaps them together in his palm.

The murmuring of the crowd gaps as a hush of expectation takes hold and folks lean forward to crane their necks to watch, and Charlie flicks his wrist upward in a trusting high-pop fling of the dice from his fingers into the stunned air, spinning and flashing.

A tiny muffled clatter sounds as the dice land and roll once to rest against the far wall, and there's a momentarily unreadable gasp from the crowd that Charlie does not need to read, because already he knows that the first come-out roll of the night means nothing.

"Craps, two craps. Line down, pay the field, pay the field."

When it seems evening has unaccountably arrived, Charlie holds up his last four five-hundred-dollar purple chips from his dwindling stake. Drunk again, beyond exhaustion, he eyes the stone-faced table crew and intones, "Four three, five two, six one. Any of the above, please. Or the reverse. For the lucky man, for I am a lucky man. Thank you very much."

He knows bad luck is a pestilence, like a cloud of tiny flying creatures that will blot out the light from above, but ultimately pass; luck will return to him, but he must be there when it happens, dice in hand, money spread on the table, a rod to conduct the lightning when it strikes, splitting the air between sky and earth. And so he continues on, wishing he could stop the merciless scourging, staunch the hemorrhaging, somehow slow the terrible painful pace of loss.

The last of his fans have turned pitying, shaking their heads, eyes rolling in dismay. Everyone suddenly knows better than this big loud guy who yesterday could do no wrong.

A horse-faced woman across the table has her head thrown back, laughing, all dark fillings against pale teeth and red gums and twitching tongue and Charlie stares at her transfixed as the sound of her laughter disappears in the *csssshhhh* of coins clattering into a slot machine tray.

Ice clatters into a jumbo soft drink cup.

Charlie slowly and carefully lifts his gaze from a wafflelike print of iced tea on the dry linoleum between his table and Hank Carline's body.

Gssssshhhh! *From behind him, Charlie watches the gunman blast root beer from the drink dispenser into his jumbo cup of ice. And then*

the man hesitates, and presses his cup beneath the Diet Coke dispenser
for a final blast, achieving his optimum personal mix.

Suddenly, from elsewhere there's quick, softly muffled impacts, a
flurry of footsteps. The gunman spins toward the kitchen, jerks his gun
up and BLAMM! BLAMM! *Two shots ring out as he fires. And then*
*another—*BLAMM!—*off in another direction.*

❦

Kathy's phone rings with that chirpy chimey sound, one of eight you
can choose with this new digital cordless multi-handset unit Charlie
brought home and hooked up and then gave up on with a goofy shrug
when it wouldn't cooperate with their fax machine. Kathy stirs and
then sits bolt upright, yanking it off her nightstand, fumbling for the
talk button.

"Hello?" Her voice is thick from sleep. She blinks at her alarm
clock and rubs a hand over her face, still half-drugged by exhaustion,
surprised she has fallen asleep so early.

On the other end there's a softly drawn-out inhalation, and then a
silence that can only be Charlie's silence, because who else, and because Kathy knows by heart the timbre of that quiet uptake of breath
that drops from faintness into inaudibility and begins again, rising
above the digital emptiness.

Kathy tries again. "Hello?" And then, in an awed desperate whisper, "Charlie?"

There's tiny click on the other end, and Kathy sits there in bed, listening to the dial tone of the lost connection, like a nerve impulse
from a phantom limb, a chord of calibrated empty noise over the
miles of wire between her aching hopeful self and no one at all.

moths ~

The Children ∼

In the dark hall that passes the wide arched entryway to the living room, Jimmy steps silently, listening for any moves within, though with the TV up as loud as it is, he's unlikely to ever hear his father climbing out of his Barcalounger and turning to possibly spot him. Flickering light and the noise of explosions fill the little room, panicky sound and motion that bounces off the fake-pine paneling and makes Jimmy wince as he moves quickly past, unseen.

The next doorway is the kitchen, where even this late his mom stands at the sink, her back to him, washing or rinsing, scouring or wiping, the tap hissing and spattering. Her face is only just turning as he hurries past and he decides not to think about whether or not she has seen him, and just continue on soundlessly, now or never, like a covert mission past the last waypoint. He doesn't even pause at his parents' bedroom door, but glides straight in, checking flank positions, eyes darting side to side, over their white particleboard dresser and their futon and leatherette ottoman until he sees what he's looking for—his father's totally eighties acid-washed old Lee jeans, carelessly folded and laid at the foot of their queen-sized bed.

He extends his hand into the space between, reaching to touch the worn cloth of these jeans and start to pull them closer.

"Honey, are you looking for me?" His mother is there in the doorway, smiling faintly, her question innocent of all suspicion, of his trembling hand yanked back as if burned as he turns to nod, wide-eyed.

"Can I fix you something? You barely touched your dinner."

He nods again, and her look is so loving that guilt and shame make his ears burn and his face flush as he looks everywhere but at her.

"Come on, then." She smiles and turns and he takes a last look back at his dad's jeans so far out of reach there on the bed, and then follows her out to the kitchen for another bowl of tomato soup and a grilled cheese sandwich he doesn't want, that in fact make him feel like laughing out loud and at the same time crying because it's so sad that these dishes—safe, comfortable, dependable—are so completely the opposite of how the world really is and will always be.

From the living room, the sound of television laughter pauses and returns in a rhythm like distant surf as he stands again in his mom and dad's room, an hour later, having crept along past the row of open doorways down the hall from his own, soundlessly and quickly. There are PlayStation "Medal of Honor" missions where you die if you don't sneak past, stealth-mode, because the opposing force is overwhelming, at least until you procure superior ordnance.

Jimmy hesitates at the dresser, unwilling to paw through these drawers and leave a sign of his searching, how dumb would that be, and besides, his mom or dad could walk in at any moment and interdict. He crosses to their closet in small careful steps and gingerly slides the mirror door on its balky track.

His father's jeans hang there, faded and wrinkled at the back of the knees, on a bolt hook a few inches inside the jamb. Jimmy slips a hand inside a front pocket and grimaces in frustration: it's empty. But when he checks the other, his hand emerges with what he seeks: shining dully, the small padlock key.

❦

Anne's eye is bloodshot through, like glaze with red jagged crazing from the hours of dry forced-air heat blasting into her bedroom, as she has lain awake in her bed, staring upward, barely blinking. Now her hand shakes as she applies Midnight Black Maybelline liner to the edges of her eyelids, extending it outward a tiny extra bit toward her temples, Cleopatra or Brit sixties style, like she saw in an *Allure* magazine, on a singer/actress whose songs Anne doesn't love but who is really gorgeous and goes out with black rappers to all the big movie premieres and record release parties and talks in interviews like a surfer chick/black homegirl combined, saying "down with that" and "what's poppin'?" but also "dude" and "like."

Anne's mom has gone to her widowed women's support group at the YWCA; she had knocked on Anne's bedroom door and reminded Anne she was leaving, already late in fact, and to reheat last night's leftovers, she'd be back in a few hours. Anne hurries, applying dark lipstick now, blotting it with a tissue in her unsteady hand, knowing these few hours ahead of her will clinch the shift in her standing; it will change the looks on the faces that still swivel to gawk at her in the halls and in homeroom, create a seat for her at the quad squad lunch table, and admit her into a state of at least outward belonging to these shallower girls, who've lived silly lives sheltered from the truth of tragedy. They don't understand, will never, how it reveals itself afterward, in the absence of so many little small ordinary moments, like the way somebody now gone once made you giggle, or the time you watched them through a window and they didn't know it, and they sang or picked the inside of their ear with a housekey.

Suddenly the vague light above and behind her seems to flicker with a faint shadow, but she turns to see nothing but the empty doorway to the hall and the phone stand and the Monet *Waterlilies* print her mom bought mail order to match the paint scheme there.

She turns back to the mirror to finish her lipstick. She has slipped on a tube top her mom doesn't know she bought months ago at Wet Seal in the mall; the tight-ribbed fabric bumps and bunches around her cheap bra, but she yanks a jean jacket over it and buttons the bottom button. The jean jacket and tube top are both short enough to afford glimpses of her pale, flat belly over her Gap jeans, which are not real low-risers so that her pelvic bones stick out like some sluttier girls wear, but are low enough to still be in, and semi-flared. She looks a little skinny and too white even to herself, but in the magazines she buys and on television and in the halls of her school everyone's belly seems to be seen, and hers at least isn't loose and jiggly and doesn't plump out above the waistband like so many do.

With a dab of Garnier Fructis mousse worked into her fine thin hair it hangs in sticky clumps as if it's dirty, and she has lined her lips a little bigger than they are, another magazine tip, for the sort of just-awakened tousled look, except for her too-small eyes and her still-too-thin lips and fleshy nose she's covered in base so the pores don't look so big. Blush along her cheeks almost creates the "cheekbone shadow" that she wishes she had more of naturally, who doesn't, but the wide flat planes of her face at least save her from the round un-formed look of a preteen girl or a really sad case "late bloomer." She sucks in her cheeks and turns half-sideways to the mirror, dipping her head slightly and raising her gaze to consider herself as she might a new girl in school or a stranger from another school at the mall or the movies, midpopular, pretty much blending, not a prude but not a CT.

Tonight her furtive way takes her down half a dark street of other homes, past that barking dog driving everyone nuts and under windows lit from within by blue television light, battered by winter moths, through the Hartnell's backyard into the Simonsen's with its rusted Weber grill and overflowing recycling bin.

At Mitch's, reddened eyes slide toward her and away as Anne steps into this suburban living room pounding with rap music and filled with shouting, laughing high school kids standing, dancing, sitting on the floor, each with a joint, cigarette, or beer or combination thereof. Her made-up face is too white, and her low jeans and tight tube top and jean jacket have only made her look gawky, put together with pieces that don't quite fit.

"Howard totally said you wouldn't come." It's Traci, shouting over the music into Anne's ear. Anne turns to face her and Howard, who nods at her with raised eyebrows, doing an impression of being impressed. He trades smirks with host Mitch, a diminutive stoner wannabe with a peach-fuzz goatee.

Anne swallows back her panic and fixes Howard's eyes with her boldest gaze, as she reaches down and unbuttons her jean jacket.

She keeps a wry little smile fixed on her face as Howard leads her upstairs, where cheap rock paraphernalia clutters Mitch's bedroom: posters, an electric guitar, and a little Pig Nose amplifier surround the single unmade daybed, where they lie down together, fully clothed.

Howard grinds himself into her, whispering, "Touch it again. Come on." He grabs her hand in his, moving it lower to where he is hard to bursting, a tiny spot of wetness dark through his pale jeans.

Anne's eyes are shut, but nothing sexual stirs in her to match his urgency. If not for the abstract calculation of benefit to her reputation, she would twist her hand out of his sweaty grasp once and for all, because the nervous little crush she had on this conceited jerk has disappeared beneath the enormity of her larger task, to protect the real truth of a human life forever.

Anne's eyes remain shut as if sealed, as if opening them and admitting the bright light of this suburban teenager's bedroom will open the eye of God on her and her shame and guilt, the ugly hidden things she cannot allow light to touch. Downstairs the rap has changed to rock and the pounding bass and drums of old U2 surge up through the floor and walls with the faint words she has almost forgotten, "someone you could lend a hand in return for grace, it's a beautiful day," whatever that means, not that it matters anyway, because Howard has her hand trapped so tightly in his.

Under the table, Anne Hagen's hand holds her father's in a white-knuckle grip. The cuff of his Red Carpet Realty jacket brushes her wrist as she stares out at the pair of tan suede shoes that slide into a stance, shoulder-width apart, toes pointed vaguely at her and Jimmy Jaspersen faintly breathing there beside her.

BLAMM! *At the sound of a gunshot, her dad's hand jerks uncontrollably, like some kind of frightened animal and not something attached to someone sitting there.*

Anne's eyes spring open. She twists and yanks her hand from Howard's grip and flees, whimpering.

Horror at her own loathsomeness sends her feet plunging down the carpeted stairs and through the living room crowded with teenagers, and past even Lori Carline suddenly there, of course, comember of the dead dad club, on deck for the big sympathy come-on. Lori turns dull surprised eyes on Anne as she rushes by and past them all, she is past them all, who betray and belittle one another behind their backs by the minute but never truly glimpse their own pathetic worthlessness.

Anne's blundering way home takes her through the same yards and down the darkened half-street past houses to her own, where she slips inside, and where the face that looks back at her from the bathroom mirror is someone else's, all caked cheap makeup, darting bloodshot eyes, lipsticked mouth like a narrow gash, the clown face of a poser and a total loser. She blasts scalding water into the sink as she scrubs off her eyeliner and blush, breathlessly, frantically, until her face is pink. A thought slows her, and she stares at herself, only now seeing it, what must be done, once and for all.

Anne finds the flashlight in the kitchen junk drawer, and slips back outside with it. With a gnarled stick of deadwood from the woodpile, she batters the side of a wire pigeon coop. The bird within beats at the air, its own blind fear smashing it against the side of the coop again and again until it finds the open doorway and finally bursts through. Anne stands there, watching the shadow flee zigzagging away into darkness.

She opens the next coop, and the bird inside regards her with its black red eyes that are both frightening and fearful, because they have come from that unnameable day to torment her like the Furies themselves. These are the dark shapes flickering at the edge of her vision. These are the shadows flitting across the sunlit ground or even at night in other shadows that have no origin when she turns to look, and this is how she will send them to other towns of other homes and people to remind them of their own secret deepest sins, that they may seek and maybe find forgiveness, because the first step is admitting you have a problem.

She lifts the stick and smashes against the side of the coop, and again, shutting her eyes, swinging blindly.

Laraby ~

Downstairs at their big stainless Wolf range, Laraby sautés chicken breasts with olive oil, garlic, and sun-dried tomatoes in a copper-clad pan. Jan paces their combination great/dining room, on the phone, and as she crosses in and out of his view past the doorway he hears her soft voice patiently insisting, "No, no, the plumbing contractor is due to start in *April . . .*"

Laraby pauses to check the chicken breasts as always, with a paring knife cutting a deep but tiny slit in the crisping skin to see if the juices run clear. He removes the pieces from the sizzling pan, sets them on a platter, and then he moves out of Jan's possible sight-line.

His hands are sure and steady as he pulls the syringe of Statrophine from his pocket, eases off the plastic cap, carefully injects a chicken breast, and another, and plates them. And then he replaces the cap on the syringe and quickly pockets it again, moving back toward the center of the counter workspace, his *mis-en-place*. He plates another chicken breast, and then sprinkles a pinch of sea salt, thyme, and a soupçon of sage over all.

Over dinner, Laraby can retain nothing of Jan's conversation; his mind is incapable of absorbing or holding a thought as he watches his wife sip her wine, talking animatedly, tucking into a piece of the chicken on her plate. Sounds have not ceased; they have become meaningless insubstantial confetti, but for his own blood roaring in his veins as his heart beats hard, fearfully, mercilessly, against the urge to throw himself across the table and fling her dish away and against the urge to nod instead and smile and watch her, gauging her intake with quick careful glances.

Jan pauses, her fork in midair with a neatly cut slice of chicken breast glistening on its tines, as she speculates about the coming months, and the months after those. "So maybe we could delay painting the spare bedroom until we decide if this is going to be the year—"

Tonight when the pain begins behind her eyes, taking root in earnest, it sends her clawing once again through her medicine cabinet.

Laraby appears in the doorway. "Your head again?"

Jan stops and nods, biting her lip.

Laraby knows this is a brand-new pain, a confident throb, hinting at reserves of strength it can and will bring to bear as the minutes crawl by more and more slowly, until time itself threatens to stop in a crescendo of white noise. He's had his own bouts of migraine, back in med school, when sleep deprivation and too much refined sugar–filled food sent his blood sugar levels spiraling and his blood pounding like a hammer behind his eyes.

"Thought so. Here." He hands her two pills he has already taken from a Molodil sample package.

Her hand trembles as she slips them into her mouth. She tilts her head forward to stretch the vertebrae in her neck, wincing.

He turns the corners of his lips down, fondly pretending to scold, "You tell me right away next time, young lady. No secrets."

"As if you don't have enough patients." She smiles weakly at him, a look that turns worried. "You think something's up with me?"

"Postdesign, prepermit home-building anxiety." He lowers the light dimmer switch and caresses the back of her neck, gently rubbing. "Causes dilated blood vessels—headache. I've given you something to constrict the vessels. A vasoconstrictor. Sublingual, same as before."

Trying to make light: "Ohhh, are you playing doctor with me?"

He winks and starts to turn away, but she grabs his face and gives him a kiss. "My brilliant beautiful husband. Of whom I am proud." She puts her arms around him and pulls him close. "Thank you."

He shuts his eyes, exhaling, almost shuddering, as her praise hits him like a drug, a sweet joyous warmth rising up and spreading from within.

In the long late hours of the evening, beneath the covers of their bed, Jan moves gently over her husband, kissing him softly, then hungrily. Eyes shut, Laraby clings, and again it's her sheer physical need of him that strengthens his own of her, which lately has been so far from love, which has been too long a wide dark tide of yearning he has fought against and refused to let carry him, out of fear it will leave him stranded.

Charlie ~

Setbacks happen on the way to greatness, the road to success is paved with potholes, if it was so easy everyone would be rich: Charlie knows these are not mere platitudes but figurative expressions of deepest wisdom earnestly believed by those who have been there and done that, who have lived and loved, who have had the courage and conviction to risk it all one hundred and ten percent, putting their money where their mouth is.

He laughs out loud, his step quick and the catbird smile on as he strolls past the dice table this time, catching the eye of Vic the Stick, who gives a tiny sideways nod in the direction Charlie already knows to go, where another chance at achieving his ultimate good luck awaits.

As Charlie swings through the casino men's room door into the heavy hush of the mirror and faux marble and gold-accented room, he channels some television version of a Las Vegas hustler on the move and in the know, with tiny twitches to some syncopated inner rhythm, all winks and snapped fingers and shot cuffs.

Angelo, the little Filipino attendant, is there, slipping a little Spanish paperback into his red jacket pocket and standing with a somber nod and a tiny "at your service" bow.

A step behind Charlie, one of the security guards enters, one he's seen all week. They have all regarded him warily, Charlie knows and understands, since they are finely attuned to anything or anyone out of the very lucrative ordinary everyday action of this place. Charlie has been a borderline case, attracting a crowd of people gawking in dumb amazement and finally pity instead of tossing their change into quarter slots or playing dollar blackjack until they hit their downside limits. This guard looms as tall as an NBA forward, with sleeves too short and a smudged mark like a bruise on his jaw. His crew cut's buzzed short enough for scalp to show through, spotted with angry patches of eczema.

Charlie winces into the mirror, touching the Band-Aids over his graze-wound, sure to be a conversation-starter or icebreaker, as it were. The guard steps up to the next sink and washes his hands, and indicates Charlie's forehead with a sideways nod, everyone nods at everything. "Nasty."

Charlie lifts an eyebrow and points a thumb at himself. "But I won the bet."

The guard must have some piece of the vig, because he moves it right along: "And you figure it's just a matter of time before you win another, right?"

"With a little help from my friends." It's prime Kojak by way of the Beatles, ghosts of the Rat Pack gone to the grave, a hip rejoinder of jazzy repartee between two seriously with-it cats.

The guard snorts. "From your friends. Talk to the hotel, they'll take a marker."

"They're already my friends."

The guard smirks like a nightclub comic at a heckler. "Where you from?"

Charlie presses: "Why? Are you my friend?"

Now the guard does a prissy little pout of distaste. "Sorry, not me. And the ones who may be willing to stake you? They're not your friends either. The vig is thirty plus, depending on collateral, and the late penalties could make you older than your years. You're staying here?"

"Second-floor, blue suite. You drop enough—"

"You get some touch, they comp you, yeah. But not my friends, understood?"

"Understood. I just need twenty-five—"

The guard shakes his head at Charlie, like he's buying on the street and holding up bills like a rube. "Tell them about it, okay?"

Standing before his Archenault Driver Training Taurus, under the Powatan parking lot arc lights, to Charlie the lips of these two bagmen look purple and their faces sickly pale. They are a sad Mutt and Jeff, an older-looking tall guy in a long belted raincoat and a Hawaiian shirt, and a short fat one in a jogging suit not unlike Charlie's, though without the rapper-label pedigree.

Protocol demands a short and fact-filled conversation, in which Charlie agrees to the rules as they are explained in a heavy Boston accent by Mr. Tall, with oddly formal syntax, "This is a loan for thirty-six hours for thirty percent vigorish. We will find you at the end of said period and expect full repayment, and vig, in exchange for return of collateral and a pass. Questions?"

Charlie shakes his head, trying not to look wide-eyed at these two, wondering if they're "packing" or "strapped."

Leisure Suit gives a little nod at Charlie, and produces a wrinkled envelope bulging with bills.

Charlie hands him his car keys.

Two Bombay gin and tonics later, in the Powatan Pow-wow Lounge, Charlie pulls a crisp C note from the wrinkled envelope he holds in his lap and pays "Thad!" the bartender, who clears Charlie's glass and sets down a tall fresh one.

A purposeful choreography ensues: the bartender moves away down the bar, wiping a shot glass, as a woman comes up and slips onto the stool beside Charlie. Late thirties, in jeans and pastel heels, bangle bracelets and cleavage, she makes a show of looking around with a big glad smile, as if she has never been here before and is deliciously thrilled at the privilege.

Charlie eyes her thin face, her wide nose and garish lipstick. He imitates an elaborate courtly bow.

She rolls her eyes, but then she laughs and nods at Charlie's tray of chips, because everyone nods at everything. "Feelin' lucky, huh?"

Rhyming again. "Come and gone, off and on."

She smiles at him, a crooked uptick at the corners of her lips. "I've been known to change one to the other. And that's a sure thing, sweetheart."

In his nautical-themed motel room, Charlie lies back on the big king bed, feet flat on the floor, head raised, singing drunkenly to this hooker who kneels between his knees. "Luck be a lady tonight . . ."

She giggles, a sound that turns muffled.

He struggles a little, weakly, but her hand on his chest presses him back. His eyes close against the too-bright night table lamp they have left on, and the idea of the sexual urge he can almost feel, that he wishes he could feel, dissipates instead beneath his greater need, to prove his sole connection, his unique and solitary whisper, from his lips to God's ear.

Sweat dampens Charlie's hairline as he concentrates, chanting softly in a desperate whispered mantra: "Lucky lucky lucky lucky . . ."

"Hey! Hello up there? Anything workin' for ya?" The hooker between his knees glances up, humor and suspicion vying. Charlie just keeps on, eyes closed, muttering: "Lucky lucky lucky lucky . . ." until the word loses any meaning at all and becomes a sound he must repeat in order to prevent some massive calamity, perhaps even the destruction of the entire known world.

Her judgment reaches him, finally, a single spat-out word, ". . . freak." Charlie remains on the bed, eyes resolutely shut, muttering, hearing her footsteps and the rustle of bills, and, "Just what's mine. See?"

Bills float down around him, like a brief blizzard of good fortune.

The door slams, echoing like a gunshot.

Charlie's eyes snap open, wide with fright as he lies there gasping.

Carla ～

In her blue dress, Carla bends to drape a red kerchief over her table lamp, and light a few vanilla-scented candles she has set out with a few magazines on her coffee table. The small flames and reddish glow warm the room, but dimly enough that the carpet's stained blotches are indiscernible, and with the days' worth of clutter stuffed into her closet and under her sofa and the sink of her little Pullman kitchen, the apartment feels almost sparse in a hip, urban interior-design way, almost inviting. She has a CD of Mariah Carey in the little boombox she bought at a yard sale last year, and the high showy trills of this neighborhood girl made good reassure her; she has achieved it all, and never once traded her Jersey accent for some phony finicky fake British pronunciations like Madonna or even that old black blues singer they made the movie about, Tina Turner.

Under her armpits she feels a trickle, or thinks she does, of perspiration, but when she checks she's dry there and her fingers carry the slight odor of her Mennen Lady speed stick. She breathes into her palm and sniffs it to see if her breath has gone bad, which with the bloated sourness she feels in her stomach from the cruddy fast food she's been bingeing on, it could be and wouldn't surprise her.

He will bring Liebfraumilch or Blue Nun or Mateus or whatever that white wine from Europe was that he liked, but she doesn't want him smoking those clove cigarettes around Davy, really. He did have a cool kind of stoner laugh with one eyebrow up, and even though he turned out not to be enrolled at the JC after all, plenty at Closkey's weren't, and they knew some of the same people, Sharon and Doug who since moved to California, and Jenn's boyfriend Scott, and he also definitely had opinions about movies and world politics, when plenty couldn't be bothered to think twice about anything. He played some drums, too, or bass maybe it was, and his band had made a demo in Detroit, was the rumor, and roofing was a low-stress way to work outdoors until they heard back. Besides, face it, not everyone can be rich and save lives for a living and still be sweet and a little shy, or have calm blue-gray eyes that secretly seem sad.

Sharp knocking on her door startles her, though she has been waiting for it for what seems like hours. She swings it open fast to stop the noise so it won't wake Davy, though he has slept a different sleep all day, deeper and motionless, snoring as if drugged. The exterior floodlight over the concrete patio shines at an angle into her eyes, silhouetting her visitor's head in a nimbus of light, but even so she knows there's a smug catbird smile on Zack's face as he stands there waiting.

In bed, naked and gasping, Carla presses her face sideways into her pillow. In a clumsy faltering rhythm, drunk and grim, Zack pushes in from behind, swaying a little, clinging for balance.

Her new blue dress lies in a wrinkled heap on the floor.

Carla shoves herself against him, again and again, but what began as a helpless, almost disembodied heat has dwindled beneath the weight of a deeper need, to be spoken to, to be touched, in any way at all, by anybody. Zack's breath on her neck is sour and warm, his hands sweaty and tugging angrily at her breasts, hurting. A twist of dingy sheet looks like a question mark, but the light of the silent television flickers over them like a strobe in a dance club, and she shuts her eyes.

Carla hears Davy fussing again and again in his bassinet but she knows if she can just make Zack come quick before he curses and rolls off that he'll lie by her with his arm across her while he passes out and she can pretend it's Laraby's arm, or even that it's that pretty nurse at the hospital who liked her diaper bag and her in a slumber party in some warm attic with bunk beds like back in junior high school. So she shifts her weight forward onto her arm and reaches with her free hand to bring him as far and fast as she can before it's too late, before everything is too late because nothing can be the same as it was, no matter how bad she wants to see the bright clean lights of a simple place like Carby's Restaurant and hear the laughing chatter of customers from their booths, and see cranky Hans the cook with his broad sweaty unshaven face and greasy apron and spatula.

But Davy coughs and then begins to squall and there is not enough time in the world to restore to her a momentary semblance of what her life was like, or someday could have been like, because even now, already, Zack's balance falters as his desperate concentration flags and he curses softly, "Goddamnit."

"Shhh. It's okay. God, you feel so big. Oh God." Her hand rushes him.

He continues, grunting. But Davy cries louder, held nonsense syllables shrieked, his pitch climbing through higher and higher notes, as if a scale. Zack tries to keep on, but finally: "Fuck. Can see why you never had me over. I mean, listen to that little friggin'—"

"Shhh. Shhh, now. Come on. God—"

"Fuck it. Fuck this." He's gone, rolling off and standing beside the bed, swaying, shaking his head. "I'm outta here."

"Zack, wait, come on—" She rolls over and sits there, reaching a hand into the space between them, but he's already yanking on his tight jeans and his Guns n' Roses T and fake-leather jacket. He grabs his cowboy boots and carries them out, slamming the door behind him, leaving her with the echo of that sharp loud sound like the blast of a gunshot.

Improbably, impossibly, when Davy's cries can't get any louder, he takes a shuddering phlegmy breath, and then they do.

wasps ~

Laraby ~

Laraby tosses a little, eyelids twitching with REM, as he dreams his same recurring dream of healing his father and finally knowing thereby the gratitude and admiration of his own best beloved mentor, for whom his own gratitude and admiration have never been less than boundless.

In his dream, Laraby's white-haired dad lies on his hospital bed in the deuce court service box of a perfect tennis court, surrounded by IVs and monitors, a defib unit and ventilator, with its rhythmic gentle gasping. Laraby approaches wonderingly, as if in slow motion. His hand rises as if of its own accord, moving through the strange light to ever so gently touch his father's forehead. The old man's eyes spring open, and he sits up, sheet draping like an elegant toga. He nods with fond pride at his son, climbs off the hospital bed, and walks away into brightness, leaving Laraby staring after him in amazement.

Laraby wakes before his digital alarm clock goes off. He switches it off, and turns to study his sleeping wife, smiling faintly down at her. Living creature of beauty, she breathes evenly, deeply, a tiny pulse beating in the dim hollow between the small delicate bones at the base of her throat.

In these moments in this silent house, Laraby feels new wonder at his adult life of attainment. Surfaces subtly reveal choices, afforded by the rewards of hard-won accomplishment: touch-dimmers instead of toggle light switches, Brazilian cherrywood doors instead of hollow-core oak, woven sisal instead of the short-nap beigey Berber you see everywhere now, even Howland has it in his dopey "chick magnet" town house lair, with his mail-ordered museum gift-shop posters and celebrity chef cookbooks.

Laraby stands soundlessly and moves naked into the bathroom, quietly clicking the door closed to brush his teeth and run a buzzing electric razor over his face. He catches his own eye in the mirror and focuses instead and resolutely on the stubble along his clenched jaw. Smooth, his skin gives back the pale light, softly shadowless.

This morning he believes in how easily and fully he has come to occupy the space the world has made for him, and that he has nevertheless made his own. He imagines, and by imagining wills into being, a sort of confident calm, a new balance that informs his quiet sure steps into his study for his bag and back out again and downstairs to the kitchen for coffee.

Laraby gazes out, through the square bay window behind the sink and dish drain, at the shadowy line of transplanted Norfolk pines guarding his side yard, so still in the held breath of night's last darkness. The high roofline of the house next door looms vaguely behind, a shallow peak barely silhouetted against a lighter dimness.

Dawnlight emerges from the leaden sky, slowly, surely, from everywhere at once it seems, illuminating all, finally. His is the posture of deep reflection before resolution, of weighing human consequences and divining courses of action, through tragedy and triumph. In the best interest of all, after all. And because the choice is truly his, with all the undeniable diamondlike hardness and clarity of fact, his and his alone, he will choose.

Laraby pulls the old capped syringe and Statrophine bottle from his bag, and carefully wraps them separately in thick wads of paper towel. He stuffs them into the stainless Bosch trash compactor, closes the smooth door with its expensive heavy little *click,* and flicks it on.

Carla ~

Carla fidgets, looking on while Dr. Laraby checks inside shrieking Davy's wide-open little mouth with a tiny flashlight and tongue depressor, listening to the telltale click and catch of snot from his sinuses or throat or inside his tiny reddened nose.

Laraby's hair along the back of his neck just touches his shirt collar, fine and shining, like a child's, the hairs separate but curving together to almost curl, maybe they would if he let it grow, though Carla likes it short because his neck is so perfect, smooth and white as a statue's.

Laraby looks thoughtful. "Some respiratory congestion. And some dehydration here. Could be a fluid imbalance from missed feedings."

Carla feels her heart surging. "Missed feedings? But . . ."

"Everybody misses one. Could also be he had the runs and your sitter didn't tell you . . . and then he got behind on his electrolytes."

Carla sees the opportunity to agree, "My sitter. Yeah. 'Cause I know I feed him. All I do is feed him, and—"

"Okay. I know. Now, that clinic pediatrician you called?"

Davy's shrieking gaps as he pauses to inhale, and Carla is quick to fill the space: "Called, yeah, but maybe he got back, maybe not, I don't know." Her gaze flits around the room, but there's nothing to really look at that makes any sense besides Laraby or Davy himself, and when she looks at Laraby again her own voice sounds funny, tight and too high. "I took Davy out, he was cryin' so hard—"

"It's okay. We're just going to feed him till he's nice and sleepy and then we'll keep an eye on him the rest of the night. It's frustrating not to be able to help him when he's like this, but it's nothing life-threatening, believe me."

Carla blinks at Laraby, and then she steps into the opening his plan presents to her. "Will . . . you be here?"

"Graveyard shift, till noon. So don't worry. Go on out there—down the hall at the end—and I'll get him settled in."

"Okay. I will do that. Thanks." She smiles at him, but from the way he looks back, kind of blankly curious, it maybe wasn't the shrugging kind of half-embarrassed look she meant, and now he's simply watching her, waiting out the unbearable seconds.

She fills them. "But, Doctor Laraby?"

"Hmmm?" His tone is absent, professional. Where else is he, when he should be here, since everything has brought them here?

"Don't you think . . . everything happens for a reason? Us, here, after everything?"

Laraby blinks at her, no clue. "We all want to believe it, I know that." He gives her a reassuring smile.

She smiles back at him. And because she must and who wouldn't, she steps forward and gently and chastely embraces him.

He blinks, thrown, a hand floating up to pat her back. And then suddenly his eyes shut tight, lids quivering, as he fights to keep from pulling her in, from clinging.

For a strange moment they stand that way, until she steps back because she doesn't want to ruin it with too much too soon, and he says for what can ever only be the exact same reason: "Go on now, Carla. He'll be fine."

She won't look away, and maybe even though he wants to out of bashfulness, he's too nice and now that they both know that he knows she was at Carby's, finally, they give each other what later they might see as their real beginning, a shy smile, after all. If only she can find a way to make it so.

The Children ～

This morning Abler runs the defroster in his little Yugo while he waits half a block away for Bob Jaspersen to pull out of his driveway in his big-dude pickup truck, the Ramcharger or Tucson or Sonora, "like a rock," like the old native son Bob Seger's song says. Jaspersen's a hard case, definitely, all failure-to-grieve, emotionally shut down, won't feel his own pain so he can't feel anyone else's. Jimmy's silence must work perfectly for him, no challenge at all to keep on keepin' on. Most likely the mother, Lydia, doesn't get to say much, either, pretty much ever.

Withdrawal's pretty high up on the not-so-short list of defense mechanisms, where the goal is to avoid communication in general, silence being a key symptom of, in this case like father like son. But for Abler something still doesn't fit; Jimmy's fear in their first interview seemed too raw and available, as if at a specific consequence for speaking, and Anne's sudden religious hysteria has sounded to him way too purposeful, dependent on a few key phrases and a spacey demeanor, hastily assembled.

The throaty roar of a big engine makes Abler look up, just in time to see Jaspersen's backup lights flicker and smoke billow in the cold from his gurgling chrome dual exhausts. Jaspersen backs down the drive and K-turns off down the street the other way, thankfully.

Lydia is at once glad and puzzled to hear her doorbell ring in the middle of the day, knowing it means the sound of a human voice, but at a loss as to whose. Part of her absurdly hopes beyond hope that it's fate intervening somehow, Bob returned from the metal fabrication shop with flowers and a sudden and complete change of heart, or a team of doctors, or even redecorators or a talk-show host and camera crew with prize money.

She swings open the door to reveal Ron Abler, all rumpled chinos and smudged glasses and clipboard, and she turns defensive before he can speak. "Oh! I know we haven't called, but you see, we're up for a family medical policy? As a benefit down at Bob's machine shop? So if they see—"

"No, I understand, but I promise you there won't be any medical record. I just want to help. I just want to talk to Jimmy. Is he any better?"

In the dimness of his closet, Jimmy brushes aside dust balls and the dried-out husk of a dead wasp, and pulls the stolen key from the pocket of his Old Navy drawstring pants to slip it into a crevice between the fake tongue and groove lap of two "pine-look" wall panels. To him this key means a choice, that he can someday make or never, but it's a kind of regaining of command and control where there has been so little, and where if there ever was, it was the cruelest lie anyway, a joke.

Hours have been like years, sitting in his bedroom afraid to but unable to stop thinking about where things will end. It's like an old-school PacMan maze, where every turn is a dead end, or like Minefield, where every step can be your last, or a bottleneck paintball ambush set up from a hardened redoubt, with the field of fire meant to inflict maximum casualties. He's afraid even to IM Anne anymore, because she has this power over him, but he has this power over her, too, and it's all a trap with no means of escape, no matter what he writes to her.

He remembers her face laughing; which was when he was always able to stare without her noticing, to see her small even teeth and watch her hand come up to tuck her straight hair behind her ear and see her eyes get small as her face changes and her laugh comes out, the sound he has loved for so long, and for so long coaxed from her.

He wants to give in to his sorrow for her, but he's too afraid of her now, and so he gives his sorrow to his mother, who seems lost and trapped, too. Being silent has let him watch, more than ever, and he sees how his dad keeps his mom that way, also, with every little look and frown, and his own cold silences, which are always judging and angry. His dad is unhappy, basically, and by being pissed off at everything on earth twenty-four seven, he's like a clock stuck at twelve that's right twice a day, and so that justifies all the other hours of being wrong.

Jimmy runs his hand over the tiny crevice that holds his treasure, and retreats out of the dusty back of his closet into the light. He quickly slides shirts on hangers together behind him, to cover the wall where he has hidden this secret choice of his, like a kind of last best hope, safe beyond possibility of discovery.

Good thing, because even now he hears voices from the front hall, a sortie or approach, and he moves quickly and silently out of his bedroom to reconnoiter.

In the foyer, his mother's back is to him as she faces out the front doorway, murmuring to that man, Abler, from the hospital, who stops and looks at Jimmy with a quizzical little smile.

Jimmy's mom turns, too, surprised. "Honey? What—"

It's not a betrayal, really, Jimmy knows, because why would she not believe that this weird guy, with his phony soft voice and concerned looks, actually means well?

Jimmy does a little circle, turning away toward his room and then freezing momentarily, and then he sees them—the car keys there on the foyer table—and he grabs them and shoves past Abler and his mom out the door into the front drive, where he jumps into Lydia's van.

Abler stands there, momentarily stunned, but Lydia shouts after him, "Jimmy!"

Jimmy turns it over, peels out in reverse into the street, shifts into drive with a jerk, and screeches off, gone around the corner and out of sight behind a row of other houses.

The world seems too bright, too loud, too filled with blandly curious faces that seem to turn to watch him go by. Faces like Abler's with round earnest eyes filled with good intentions and mouthing gently prodding questions, belonging to people who always want to shift the arrangement of the way things have to be, no matter what happens to everybody because of it.

Corners loom, full and T intersections and Y junctions, and why anyone should go one way more than any other has to do with their own operational priorities, which are usually getting and spending, but also with the other people in their lives, which overlap anyway, but all boil down to love or money, all. As he drives his eyes flicker over the telephone poles and sagging wires of these streets where love or money makes every car or pedestrian in sight or anywhere else turn right or left, or go straight or stop before the sad dead lawns of the single-story houses of this town, where love or money wakes someone up in a nightmare or makes them feel safe enough to finally sleep, or lifts a hand to stroke, or to smash, or turn upwards, empty, asking.

What in this moment dictates his objective, his route to a destination, as if one can be imagined ever again? Among all other people, who is there to love him, finally, in spite of everything?

As he drives screeching around a curve, Jimmy performs a sort of mental inventory, a terrifying mathematic as he discounts one ally after another: fear of his father drives his mother deeper and deeper into her small trapped life, until even the words that come out of her mouth are his father's; his father's own stubborn grip on bitterness prevents pity or sympathy or love. Even Anne is as afraid of Jimmy as he is of her. But the more desperately they seek escape from each other, the more tightly and irrevocably bound they are, which may be a kind of love, too.

He turns left into a littered trash bin lot, beside a boarded-up liquor store, where he sees a phone booth, glass spider-webbed and zigzagged with black spray paint.

When he climbs out of the truck and slams the door behind him, he catches a glimpse of his face in the side mirror as it flashes by, a white stunned oval floating in vague colors, and a sound he doesn't want to hear again comes back to him from some other elsewhere, at once foreign and familiar as a sudden memory or recurring dream.

There's the clatter of ice into a cup as Jimmy stares out between the legs of their booth's tables, at the back of the man who stands at the drink island, now pushing his big plastic drink cup against the root beer dispenser first, with a click and a thick hiss of soda, and then the Diet Coke.

In a high convex mirror on the far wall, Jimmy sees clandestine movement: in the kitchen, the cashier or counter girl begins creeping slowly, slowly, out into the open, from behind a door, sideways along the rear shelf.

The gunman turns his head, ever so slightly and just as slowly, as if to look back.

In the convex mirror Jimmy sees the counter girl's hand reaching, stretching out into bright space as beneath their table Anne's dad's hand reaches slowly for Anne's, even as the gunman's head keeps turning ever so slowly, slowly, until in the high convex mirror Jimmy sees the counter girl grab something from a shelf and carefully and quickly retreat again, just slipping back behind that door and reassuming her covert position again.

There's a quick flurry of footsteps and the flash of dirty white cloth from the kitchen as a guy, the cook it must be, stumbles out a rear kitchen exit. The gunman spins toward the kitchen and jerks his gun up for a short burst of suppressing fire—BLAMM! BLAMM! BLAMM!

Beneath the table of their booth, Anne doesn't dare a breath. At the edge of what she can see without moving, she sees past Jimmy out to the dining area where the gunman grabs napkin and straw from the drink island and scuffs away to an empty table. He carefully wipes it down, before he pulls the straw from the wrapper, jams it into his drink, and sips with a soft gurgle.

Slowly, her dad's hand finds hers, and she grasps it, hard and steady to say she will not let go.

Brrr, brrr. A phone begins softly but insistently ringing, opening Anne's eyes as she realizes it's ringing in fact not a yard away on her desk, but just out in the hall between her bedroom and her mother's, from where she hears her mother pick up and speak softly, even hopefully, into the receiver, "Hello?" And then again, "Hello?"

Anne steps to her closed bedroom door, to hear more clearly her mother's soft curse and the click of the hall cordless handset back in its charging cradle. She knows and grabs her jacket quickly and is there to pick up her own extension when the phone rings again right away, yelling out through the shut door to her mom, "I got it! I got it!"

Anne holds the phone to her ear, narrowing her eyes in fear and suspicion. "Hello?"

Nothing.

Gauging the silence, she asks as if she doesn't already know: "Jimmy?"

She hears his sharp shuddering intake of breath, confusion becoming panic.

"I didn't see anything from you. Can you mail me? Is it that man Abler? Is it him?"

Silence.

"Okay. Meet me. Tompkins Park. By the bridge. I'll be there. Now."

Silence. And then *click,* and the buzzing chord of the dial tone.

Anne yanks her sneakers on and rushes out, but her mom is there, always there, following her to the front door, practically wringing her hands.

"Honey? You won't be long? Where—"

"Told you, Mom. It's just another prayer group meeting. A few hours." She stops as if at a thought, and turns back to her mother, archly. "Would you like to come? You could pray, too. For Dad's memory? Of his courage?"

Doris wants to reach for her and shake her until she cries, but she knows better. "Honey, I miss him, too. I do. And I want so much to talk to you, sweetheart. About that. About—"

"I have to go. "Anne gives her mother a wide impatient smile.

Suddenly her mother's hands flash out, gripping her shoulders, fingers digging, her lips tight and thin and ugly as she shouts, "Stop it! You think all this gives you permission? Is that it? I lost my husband! Who do you think you are, with this dimestore televangelist crap? God picked you? So maybe some boy will, too, finally, or Traci or the others—"

Anne glares and twitches out of her mother's grasp. She sidesteps and opens the front door to reveal Ron Abler, just lifting a finger to the doorbell.

Abler speaks rapidly, flatly, "Thank God. Jimmy's run off. His mom thinks you might know where he is."

"Jimmy?" Anne says his name slowly, as if it's a new vocabulary word. Doris simply stands there, looking from one to the other.

Abler presses gently. "Have you heard from him? Do you know where he is? They're worried sick."

Anne smirks at him. "He won't talk to you. He'll never talk to you."

Fear and suspicion cross Doris's face in the same instant. "Anne? Why would you that say that?"

Abler gives Anne a confused little smile, as if she has performed an impressive amateur's magic trick. "How do you know? You know where he is, don't you?"

Anne starts out the door past Abler. "He'll run from you. You can't help him."

"Then maybe I can help you." Abler grabs her wrist, before he can stop himself. "Wait, now. Please."

Anne looks down at his hand gripping her wrist, and then up at him, a flat gaze of hatred. Doris looks helplessly from one to the other, horrified.

Anne smiles pityingly, yanks her wrist away, and walks.

Doris and Abler watch as she climbs into the car, slams the door, and peels out backward down the drive, and onto the street.

"Should we follow?" Doris spins toward him, helpless, near tears.

"She's right. He'd run from me. She's the only one who can get him back." He stares out at the street, as if Anne has left some clue there, as to how to reach her.

"But who's going to bring her back?" Doris wants to know. "Who's going to get my daughter back?"

Charlie ∼

Out in the bright dining area, Charlie Archenault is a statue, only lifting his gaze ever so slightly to see the gunman pace slowly by, and sigh to sit with his upsized drink and straw at a nearby table, leaving behind a footprint of spilled iced tea shining in the flat white light of day from the windows.

In the glare of morning through his open curtains, Charlie shifts and brightness stings his eyes, crusted nearly shut. All is whiteness, shifting and painful, blurred by his snagged eyelashes as he shuts his eyes again and rolls his creased swollen face deeper into his pillow. But scratchiness along his legs and arms will not let him escape back into sleep and he moves a hand to his thigh to find stiff paper there, a bill it would seem, and then another, and another.

He forces his eyes open until the whiteness resolves into shapes detailed enough to become his own ugly motel room, his bed, in fact a bed of bills, two hundred hundreds, less two for a new leisure suit and assorted toiletries, incidentals and libations, and three for last night's services performed but not quite consummated, as it were.

A twinge traverses his vertebrae into his shoulder blade, on which he has slept too long and hard, drugged by the bottle of crème de menthe the Powatan Thunderbird Casino Motel bellboy fetched for Charlie and his erstwhile consort for one of those spent hundreds.

Today Charlie's touch with God has turned Job-like, but he believes with the faith of the faithful; it's all for just cause.

A rolling flutter of gas roils his gut, squeezing his heart in his chest like a fist, sharp as angina, seeking escape. His head, also, joins in with a searing pulse whose rhythm nearly corresponds to the whisper that leaks from his pasty lips, "Fuck, fuck, fuck, fuck."

He appears to think for a moment, and then simply leans over the edge of the bed and lets it all come up, the beige lumpy batter of chewed bar nuts, the syrupy mucus of green booze, in a single shouted nonsense syllable. Tears sting his eyes as the noxious stink of his own bile hits him and sickens him again and again, as he aspires to the state of purity required for the receipt of God's own good luck.

Which is when he hears it, the sound from the bathroom which should not be but is, which is the rich gush of water into the Jacuzzi tub and the blast of the air jets, suddenly and unaccountably working.

From the doorway, he blinks in at the noise and brightness, a hundred-dollar bill stuck to his shoulder, foulness in his mouth.

When Charlie has held his head under the blasting cold Jacuzzi tap, and the stabbing behind his eyes has returned to a throb, and the clenching in his bowels and stomach has begun at last to ease, he shuffles back out to the bedroom to part the drapes, but no memory prepares him for the rushing tumult of the outside world. Billboards blare in the ugly dull sunlight, motion and sound surge in the air-brakes of buses and the rush of semis roaring by on the freeway, scattering trash in a whirl of road wind.

Through the big picture windows, from his table Charlie can see birds in the sky, wheeling in unison this way and that above the sparse traffic on Route 84 where the guy from out of the kitchen, the cook, has run from the restaurant crying like a kid in a tantrum, shouting and waving his arms at the swiveling shapes of faces passing in cars.

Sunlight streams through the two bullet holes in the rear kitchen door, cutting shafts in the smoke from whatever's burning on the grill,

probably something high-carb and fat-heavy enough, without all the
burned carbon stuff they say is carcinogenic now anyway.

From the corners of his eyes, Charlie sees the third bullet hole gaping
from the shoulder of the life-sized cardboard Carby's Cowboy, his weird
white grin and his own gun pointed nowhere.

Charlie has brought last night's dregs of crème de menthe to his lips, but he hesitates now because the coaster stuck to the bottom of the smudged glass says something interesting, a message meant for him, finally, which in fact says all when he peels it back and stares down at it: "Your time is now."

Charlie rushes hobbling across the oil-stained asphalt between motel and casino with a twinge under one eye, clutching the bills he has frantically collected from around his room, back in the same wrinkled envelope from whence they came.

Seven steps take him from in front of one parked tour bus to another, shorter steps than usual, to be sure, since a swollen ache like gout has inflamed the toes of one foot and makes him drag it slightly sideways.

Shadows cross the lot as wind blows clouds across the sun, and the light flickers in Charlie's darting eyes as images battle their way in, the big billboard "Go 4 It!" with the unimaginable beautiful teeth of the model bending so her hair hangs in a single lush lustrous wave, "Just Do It!" on a semi blasting by, above the spiky hair and perfect beads of sweat on the tanned face of a swimmer or jogger who is so young they will always be that young and their lives will always be that effortless. "No Limits" shrieks a poster on a tour bus, its brakes hissing as it stops, door sighing open. But Charlie doesn't stop to see who alights from within, because a deeper pain has begun in earnest in his foot, pulsing urgently, because he is running faster and faster now, clutching his envelope, toward the wide front doors of the casino.

A pebbly depression in the asphalt catches the side of his foot, and his rushed clumsy momentum brings him down on an arm and a knee, the other hand flung out, grasping at nothing. His envelope of bills skids along the ground for a good few inches, and comes to rest just out of reach, bills splayed from the opening, as if by a dealer making change. The bills seem to hesitate, and then flutter ever so slightly, before taking off in a gush and skitter of wind.

Charlie lets out a sob like a laugh, but he does cry, finally, as he stands there to see proof of his own personal providence, the dark Hindu family in their bright silk robes of yellow and blue and green who at first appear to bow and run, bow and run, again and again across the near corner of the Powatan Casino parking lot. The children squeal delightedly, and the elderly smile and join in, strange earthly angels plucking Charlie's windblown bills from the cyclone fence and from the asphalt where they lie briefly, flapping weakly before taking off again, as if in momentary respite from the rigors of commerce.

Charlie wipes grateful tears as each approaches with a timid smile and a nod and bow to return to him a portion of his bounty, that he now knows is the sole opportunity in his life to provide a life worthy of his family's love and of himself, since he has twice been spared the worst and lived to tell.

bats ~

The Children ~

Jimmy has pulled the van up by a few sparse trees near the old railway trestle bridge in Tompkins Park. Long out of use, the bridge spans a shallow weed-choked bend of river half a mile downstream from the bank where he and his dad fished a few days ago, a lifetime ago it seems, of days spent in his dim bedroom dreading the knock on the door that would finally bring someone, Abler, it turns out, to ask and ask and ask.

Voices reach him, the echoing shouts of two kids on bikes braving the muddy service road: "Wait uuuuppp!" "Move, dumb ass!"

Jimmy lowers himself sideways, to hide behind the high door frames and the dash, listening to their voices fade as they ride by him and the trestle bridge, past the deserted picnic area toward the park exit. Silence reestablishes itself; the day is windless, the sky out the windshield is full of high featureless clouds, empty and white like a blank sheet of paper, the sun an aching smudge of glare.

Jimmy waits a beat, and then sits up and opens his door and slides out, looking around as he softly closes the door behind him.

He walks the trestle, stepping from one oily, black wooden rail tie to the next in a limping rhythm, avoiding the loose gravel between. He has his arms folded in front of himself as if he's cold, as he approaches the middle of the bridge. He pauses there, and looks over the edge at the dirty water, some sixty-odd feet below.

Jimmy climbs up on the wide rail of the trestle bridge, and spreads his arms like wings. A light breeze has arrived to flutter his shirt-sleeves and cloud his breath with its cold. His skin is blotchy with tears as he looks out into the broad sky, which he longs only to enter, to fly off and remain borne by the currents of pure air among sunlit clouds, or to light again in another world where the opposing forces of truth and of lies gather on a vast plain to face off, and heroes win the day.

Suddenly, from behind him, "What are you doing, Jimmy?"

He turns his head to look at Anne. He smiles sheepishly through his tears and flaps his arms like wings.

She glares. "You do anything stupid, and I'll tell everybody why. Because of the truth."

His smile fades. He lowers his arms, trembling, eyes wide. But she wouldn't dare, couldn't possibly risk his own retribution, unless she saw inside him, how he could never allow himself to betray her.

As if reading his mind. "You think I won't? I'll tell just how it happened. So everybody knows."

He shakes his head back and forth, shutting his eyes.

Suddenly, she's there, grabbing his shirt, yanking him back off the rail. He falls hard on his side, onto the railroad ties of the bridge. She's on him like a fury, gripping his wrists, her nails digging into his skin as she hisses in his face. "Then we're going home. And you're going to keep quiet. Understand me? And there's nothing that Abler guy or anybody can do."

He swallows, mute, trying in vain to grasp it, how he could have even dreamed of escape, of flight, when his secrets and hers keep them bound as surely as if they were chained to each other, like the helpless hands of a prisoner.

Finally, his silent nod promises more silence, always, and suddenly her glare is blurred with tears from some near-forgotten place flooded with them, as she grabs him and clings with all her strength to whisper fiercely: "Jimmy, Jimmy, we're still us. We'll always be."

He holds on, hard as he can, as if against some vast force trying to tear them apart.

As Anne and Jimmy step from the Hagen van, returned to his mom, Jimmy's eyes nearly roll in his head in an effort to avoid anyone else's, because almost anyone could see too much at any point; too much can be accidentally revealed, secrecy too easily breached.

His mom grabs him around his narrow bony shoulders and can't stop the grateful tears streaming nonstop down her cheeks, nose running. She pulls back and peers at him again, as if to be sure, and then lets go and grabs Anne in a sudden hard embrace. "Anne. Thank you. Thank you. For bringing him back."

Anne gives her a stiff little smile, and her voice comes out low and whispery and strange, somebody else's all over again. "Mrs. Jaspersen, pray with me and Jimmy. Pray with us now to honor my dad and Jimmy, too, for their courage—"

"I do, Anne, and I thank God that—"

"Right here. Now."

Jimmy glances in dim surprise at Anne and then quickly away, eyes welling again, darting at sky and trees, down his street of parked cars and small defenseless homes that looks the same but never will be, at anything else but his love still lost to him after all.

Lydia releases Anne, backing up a step, blinking at her. "Here?"

Jimmy sees his mom's wariness can't resist Anne's solemn nod and begging gaze; she pulls Lydia into submitting out of gratitude for his return, just as she has made so many submit lately, out of fear or guilt, or just pretending to go along, delaying in case more advantageous conditions develop and afford better opportunities to engage. Will there be any, ever? Have those moments come and gone?

Jimmy hesitates and then joins them, and the three of them kneel there in the cold, on the Jaspersen's dead lawn, as if awaiting a coup de grâce from behind.

❧

The purposeful silence of the crowd gathered this evening unnerves at first, but a few moments into praying, Anne finds herself imagining a rhythm in the shallow breathing and tiny stirrings of the school prayer group, tonight swollen to three times its previous size, standing-room only. Lori and Sue Carline are there, Traci and a few others from the quad squad form a group, and there are more than a few kids Anne doesn't recognize, likely guests from other schools nearby who have heard or been invited. All heads are bowed as they pray.

Sitting at a school desk turned to face the crowd, Anne prays that earnest trust in God will transform all, and all that we have testified will be transformed into truth. Or unto? Well, truth and God and witnessing definitely, because why else would that day have happened, and Anne be there for people to believe afterward? So it all makes sense, in a way, even if the way slips away now and then and feels hard to exactly explain, which is the way God works anyhow, isn't that what they're always saying? So even that it doesn't make sense makes sense, which is truly pretty cool. And definitely true.

A muffled cough sounds from the back of the still room, and as Anne prays she opens her eyes a sliver. Between the blur of her eyelashes she sees a girl she doesn't know tuck a strand of hair behind an ear, a boy red-faced stifling a laugh and Howard last at the end of one long row, pretending to pray.

He winks at her.

At prayer's end, down the broad front steps of Hunt Landing High School, Anne and the others move in small murmuring bunches as mothers pull up in their minivans and SUVs to carpool their children home. Most stand well back from Anne, regarding her with shy hopeful smiles.

Sudden brightness turns heads as a TV news crew seems to appear from nowhere, dragging camera, cables and glaring key lights to quickly corner Anne where she has traversed the lower steps, on her way to the parking lot.

The reporter is a tiny woman with a boyish, urchinlike hairdo and darting black eyes, and as the prayer group closes in to listen, she lifts her microphone to just beneath her chin to ask, "Anne, are these people friends gathered to honor your dad? Or is this part of a bigger movement back toward belief in God?"

Lights brighten around her, and Anne keeps her eyes wide, unblinking, as she steps into this moment that has always been there, awaiting her arrival.

Carla ∽

Carla's dinner is burning, a hamburger patty blackening in a pan and spattering grease because she's distracted by that Hagen girl on her TV again, blinking stupidly into the camera before answering the reporter in that phony soft voice, "It's both. No one should be alone with their fears and doubts. Not when we can have faith together, each and all of us. We call out, our voice is heard."

Carla kicks away some bit of strewn trash that tickles her dirty bare feet, just some crumpled paper towels and maybe a Mickey D's container and a milk carton that have overflowed from the pail she's been meaning to empty, as she steps closer to the TV for a last look at the Hagen girl and the crowd standing around staring at her like she's a TV personality or somebody, for God's sake. Is that all it really takes? Your dad gets killed: zap, you're famous. Maybe it's a kind of consolation, like since you had such bad luck, God evens it out by making everyone at least pay attention to you for a while. Not that it balances out, but it's a start, maybe, to at least have people look at and talk to you, instead of either feeling like a ghost or having them look for the wrong reasons—not such a bad problem to have, anyhow, there are lots worse, for sure: Africa, Iraq, Katrina, diseases even the best doctors can't cure, plenty to see on all the medical shows, every week losing someone, in between scenes where they flirt and smirk and get jealous.

Now there's that Hollywood gossip show with the echoey theme music and that blond lady who's not really so young though plenty cute but, sorry, what a ham, anyone can see. Her face is even a little frightening, with so many expressions as her voice lands on parts of words, "*su*permodel," "*re*hab," "prem*ier*" and her eyebrows go up and down and her head bobs and tilts with showy phony concern as her smile appears and disappears. Commercial, next, *pfffft,* there's the other Hollywood show, same story, swear to God, no exclusive scoop here, just the same tilted shuffling look at that skinny starlet party girl with her hand up, laughing and angry at the same time.

From his crib, there's the small sounds of Davy twitching and fitful faint sighs and half-sobs with a cranky edge, almost like maybe something in particular is bothering him, a pajama leg chafing, or diaper mess, but probably really not. At some point, lots of child experts agree, tiny discomforts are a part of life, and we're all way better prepared to tolerate a few sooner rather than later, not that he's really feeling any, in his Costco crib that cost a week's salary and tips, with the foam pad and moisture-repellant "Happy Feet" pad cover and blanket she's washed and washed with plenty of Bounce fabric softener, and the hypoallergenic type at that.

Half his tiny curved lips seems to smile and he finally quiets, for a second anyway, but these noises can go on for hours while he's half-asleep and dreaming of whatever babies dream about. A good question anyway, because they say you dream about stuff from your day that you didn't really notice, but in his case that would be what? The lime-colored painted dowels of his crib bars, or the nub of his "Robotz" pajama sleeve rubbed against the side of his face? Or how she smiled down at him and brushed her fingertips along the side of his head and his sparse brown hair, whispering, "love you, love *you*" to him over and over again?

Carla turns back to her little Pullman kitchen, where greasy smoke now billows upward from the pan. Memory slows and finally stops her as she stares at the blackening lump of meat.

A Carby's Cowboy Special burns to black on the grill.

Smoke rises, cut by shafts of sunlight streaming from the two bullet holes in the cheap back door you had to slam to shut tight.

On the other side of the counter, a third bullet hole has ripped through the big cardboard Carby's Cowboy, high on the shoulder, wouldn't kill him.

In the kitchen, stuck between the open utility room door and the wall, Carla stares down at her cell phone, the LED message blinking on its face, "signal faded." Her eyes sting from tears because it's so stupid, what she's done for nothing, and nothing times two is less than.

From the dining area, there's that soft gurgle of someone sipping a soft drink, and now all of a sudden that tinny U2 "Beautiful Day," all trebly echoey drums and ragged voices.

Carla jerks her head up to look again out through the mesh grille of the open pantry door she stands behind, out at the dining area floor to see it: enough of a cell phone sticks out of the dead guy's pocket to know it's ringing that song.

She lifts her gaze to see the back of the gunman's pink balding head as he sits at his table drinking his drink through a straw, noisy, too, like he doesn't care who in the world hears him.

And then the dead guy's cell falls silent.

Charlie ~

At his table nearby, Charlie lets out a long silent breath of relief.

But of course now: Ble-eep! Bleep! Bleeep! *The dead guy's voice message alert goes off, a quick peppy melody of digital tones.*

And the gunman sighs and stands.

*Charlie watches him move slowly across the room, away from him, one
Hush Puppy leaving a telltale wafflelike print behind, this time of blood.*

Red dice land, bouncing and rolling, the white dots an uncountable blur as sides present themselves and flash away, until finally the dice rest flat upon the green felt to expose the roll's outcome.

Vic the Stickman could be a ventriloquist, his face immobile as he narrates, "Seven out."

Across the table, balding in baggy jeans and a turquoise polo shirt, the roller stares unwelcomingly at Charlie, who lingers a step away from the rail, half in the aisle, still clutching his envelope of bills as he gulps down yet another mai tai.

As they take his odds and pass line bets, the roller takes a hundred-dollar black chip from his dwindling stake, and drops it onto the pass. And then he tosses down another five, which rolls on its edge in a little circle. "Five dollar yo for the boys."

In ugly glasses and a white shirt a size too small, the boxman slaps the chip flat with his palm. "Fi dollah yo. Thanks a lot, sir," he says, but when his eyes look up, they meet Charlie's and he's not smiling.

"Hon? I can't getcha another unless you play." The waitress is back, so soon, again pulling Charlie's focus from the rhythm of losses and wins at the table, which he has just been beginning to almost control, little by little.

"Sir?" The boxman again, a new guy, "Chuck" from "Beantown!" who doesn't know better. "If you're not gonna play, I'm gonna have to ask you to back it up."

Charlie's smile is fearful, but he chuckles as he steps back, clutching his envelope to his chest. He turns, finally, and shuffles down an aisle of slots.

Bits of conversations echo like a B movie sound track: a husband works a toothpick between purplish lips, scoffing at his wife, "All day to lose a sawbuck, the way you keep at those nickel slots. Just put it all down and let it *ride!*" A girl barely in her teens rolls her blue-shadowed eyes at a boyfriend in a low-slung cowboy hat and football jersey, whining, "Come *on,* Duke, ten!" A hatchet-faced woman with orange hair glares at a sullen bowlegged man, "Stow it, Buster." All fade and surge as laughter bounces off walls, without origin or end. Dealers smile with benign goodwill as if drugged, Muzak dimly soars as the crowd bunches and gawks by a high-roller blackjack table, or the grinding bell of a big slot winner, or a shout of innocent joy from a coffee shop Keno player, back on big street.

Charlie's eyes dart over all, flickering over logos and faces, jewelry and tattoos, for an omen emblazoned anywhere, a sign from above or within or wherever, that this is his all or nothing, now or never moment to ascend from dream to destiny.

Kathy's at her kitchen desk with her checkbook, on the phone, pencil in hand as she listens to the automated voice recite her recent savings account activity, "a debit for eight thousand dollars on March 22, a wire transfer for twenty-five thousand dollars on March 26. Press one for five more transactions, press two to—"

She hangs up, staring off, numb.

She pictures the missing money as neatly bound stacks of bills in a shining metal suitcase, like a drop in a parking garage, for diamonds or dope. Twenty-five thousand dollars was Charlie's uncle's bequest and what was left of their own meager savings, all of it, their lock against the wolf at the door, their start on Beth's college fund, their chance to maybe trade up if the right condo came along, if rates kept falling, if the local high schools finally outsourced all their driving ed programs like they'd been threatening, if Charlie's business took off the way it should, if, if, if.

With a gnawed fingertip, Kathy smudges a tear from the corner of her eye. She lets out a shaky sigh, a chuckle of dismay. And then she sits a moment, perfectly still, staring off, as if at a thought that becomes a decision.

She pulls a card from her pocket, and dials the number off it. *Brrr. Brrr.*

"Hunt Landing Police."

Kathy hesitates.

"Hello?" The voice repeats, annoyed, "Hello?"

Kathy disconnects, and sits there without moving for another moment, thinking, Charlie, Charlie, Charlie, his name like a rueful chant of love and regret. Whatever his secret is, she has to trust him, has to believe that it's all beyond his choice, because he has always been and will ever be nothing if not innocent and steadfast.

Kathy takes a breath and dials 411. "The Hunt Landing branch of Interstate Bank? Right. Thanks."

She jots down the number. Disconnects again. Dials it. *Brrr. Brrr.*

"Hello? Yes, I wonder if you could verify the recipient of a wire transfer? Just to be sure?"

Laraby ~

Again heart patient Sam's flat-lined monitor fills his room with its baleful tone, and with other rushed fearful sounds: the quick squeak of crepe soles on linoleum, breathless frustrated sighs as Laraby shouts: "I said charge the fucking paddles again, goddamnit! Are you deaf?"

The nurse cowers, desperately working the defib controls. She thrusts the paddles at Laraby and he grabs them to shock Sam all over again, jerking back as the brain-dead man leaps upward as if to embrace him and never let go, but then flops back down again loosely, so limply his body can only be a truly uninhabited thing.

Here is absence, approaching, looming, vast, irrevocable abrogation of self into nothingness, beyond breath and sensation forever. It's all Laraby's to prevent, with his will and his hands and hard-earned skill to battle and conquer, that he may believe that he may be deserving.

He stands a step back, holding the paddles up as the defib machine recharges, whining and buzzing like some giant stinging thing, recharging.

Laraby knows this nurse, a short dark woman with a double chin and teary eyes, Ruth from Ann Arbor, is an old hand at internal, but when she looks at him her eyes are odd, wide, confused.

Never mind. He bends toward Sam again. "Clear?"

Suddenly, from the doorway: "Pal, he's had flatline EEG for days. Give him a rest, huh, Chief? Shouldn't you be down in ER anyhow?"

Laraby glares contemptuously at Howland, this rangy, light-haired Midwestern jock, with his matinee-idol jaw and idiotic sports metaphors, a high school wise-ass who lucked into everything in life with his looks. "What the fuck do you . . ."

Laraby's voice trails away, and he goes still as it hits him. He stands there blinking, first at Howland, and then at the deceased man he has tried to resurrect, against all common sense, hope, and decency. He sags against the defib unit, as if a blow has knocked the wind out of him and left him breathless.

After Laraby has visited the dispensary again, under the bright bluish fluorescent lights of the staff locker room, he and Howland doff scrubs on opposite ends of a bench. Howland stretches his neck, whistles, pops his knuckles and yawns with showy fatigue. Laraby's silent and taciturn, his eyes hooded, furtive, as he yanks off his gum-soled Bean-catalog mocs and tosses them clattering into his locker.

Sam's death weighs on him, as if the secret of his own incompetence has become unwieldy, the evidence more and more visible until it's undeniable, until even the janitor buffing the linoleum and the part-time nurse's aide from the junior college must know and shake their heads in dismay behind his back. For the briefest of seconds, Laraby considers the comforting old chestnuts of common wisdom: you can't win 'em all, makin' space for the race, had a good run. But in the end, what on earth keeps these from becoming facile, basest rationalizations for failure? Other than refusing them altogether, what guarantees they won't become excuses for the staph-infected intubation wound, the nicked intestine?

Howland sees Laraby's mood and offers his smug cheerful sympathy: "Hey, no harm, buddy. And not to go beyond these walls, count on it." He pauses, as if thinking, and adds as if it just occurred to him, "You'd return the favor if I went a little OB. I mean, if we don't watch each other's backs, who will?"

Laraby turns his head slowly to stare in disbelief at this loud-mouthed swollen-headed cretin so blatantly buttonholing him, just out of residency, who has never missed a chance to flirt broadly with Jan and undermine Laraby at every possible juncture in a year of workdays. Likely as not, Howland clued hospital heads Gretchensky and Carlson in to Laraby's "overly hopeful" treatment of the GSW vics from the Carby's Restaurant event, probably why the report got yanked and so scrutinized to begin with.

Howland meets his glare with a defensive blink, and then a steadfast defiant gaze, standing hard by his self-serving little quid pro quo formulation.

By the arc-lit darkness of a 76 gas station pump, breath steaming in the cold, Laraby grabs the little red plastic jerry can from his Mercedes trunk. He swings the can as he strides a few jaunty paces to bend and remove its cap, swipe his AmEx on the pump, press "performance," which is really the low-test stuff, and take down the heavy greasy nozzle. He jams it into the gas can's dark mouth and presses the handle lever, hearing the guzzly splash and swirl of liquid within. Looking around, he whistles a little, and then he has to chuckle, it's so like urinating in an empty men's room.

He stops at seven oh oh, smack on the dollar, everybody's game, because these days what isn't a game? Cell phones now come with Tetris or Blocker or Gog, Japanese cartoon-looking characters blipping and chirping, miniexplosions of tinny static. Television has made games out of "surviving" a judge's scorn for your singing, or a voluntary stay

on a tropical island of confiding schemers, or the rejection of a potential date, as if any of these were life-threatening. Laraby can't watch
this stuff, though he has seen even Jan roll her eyes at one of these
shows, but then settle into the sectional a little deeper to stare for a
moment. At what? Was it the toned tanned abs of the guys with their
surfer jams and Crest Strip smiles?

Traffic clogs a few intersections, but Laraby pulls up at the construction site in under ten minutes, as the sky darkens to a pall over the
lot. He sits for a moment, looking out at the shadowy framed structure that will be their new three-bedroom, three-bath custom home,
with outbuilding office and guest loft, in three month's time or so, if
the subcontractors can just stop pointing fingers and avoid that flu
they seem to come down with every other Monday.

He climbs out, collects his jerry can from the trunk, and approaches the perimeter cyclone fence, a barrier to nobody with the
will to climb it. A sweaty tightness grips his neck and shoulders for
a brief second and he exhales noisily, shaking his head at nothing
and chuckling a little as he opens the gate padlock with the little
key Jan has given him, with her instructions. He hefts the can with
a little swing, feeling the weight of the gasoline sloshing side to side
within.

By the porch side of the framed house, beside a concrete footing,
Laraby finds the portable generator right where she described it,
when she asked him for this favor for their sick framing subcontrac-
tor. He unscrews both caps and pours the gasoline into the tank to
power the security floods, so Jan can walk the site after dark if she
wants to this week, measuring, adjusting. Dreaming.

Back in his driveway, in what has become a ritual meditation upon
each of his failures, Laraby sits again in his little Mercedes, bucket
seat reclined, his windshield full of vague darkness dotted by stars
and the blinking lights of a passing plane. A shadow flaps from the
eaves to the bare trees and back again, worrying the dim light from
the streetlamps before it disappears.

Certainty and fear of his own ineptitude grip his diaphragm, stopping his lungs from a clean complete breath, suffocating him slowly but as surely as dead hearts suffocated Sam, his dad, that gunshot Realtor with the aorta that wouldn't take a suture, the lungs that wouldn't fill, the body that would not be healed, that he could not heal.

Little by little, his panicky breaths begin to slow, as he balances the worst with his recent success, factoring it into the familiar arguments of self-judgment and verdict; Jan's beautiful face looms in his memory and imagination, her eyes shut, lips smiling faintly as she clings beneath him.

He raises his seatback to its memorized driving position, and slips out of the car with his black leather medical bag full of med samples.

mantises ~

Charlie ~

Just two doors down from Charlie's semidetached town house, next to the next duplex over, Rosalee's a plump Honduran widow in reading glasses and a duster, quick to make Beth giggle with her fond clucking, silly bug-eyed faces and grins. Kathy has left Beth with her before, no drama, when Charlie got delayed and Kathy had to drive her dad in for a dialysis appointment. She's already called Rosalee three times today, getting no answer or answering machine, which is not so confidence-inspiring, but tonight when Rosalee finally does pick up, Spanish TV blaring in the background, it's a relief.

Now she holds Beth on her hip as Kathy takes a shaky breath and does a quick mental inventory of all she's leaving for worst-case scenarios: cell phone numbers, physicians' numbers, two hundred dollars in twenties pilfered from her and Charlie's emergency kit in their garage—their "nuclear war" stash, he liked to call it, which she had nagged him into creating after 9/11 and the weeks of anthrax scares just after.

Kathy has her Yahoo! map downloaded and her route marked in red flair-tip, along I94 across the state, then south via smaller state highways and county roads to the Powatan Thunderbird Gaming Casino. Across the state line deep into Ohio, it's in farmland Kathy remembers; as a teenager her folks drove her in their station wagon to summer camp that way, past rusty grain silos and low green hills covered with alfalfa and sorghum and soybeans, dotted with tiny untroubled enclaves of vacation cabins and retirement trailers crowded around weedy little lakes.

On her little map, smudgy from her cheap little inkjet printer, Powatan seems a factual enough place, with a discernible location in the real world, but no aspect of its reality gives a hint why Charlie would leave without a word to anyone, to go west instead of east, turn south instead of north at any of hundreds of exits and entrances and crossroads, to arrive at such a destination.

Kathy leans to kiss Beth's forehead, to take in her faint odor of baby shampoo and soap and sleep. Beth blinks at her, reaching out a tiny hand with a small cranky noise.

Rosalee smiles and nods. Kathy turns away to grab her little suitcase, but hesitates by the front door, turning back, "I'll call in a little while. Oh, and if she wakes up and won't go back to sleep—"

"Bosco. I know, I know."

Kathy takes a breath; she opens the door to leave, and then stops, turns back and grabs the framed photo of Charlie from the foyer table.

Charlie's feet ache, but he keeps on, sliding one in front of the other, eyes side to side, on the lookout for luck. His shuffling steps have created a sort of circuit by now, laps marked by the "McHale's Navy" quarter slots, and the roulette machine row with a big flatscreen video of a *Shrek*-like cartoon lady croupier winking, all the way back around by the buffet line and the VIP Club to check again on the dice table action.

Finally he slows to see the dice flopping onto the green felt and rolling to rest and reveal a five, and then the blessed six: for Charlie a sign surer than any that the odds are indeed changing to accommodate him, creating more and more cumulative probability, hell with that, *certainty*. His predetermined destiny draws nearer with every inch of the earth's rotation, the stars themselves align, all to fulfill his own personal horoscope of a big double odds pass line bet won, and patiently and judiciously parlayed into lasting financial freedom and security for himself and his own.

"Eleven, yo. 'Leven, pass winner, pass." This stickman is "Freddie," another new guy, with one droopy eyelid and purplish thin lips like a gash in his shapeless pale face.

Past drunk, Charlie steps up to the rail and slaps his envelope down for change, but just a bit late, because the roller across the table has already set the dice in his hand and then yanked it back and opened it to let them escape into air, even as the stickman is reaching for Charlie's envelope and the dice land and the boxman calls it, "Deuce. Craps, line away."

Charlie grabs his envelope off the felt and steps back as if struck, but his foot lands half on the foot of the waitress who has suddenly appeared behind him; he hears her soft curse and flings out a hand to grab the rail for balance and ballast, but it catches on his neighbor's stake of two-dollar chips and okay, maybe a few go skittering off, no big deal, not like the waitress's tray clattering down onto the carpet with the scattered ice and highball glasses rolling everywhere.

So of course Freddie the Stickman gives a tiny high-sign to someone and suddenly two security guards are there, grabbing Charlie either side in a classic bum's rush. Charlie blinks at one's name tag.

"Sal! Howsa! You from a small town or the big city? Hey, not talking your language? Early-bird bonus Caribbean Keno stud! Triple odds fun club discount *fever*!"

Charlie staggers, head thrown back, laughing, as they help him away from the table.

In his nautical-themed Powatan Thunderbird casino motel suite, the two security guards lay Charlie down on the king-sized bed. He giggles and digs through his pockets and comes up with a five-dollar chip. He hands it to one guard, who smirks and tosses it back.

Charlie can't stop laughing, until he is suddenly alone, crying in great breathless sobs as he sits on the edge of his bed. His face twists and he lowers and lifts his head as if davening, hands balled into fists at either ear as wave after wave of inexplicable grief overwhelm him.

Laraby ⁓

For their late dinner together, tonight Laraby purees leeks and potatoes and blends chicken stock for a pot of soup while Jan collects silverware, absently chattering, "I thought we could maybe go . . ."

Her voice fades slightly as she exits into the dining room to set the table. Laraby quickly slips a new syringe from his pocket, holds it over the pot steaming on their Wolf stovetop, and depresses the plunger, sending a needlelike stream of liquid Statrophine into the beige soup.

Jan continues on from the living room, "with a little larger spare bedroom—" as Laraby smoothly pockets the syringe. And then he checks the doorway and stifles a choked sob at a half-thought, a millisecond's glimpse of the unimaginable, even as he pulls out the syringe again, to add still another dose to the soup.

"—in case we actually decide to, you know . . ." Suddenly she's there behind him, reaching for wineglasses.

He palms the syringe, barely breathing, heart pounding. He turns to face her, puts his arms around her. She stops, looking up at him, smiling.

"What?"

His eyes glisten with desperate love and fear: "I love you is what. Do you know that? I truly do."

As she turns her face to his and they kiss, he slips the syringe unseen back into his sweater pocket.

An hour later, with last night's leftover lamb roast, Jan has eaten a whole bowl of Laraby's potato-leek soup to his few vague spoonfuls, and Laraby has once again nodded and smiled wanly during dinner without hearing a word she has said, though from her gestures and lively expression it seems her chatter could be a dialogue unto itself—vague enthusiasms countered by small doubts, each quickly resolved in favor of a future filled with infinite, simple happiness.

They stand now, side by side, Laraby quickly rinsing the dirtiest dishes before loading them into their Bosch dishwasher, Jan wiping the counters as her idle talk skips without segue or prelude to other subjects, other conversations, in the manner of so many long and successfully married.

Laraby glances at her, pleased by the quick impression, after these years. Tonight she wears a simple but expensive long-sleeved T-shirt over jeans, but her form itself achieves elegance with length of bone, slimness of wrists and ankles, the gentle but solid curves of hip and bust.

Any moment now, Laraby expects to see it: the hesitation and puzzled frown at the first small twinge of vasodilation. Certainly the dose was adequate, no worries there, and at a typical absorption rate, the first effects should occur momentarily. Too bad, of course, that he couldn't somehow slip her the Molodil before the onset of too much discomfort, but then he would be denying her the opportunity to experience and express the gratitude and earnest admiration that has brought them closer of late.

Brrr, brrr. Their phone rings, an expensive-sounding purring tone that Laraby has loved for its softness, but which tonight jars and distracts, just when he needs to be most focused and watchful.

"Just let the machine—" he begins, but Jan is already scooping the handset from its cradle.

"Hello?" She smiles at the cabinet in front of her, and then, "Oh, hi! Sure. Hold on a sec, I've got him washing dishes. Why should it all be about saving lives?"

Laraby is just reaching for the leftover soup, but she has already turned to him with a hand over the mouthpiece and a raised eyebrow to stage whisper, "It's Travis, honey."

Possibilities loom in Laraby's imagination, none welcome. Is it something about what happened with his patient, Sam? Has the prick Howland opened his fat mouth, letting it drop nonchalantly but nonetheless like a pall over Laraby's ER tenure?

Absurdly, he smiles and points down the hall. "I'll take it in the study." He grabs a paper towel and exits, drying his hands.

As he steps down the short hall, he hears Jan's sweet voice behind him, murmuring, "Travis? Say hi to Angie for me. Tell her I haven't forgiven her for that line call, our last match."

In his study, Laraby flicks the light on and picks up the phone, and as he listens to Carlson's bland questioning, his first impulse is a small surge of pride that his opinion matters, but his next is the queasy recognition that here it is: the commerce of words spoken or not, the price of Howland's silence. Laraby paces, stalling and making sure. "My take on Dan Howland? Well, he's—wait, Travis? Did he put me down as a reference? Or . . . no, no, it's fine, it doesn't matter. Not at all." Laraby winces, and then offers up his part of the bargain. "He's . . . top-notch. Great candidate for GP attending. Sure."

Tonight the two little sublingual Molodil press easily through the foil of the sample pack Laraby has pulled from his black medical bag. Propped up in bed, Jan is pale, carefully motionless, her eyes resolutely shut against the small light from her dimmed night table lamp. He gently lifts her hand and turns it, placing the pills in her palm, holding a glass of water with a straw at the ready, for her to sip.

She takes the pills, letting them fizz and dissolve under her tongue. Weakly, she embraces him, and he shuts his eyes to let her softly murmured praise spread through him like the warm tilting wave of a Percodan or Fentanyl, not unlike, in fact, her own imminent relief from pain.

He knows he's not far from the moments when she will convey her thankfulness, sweetly at first, and then with a quickening urge he'll answer with his own, but only after all of her asks, her gasping breaths, her long torso pressed against his, her fingers pressing into his back and buttocks as she clutches at him. It's their duet, melodies ascending in counterpoint, climbing together, drawing them always nearer and nearer.

Later in a blissful doze, they float in the stillness of their bedroom, Jan's head on his chest, while Laraby gently and slowly strokes her hair, over and over again. A pool of moonlight from their window illumines their tangled bedclothes with silver, deepening the shadowy hollows where they lie, legs entwined and their deep slow breaths in rhythm, as they let whole moments pass in peace, without purpose or comment. For Laraby there are no moments as tender as these, shared so quietly yet completely with an invalid he has healed, as if in answer to her prayers, whom he will never fail to heal, serene in his place in her life and in the estimation of all.

The Children ∾

Alone in her room, Anne has switched off her computer and her TV and her new Fergie tracks on her iPod shuffle, to kneel and give voice to her secret but truest hopes for herself, and for all the innocents in this world, because chosen by God or not, we are all God's creatures great and small.

"To rise above our limits . . ." she prays. "And find peace . . ."

In this moment she longs to believe in her words and the longing they hold. "To find freedom . . . and avoid pride and temptation . . ." Her eyes shut, she asks God that all may be liberated from earthly desires and their consequences, because what else is there anyway, that always ends in so much sadness?

Her voice is faint as she continues, for bravery and courage for everyone. "To face fear . . . borne on the wings of joyous angels . . . above all the sins of this earth . . ." She imagines her words as ghostly flying things, rising up through ceiling and roof, climbing the vast darkness of night to the vault of heaven.

"Our Father . . ." Her voice grows fainter, a confidence among the millions rising up from all the corners of the earth to reach Him, if only they are whispered by the pure enough at heart. "Grant us the strength, in the name of Thy only Son."

She thinks, and tightens each hand's grip on the other. "And send a sign or someone, something, please . . . unto me. So I may know thy will. Amen."

She remains motionless, as if listening for a voice, a reply, or just an echo of her prayer.

Later the trembling blotch of light from her flashlight faintly touches the pigeons returned to their open cages, the colorless gray of their gripping talons, the depthless red of their eyes, their restless dirty wings.

In her nightgown, Anne stares at them, dazed. They are too much like us, lost and seeking, fleeing and returning, free to fly but trapped somehow, always.

Jimmy doesn't care what time it is, because time is measured in mission progress and tonight he's made plenty, having infiltrated his brother's bedroom and closet and secured the USMC fatigue shirt he now wears over his T and a pair of easy-fit Gap jeans and dark Nikes he can run in.

At his little HP desktop computer, Jimmy finishes his final IM to Anne and clicks his mouse to send it flying, out across the dark vacuum of cyberspace. He switches the machine off, because there's no reply necessary to a statement of fact that it is not a question. There are no choices now because there are no options, though tonight some cowardly weak part of him still hopes some great catastrophe will finally overrun the events in his own life, by wrecking everyone else's: a terrorist attack with nuclear weapons, or sprayed smallpox, or a railroad nerve gas spill like the one they faked in the movie *Close Encounters*. What a relief any of these would be, every adult nearby indefinitely preoccupied with other more important problems, until they forget all about what happened and forget they ever meant to ask anything about it, and Jimmy can slowly speak a few more words each day without demands for more, until little by little, he and the world are restored.

Meanwhile voices reach him from the kitchen, his parents arguing, muffled by the cheap Sheetrock walls to murmuring, but not near enough to be unintelligible, never enough.

"Ed Sykes had a sister-in-law wouldn't talk, but *she* came around." His dad's emphasis is wheedling, blaming.

Jimmy feels his throat tighten up with anger. Has his dad ever once stopped to wonder why he can't talk? That maybe for good reasons, like loyalty and chivalry and love and honor, he needs to be brave enough to remain silent? Never, of course, not for a moment.

His mom comes right back. "I can't listen to this. I won't. If it was Michael you'd get a doctor quick enough, job be damned—"

Jimmy steps to his bedroom door, opens it a crack.

"Oh shut up," he hears his father say. "Who do you think you're impressing with your hysterics? Maybe that Abler character from the hospital or the county or wherever. Maybe he goes in for all that."

Silence intervenes, and then his mom says softly, almost thoughtfully, as if the idea were just now occurring, "You're a coward."

"Watch your mouth." This is a favorite of his dad's, a dependable old standby that has always turned an argument into stony silence.

Not this time. "Fuck you," his mom says, and something inside of Jimmy expands, beyond all hope to a surge of joy, but unfounded and short-lived, because the first blow is a dull wet-sounding slap that makes him flinch with a small sob. And then there's silence. And then he hears the sound of another hit and his mother's first gasp as she begins to weep in pain and fear and utterly useless fury.

Now, finally, there is no waiting anymore, only commitment to performance of duty and achievement of objective. Jimmy steps rapidly and covertly along the dim hall to the living room, where he listens to his mother gasping and weeping in the kitchen, as his dad's blows continue to land.

Jimmy steps to the front door, and without a sound opens and closes the door softly behind him. Waypoint one, reached.

Outside, the night is damp and finally a little warmer, darkness side-lit from the oily purplish light of the streetlamp faintly buzzing across the street. He ducks down beneath their kitchen window ledge and hurries past along the stained concrete to their yard, to the squat little utility shed there.

Jimmy pulls the key he has stolen from his dad's jeans pocket and opens the lock with it, carefully, quickly, without fumbling, his breathing even and sure. He pulls out the cloth-wrapped rifle, but sets it aside and keeps on digging through the shed, finding a small object, also wrapped.

He steps back, takes a breath, and unwraps it, revealing the black metal cross-hatched "nonslip" grip, revolving cylinder and oily black barrel of a well-maintained .38-caliber handgun, gleaming meanly in the darkness.

He jams the gun into his waistband and runs, over their short drive and down the middle of the deserted suburban street, feet and heart pounding, the clouds of his breath like steam in the streetlight.

Carla ~

Davy's cries have climbed in volume to a crackling ragged edge in Carla's ears, distorting like a held note of electric guitar at a rock concert.

Shoulders hunched, fists pressed into her ears, Carla paces a tight little circle through a few fast-food containers and crumpled paper towels strayed from her recycling bin. She would turn up the TV, but that jerk next door will start banging on the walls to beat the band, and since she can't shout back and tell him to shut the fuck up without him calling the cops, what can she do but pray to God that Davy will just get tired enough to shut the fuck up at some point, because how can he not? No one can keep it up forever, can they?

As she paces, she shakes her head at the rattling din of the single syllable Davy has stretched into a wail, "*wiiiiiiiiiiiiii. . . .* " Which is exactly what she wants to know, anyway: why? Why has God picked her to punish with these days and nights of agonizing cries or awful silence she fills with television sitcoms and talk and game and reality shows? Why torment her with the flies that have appeared from nowhere to buzz in her ears and so lightly touch her that she shudders and swipes in fury at the air?

"*Wwwwwiiiiiiiiiiiii?*"

Finally she understands the hollowness in her stomach and the sour taste in her mouth as desperation, sees her tiny overheated apartment as the dead-end trap it has become, and she yanks Davy out of his bassinet and dresses him quickly in his Target snap-on Hercules pajamas. His arm snags in the sleeve but she yanks it through and snaps the cuff around his fat little wrist.

"Snug as a bug in a rug," she tells him, not that he stops yawping for even a single blessed second.

She hoists him onto her hip, grabs her coat, and leaves, slamming the door behind her and carrying him down the concrete steps toward the street and her car and wherever it will take her.

At the front door of Jennifer's peeling little house, Carla juggles squirming Davy in her arms as she knocks. Davy bends backward against her grip, mouth widening as he howls.

Across the tiny patch of dead lawn, a curtain parts in a second-story window of the house next door, an elderly woman in a hairnet scowling, blue television light flickering behind her pale fat face as Carla thumps on Jenn's peeling front door with the side of her fist. "Jenn? Hey, Jenn? Hello?"

No sounds return to her from within; Davy's cries reach a new pitch, as if it were possible.

Carla *shh's* him. "You're okay. Hush, now. Hush."

Carla clumsily ties his plastic convertible bassinet in place with the rear seat belt and drives the streets of Hunt Landing while he shrieks. Her eyes ache and she shivers as she skids past liquor stores and courtyard apartment buildings like her own, peering out the smudged windshield at the street-lit darkness, as if trying to divine a route.

But to where? In the end, where is there to go where you don't bring your own with you, where the blank slate we are to strangers can hold some possibilities, for courtesy and kind curiosity, and wherever those may lead two people who discover they may be two of a kind?

Up ahead, Carla sees a bar, a run-down cinder-block joint with a blacked-out front window beneath a retro-looking neon martini-glass sign that tilts back and forth, pink and then green, over and over again, The Tick Tock. She pulls up at the curb a deserted half block away and parks. She turns off the engine and sits, staring up at the sign, Davy's screams like needles in her skull.

Finally, Carla climbs out of her car, closing the car door behind her, muffling Davy's shrieks from within. And as she walks away from her little Escort toward the Tick Tock bar, the volume of his cries diminishes, until he may really just be fussing a little, anyway. In all probability, in actuality.

Inside the Tick Tock, Carla finds a cracked red-leather stool next to a barfly with sideburns, broken nose, slicked hair. He turns and gives her a sideways grin, exposing crooked, mossy teeth.

When they have sung songs of old together, been a ragged choir stumbling through "Sweet Home Alabama" and "China Grove," pounding in sloppy unison on the bartop and collapsing against each other in gales of helpless laughter, out on the street outside the Tick Tock, Sideburns mutters against her smeared cheek and snakes his tongue into her mouth, thick and darting, rancid with gum-rot and beer. Carla shoves him away, but he grabs her, pulling her mouth to his again. She knees him in the crotch. He falls, rolling and dry-heaving on the sidewalk as Carla stumbles away around the corner.

Carla slams her car door behind her, waking Davy, who blinks up at her. He sniffles, and then falls silent, staring, and then he begins to cry, weakly at first, and then louder. And louder. Breath clouding in the cold that on this unending night has turned so bitter.

Carla covers her ears against the sound, so loud it fills the world, and shuts her eyes so she doesn't have to see his twitching tiny chest, his face caked with mucus and dried tears, rubbed raw, but too white like tissue paper you wrap a gift in, if only you had something left to give, to anyone.

"God, no, please. Please, no." Carla whispers these words and repeats them in different order, again and again, until they are just a rhythm of meaningless syllables, forever unheard, drowned out by her child's cries.

angels ～

Laraby ~

Morning has come and nearly gone in an overlapping succession of minor ER cases—a mild sprain, a bad strep, a droplet of splashed acetone in an eye—and now Laraby paces the scuffed linoleum of the admittance area hallway, the nurse's desk phone to his ear as he explains, "Honey? I'm sorry, I've got a pedes case waiting, and a few more on deck. Lunch is out. You should just go on without me."

Over the line he hears the *ding!* of the microwave bell in their kitchen and the telltale racket of Jan opening the stainless-and-glass door and pulling something out.

He hears her laugh. " 'S okay. I am. Leftovers."

A passing nurse hands Laraby a chart, but he doesn't glance at it. Tense, he repeats, "Leftovers?"

"Soup from last night. Even better today." More kitchen sounds, a dull clatter of silverware, the unscrewing of a cap.

Laraby feels a chill prickly sweat, his pulse leaping. The phone in his hand seems suddenly weightless, alive and ready to fling itself into space, and he grips it hard. "Yeah? I didn't see you save any."

"Sure, I'm taking a thermos out to the site. Check some measurements." He hears drawers opening and closing, Jan retrieving her carpenter's tape measure and chalk, no doubt.

Laraby clings to the receiver. "Jan, why not stay home? Maybe I can get away."

"You just said you couldn't, silly." Her voice is still a college girl's. "Look, I'll be a half hour. That's all I really have, anyway. I'll call you when I get back. Okay?"

"Jan, why not wait, and later we can both—"

"Later? I'm late now if I want to get to work at all today."

"But—"

Jan laughs, as if he has been flirting with her. "Byyyye."

Laraby hangs up, paces a little circle, his skin damp and tingling with fear. He looks out through the glass doors into the waiting area, and goes still, seeing Carla Davenport standing there with her infant Davy silent and swaddled in her arms.

He steps back, as if struck by a blow.

Change in hand, there was change, turning away with a thoughtless smile at Carla, away and starting across the dining room floor to the big bright doors with his coffee to go, Laraby moves on past the man in the red sport coat just sitting with the laughing teenagers, and pauses a small beat just there at the door to glance back one more time to see if she's still looking, sometimes they do, and this one is.

Through the glass now, mother and child are motionless, as if a vision, the ghosts of our own guilt, for all our loved ones who must suffer so we can be loved more. She looks up, and they lock eyes; hers, pleading; his, horrified, as he finally understands and turns away to the station nurse, is it ever the same nurse, to quietly and quickly say, "I have to leave, have someone take the baby and check him, but keep her here. Get child services, and that counselor from county, here, now." He rushes off down the hall, lab coat floating out behind him.

Down wet streets in the rain, Laraby guns his Mercedes past slower traffic, speed-dialing his cell, sobbing in frustration at the tinny mechanical voice that comes back to him, "The cell phone customer you are calling is—" He flicks it off, flings it onto the passenger seat.

A horn complains behind him. He makes a skidding fishtail right, down a smaller street, trying to avoid County 9 and State, where there's no turn lane and one car turning left can make anybody late.

He's speeding through a blue-collar Hunt Landing neighborhood now, past single-story homes of faux redbrick siding with sagging porches and peeling eaves, past muddy yards and dead shrubs, to stomp on his brakes and stop thankfully just short of a crosswalk, where black children in white winged angel costumes hurry beneath their teachers' umbrellas, across the wet street to their elementary school and their Easter pageant dress rehearsal. Mild, reproving eyes turn toward him, looking through the streaked windshield of his car, the child eyes of angels who are our guardians, divining all.

Abashed, Laraby turns his head away, and then screeches off with a sob again, as they gain the opposite curb and turn to watch him go.

His mind seems to split into fragmentary imaginings of Jan in the drizzle as she pulls up her jacket collar and squints up at the low clouds. He can see her, there at the site of their half-built house, standing in the wet chill beneath a tarp slung between posts of fir, drinking his reheated leek and potato soup from her thermos, while she rechecks the framing and footings of the front portico, the plumb line of the bearing posts, the square of the good foundation beneath the entryway to their future home.

When would it happen? As she bends with her tape to confirm a measurement, would she hesitate, pressing a hand to her temple? The tape measure would fall to the ground, as she drops to her knees, dry-heaving, and then vomiting as her blood vessels open all at once instead of in sequence, even as his only seem to shut in a sharp unending stab of fear.

And from her raincoat pocket, faintly, the brief melody of tinny notes from her cell phone would sound, distantly and not unpleasantly as it fades farther and farther away and disappears into nothingness, as Laraby drives endlessly toward her with his own cell phone pressed uselessly against the side of his face.

Carla ~

Sitting in a plastic chair in the admittance waiting area, Carla shifts with vague unease. On the wall-mounted TV *Hollywood Squares* plays softly, and Carla squints at it with dislike, but then remembers it's for charity. Too bad those others, *Fear Factor* and whatnot, where people eat the most unimaginable stuff, aren't also, but then would people do that for anyone else? You hope so, but also doubt it, that anyone would let spiders crawl all over their face and not even move to do the slightest thing about it.

In the kitchen, hidden between the open pantry door and the wall, Carla peers through the mesh grille on the door, seeing the man with the gun in the tan jacket bend with his face downcast away from her, and bend again out there in the dining area floor, like he's bowing to an audience, but really reaching, and then doing something with his gun. Until he steps quietly, it really is just so quiet, to the booth where that guy in the red sport coat begins to weep and whisper quietly, as if finally confessing some horrible lifelong regret.

Carla looks down again at her little cell phone, which she has risked her life to grab, what for, flashing its message over and over again like a verdict, "signal faded."

His back to Carla, the gunman steps toward the booth and lifts his pistol and BLAMM!! fires point-blank, which Carla can see a little of, too much.

Carla looks instead at the Carby's Cowboy Special burning on the grill,

thick smoke curling upward, but she still can't help but flinch as
BLAMM!! the gunman shoots that man again, and mercilessly, BLAMM!
yet again.

The fly finds her cheek again, and takes off, and touches down again,
but Carla doesn't move, cannot move, to brush it away.

Carla brushes absently at her face, at nothing. She tries to focus on the
wall-mounted TV, but why did they want to examine Davy without her
even there, and have her wait in an upstairs lounge besides, something
Dr. Laraby wouldn't normally do? Today for some reason his usual
nice look of concern had seemed kind of suddenly afraid, somehow,
his eyes darting around, which didn't seem like him. Weird, how he
just turned his back to say something to the nurse behind the counter
there, the same one who was so nice to Carla that one day and liked
her diaper bag and chatted with her, and then he just suddenly rushed
off down the hall out of sight, his white coat floating out behind him.
The nurse looked different, too, through the glass straight at Carla,
talking into her desk phone with a hard blank face, whatever that was
all about.

But whatever, anyway, because Davy needs to be looked at for
sure, since his breathing has been raspy and shuddery and his skin so
white but hot to the touch, his eyes dull and staring but without really
focusing.

A commercial comes on now, with dance club–style music, for a new
boxy little SUV that looks kind of fifties, Johnnie Rocket's–like, driven
by a beautiful girl younger than Carla, in boxy interesting glasses that are
the look now, with a smug cool little smile. And then there are thin
deeply tanned vacationers who windsurf, dance, rock-climb, and laugh.
Sunlight flares into rainbows, kayaks appear. And then they open the
SUV and fold it in or out everywhere like a Swiss Army knife, a tent appearing, a hatch opening, a seat folding flat for a mountain bike, or
wait, now it's a beach and a surfboard, with a hang-glider in the background, and everyone carrying their own colorful water bottle like a
commercial for water or maybe something to carry it around in.

A phone begins to ring, *brrr, brrr,* softly, but insistently.

Brrr, brrr. The phone is ringing as Carla hides behind the open door of the pantry, watching the Carby's Special burning on the grill, sending up plenty of smoke. If it should flare up Carla knows to dump flour on it or use an extinguisher, they say water makes it worse, something that came up in the household dangers talk at her parenting class at the Y.

"Ms. Davenport?"

Carla looks up from the TV in surprise: a different nurse stands there with a policeman, which is weird, and a woman in a tan pants suit with a clipboard.

Carla stands, flustered, looking around, as if cornered.

The policeman looms like a giant, so much dark blue, with a stony face that doesn't smile and hands that hang at his sides near his black gun and nightstick, though his voice isn't mean as he says, "We just have a few questions before you can see Davy. Would that be okay?"

Carla looks from one to the other, and takes a step back. They step forward, palms out, as if to reassure her. That what? That they understand what they can't possibly ever? That they know he's a "handful for a single mom," or that at night when he's finally asleep and the TV's off and the phone lies there like some dead thing, there's nothing but sounds from outside, a car going by or someone laughing, and it makes her head and heart ache to know it can all be over in an instant and that's all there ever was and will be?

Carla simply turns and runs, off down the corridor, as fast as she can to anywhere else, her sneakers squeaking.

The cop gives chase, flashlight and nightstick bouncing against him. "Hold it!" he shouts.

Carla yanks open a door, ducking into a stairwell. He follows, footsteps pounding and their gasping breaths ringing from the polished cinder-block walls and metal stairs as they run.

Charlie ∼

Southern Ohio spreads out and away forever, all flat sparse woods and corn stubble and tiny distant farms down muddy access roads. Up all night, Kathy has driven her car from rest area to rest area for coffee and bathroom stops, and now she drones on past a sign, blurred by the streaks of rain her worn wipers leave behind: CARGILL 28, POWATAN 50.

On the seat beside her, she has her marked Yahoo! map, and her photograph of Charlie and Beth in the frame he bought her for an anniversary, which one Kathy can't recall; it has held a photo of them on their wedding day, a cornball staircase pose with him on a lower step in front of her and both facing the camera sideways with impatient smiles, and then later one of them on their honeymoon, taken by a waiter at the Acapulco Carlos n' Charlie's when they were blasted on Añejo margaritas and dizzy from jet lag. That one had stayed in the frame for years, until it was replaced by one of her holding Beth for the first time, with Charlie beaming beside her, all a little harsh from the flash bounce off the windows of the hospital room, but still it showed Beth's tiny smooth eyelids shut and her sparse hair so black it looked wet. And Charlie, of course, grinning like a loon.

Hair awry, clutching his envelope, Charlie is back as if he never left the Powatan casino gaming floor, eyes wide and rolling as he leaves a swath of misfortune in his path: slot tumblers click to a rest, three sevens and a cherry punctuated with a player's soft curse, or the groans from a blackjack table as the dealer flips over the bullet to add to his suicide king or bitch black queen of hearts, no push. A moan sounds from a roulette table, where what looks like a half-drunk wedding party has bet, hopefully not on today's date.

A girl's pretty face is smeared with ripe acne, a young buff guy's arm quits at the wrist. "Deuce, line away," deadpans Stu the stickman. Laughter reveals impacted teeth, the cheesy stink of gums swollen with gingivitis. Skull and poisonous snake tattoos adorn the flabby biceps of bikers in wife-beater T's and braided beards; bits of metal pierce teenagers' faces, like gleaming decorative shrapnel from the exploding ordnance of warfare.

Where is there luck to be had in all this ugliness? One sign, and Charlie would bet it all, since no sign may ever come again to him, no other luck as long as he or any of us live in such a relentlessly hideous world as this.

But no, what was that? Patience is all, bad luck means good is due, contrarian thinking gets us through when the chips are down, to the very second when luck and a wager intersect.

Down an aisle of quarter slots, hair-gelled young guys in rented tuxedos pass around a flask, and some bridesmaids in peach satin hang back to flirt before they all head for the "event room" or wherever it is they might have daytime weddings and such in this place. Somehow they have surrounded Charlie, or he has blundered into their group as he shuffled around the gaming floor this morning, searching for fate's last opportunity. One turns to laugh at another, and her eyes flicker with dismay at Charlie's wild hair, unshaven face, and wrinkled clothes.

Charlie turns from her look, forgetting it almost before he notices it, because at the end of the aisle, at the end of all the aisles where they meet in a circular hub of lounge furniture and a small raised stage, there beneath the quadruple odds, sucker bet Big Spin, a country-western singer in a red leather fringe vest sits at her synth 'n' drum machine, singing into a microphone. Charlie steps toward her, dazed with light, to see her simple even features unmarred by mishap or affliction, and that her lean forearm bears a beautiful tattoo of faded watercolors: the winged Harley-Davidson logo.

Like a doorway finally opening to his own private destiny, the words of her song reach him. "I can fly higher than an eagle, for you are the wind beneath my wings . . ."

Sounds cease, the world slows. Charlie steps forward, reaching inside his track suit jacket for the only weapon he has, all that he has borrowed against livelihood and limbs, his envelope of cash. He bears it through bright space and hands it to the Big Spin spinner, who smiles the smile of an angel as he speaks soundlessly to her.

She spreads his bills and then counts out near twenty-five thousand dollars' worth of chips, and then she slips the bills into a slot, no wasted moves.

She puts all his chips on seven. And spins the big garish wheel.

To Charlie, as he stands frozen there, the snap of the rubber plectrum from peg to peg is suddenly loud, as a jackpot alarm blares and someone's cell bleeps and the singer's voice seems to reenter the world of a thousand other noises, suddenly and sadly no louder or more significant than any other.

The voice message alert sounds from the cell in the dead guy's pocket,
Bleeeep! Bleep! Bleep!

Without moving his head, Charlie shifts his gaze upward, out across the room, seeing the gunman's Hush Puppy leaving a wafflelike print behind, of blood.

The gunman is half-turned away, sighing and bending, reaching as if to pick something up off the floor. And again. Again until finally he steps away, to the booth where the guy in the Red Carpet jacket has already begun to murmur softly, pleading.

At his table, Charlie lowers his gaze to his tabletop, his forearms lying there as numb as if they were someone else's, soaked in spilled iced tea.

As the big wheel slows, the rubber plectrum bends against the peg between the six and seven slots. The wheel creaks and groans, and the spinner's smile is almost sweet enough to make one think the world could still somehow be fair.

The Children ~

In daylight, the bruises on Lydia Jaspersen's face and neck vary from bluish to a deeper purplish hue, from the various impacts of Bob's fists. She stands in the doorway of Jimmy's bedroom, bleary and aching, staring in at the empty clutter and still-made bed, before turning to rush for the phone on the hall table.

As she reaches for it, her eyes find Bob, just sitting up from the living room sofa, pale, hair awry, in a tangle of dingy blanket. He glares for a moment and then pounds across the steps between them to knock the phone and its cradle off the little table, with a clumsy swipe that tangles his hand in the AC cord. In sudden helpless fury, he flings his hand around, trying to free it, kicking and lashing out, gnashing his teeth, pale and pathetic with his paunch and slipping boxer shorts.

She looks at him, unmoving, hateful, finally defiant. And as he quiets and his shallow breaths slow, his eyes search hers, desperately seeking purchase, like the hands of someone falling. Finding none, he finally turns and heads into their bedroom, where he yanks a suitcase from the closet.

She picks up the phone, setting the cradle back on the table, dialing rapidly.

Brrr, Brrr. A phone is ringing, but Anne doesn't hear it, because she is standing motionless and pale at her desk, her eyes flickering panicked again and again over the little window on her computer screen, as if by reading and rereading each word before she begins the next, she can understand some happier, less-dire meaning to the message there:

> Annie Annie Annie It's Not Over Yet It Will Never Be Never Be Never Be.

From outside her door, suddenly her mother is pounding, shouting: "Anne! Anne! It's Jimmy's mom!"

Anne rushes to her door and flings it open. Rapidly, softly, "It's okay. I know. I know where he is. God knows I do. I'll go."

"I'll drive us," her mother insists, just as softly and as resolutely.

Doris strains to see through the wipers and the rain, skidding their van around a corner onto County 9, past the shabby minimalls and the U-Haul lot, the Mediterranean-themed condo developments and vacant lots along the west edge of town.

Anne grips the dash, grim, her placid spaciness gone. "It's all right, Mom. I can save him. Dad saved me so I can save him. We can all save each other."

Doris glances at her daughter, sensing points of no return passed, irrevocable choices made, inevitable consequences come due as paths converge, Jimmy's and Anne's, somehow, with her own and her lost husband's.

Doris leans on her horn, lane-changing around slower traffic, fighting the drag on her wheels as they plunge through runoff, throwing spray across the gutters and curbs and sidewalks of Hunt Landing.

Traffic slows around a road crew, their orange vests bright in the rain as they clear gutter debris. One crew member wields a stop sign and a queue of cars forms, closing in behind them and stopped in front, as a garbage truck is loaded with tree limbs and a bent rusted shopping cart, of all things, from a storm drain.

In a copse of bare trees by the old Tompkins Park train trestle, Jimmy stands bent over, soaked and shivering in the rain. Gasping for breath, he pulls handfuls of hair on both sides of his head, moaning, his eyes shut tight. The grip of his father's pistol protrudes from his jeans pocket.

Beneath the table of the booth where Anne's dad sits weeping, Jimmy
stares out through the clutter of table and chair legs and his eyes meet
that big guy's, the one in the short-sleeved white shirt by himself at the
table with his drink spilled and dripping down.

He can only think it has all come to this, whatever this is, this day or
these trees or this bridge of unused train tracks going nowhere, as if
there were any place to go anyway, where a location could be secured,
where a perimeter might be maintained, where defenses may be successfully mounted against all incursions, out of sheer determination
that promises be kept and that goodness shall in the end and for
always prevail.

His eyes spring open, but they're a thousand miles away, tears
spilling.

Under the table, Jimmy's eyes widen, unblinking with fear as he sees the
gunman's feet approach, white sweat socks and Hush Puppies scuffing
along through scattered napkins and Styrofoam trash, a Special take-
out box, a few "Joe to Go" cups rolling.

Jimmy cowers back, pressing himself against the cool brown leatherette.
Beside him, Anne also seems to cower back away, staring down terrified
as if at something she has dropped, her hands fluttering around her face
like frightened birds somebody's flushed from high grass with a footstep
or a gunshot.

Jimmy's running now, breathing hard, his eyes staring at a distant
point only he can see, an eyes-only mission objective as secret as it is
vital, to both the short- and long-term strategic interests of himself
and of his love and loyalty to his only friend.

The handle of his dad's old army issue .38 is cold in his hand and
heavy, as he holds it in his pocket to keep it from bouncing against his
soaked thigh, and his legs ache with his weight pounding down into
his thin sneakers.

The rain quickens, spattering the sparse gravel and hardpan along the shoulder of this back county road from Tompkins Park, where it curves past equipment yards and raw fields of stubble toward town.

Abler's defroster is balky, so he drives hunched over to peer out the unfogged bottom of his windshield, until the mildewy heat clears the rest and the vague colors and shapes outside sharpen into the black wet woods and fields just outside Hunt Landing Township.

With no call left to make, no good word to say to anyone who wants to hear it, he's packed his duffel and laptop, and made his start northward to tomorrow's reassignment, on emergency loan to a little Upper Peninsula town, where an off-season thunderstorm has turned loose hillside into mudslide, washed away a low-lying eighth mile of county road, and drowned three.

To Abler, flood suggests new, specific pretexts for familiar dramas: self-loathing and guilt for trying to cross the road that became a river, bitterness and blame for the poorly engineered culvert or street drain, public safety ass-covering for the liability lawyers, all a dodge from the real and inevitable grief of losses too hard to face in the immediate aftermath. He's seen elderly couples in motel lobbies, laughing at sitcoms while their homes lay strewn and splintered by tornados, parents filing suit and scheduling depositions before their child was in the ground. Oh, how we flee pain.

Abler's cell chirps and he picks up.

His red taillights brighten in the rain as he pulls over and stops.

bird of prey ~

Laraby ~

Laraby's little Mercedes skids to a stop and he jumps out, looking frantically around, running for the entry gate of the chain-link security fence that surrounds the framed shell of their future home.

"Jan? Jan?" He shouts, his voice disappearing into the rain and the wooded hillside beyond their half-acre lot.

He spots her, lying facedown in the rain, other side of the fence, the galvanized chain link between them parceling the world into rows and columns of diamond shapes, as they did between him and his dying father, a barrier for no more than a moment, but a moment unending.

He runs around to the gate, but it's the kind that locks automatically when it closes. Terror flings his hands and feet into the links of the fence as he grabs hold, scrabbling upward, frantic.

He slips down the other side, fingers scraping across the rattling cold metal, cut and bleeding from burrs as he stumbles across the last long yards toward her.

She is cold, not breathing, pulse thready and uneven, cyanotic, but for how long? How many minutes of oxygen deprivation have passed, how far has she gone? His mind snaps shut on the possible answers, one after another, and on their attendant prognoses as he gasps in panic, fighting for breath himself.

He yanks a syringe from his pocket, tears her sleeve and plunges the needle hard into her arm, squeezing the stopper.

He bends to her again, listening for breath sounds; a faint trail of vomit runs from her white lips to jawline, her chest remains still, so still, as the poisons battle within her, one to constrict her blood vessels, the other to widen them. Her skin is still bluish, as bluish as his father's, and Sam's, and Aaron Hagen's was anyway, even before he accidentally nicked the aorta when no one could see and blamed it on a stray bone fragment. Not that it mattered, did it, all of them already irreversibly dying anyway as their EEG monitors flatlined and harmonized with the blood gas alarms, just before each TOD was notated and a sheet flipped over their dead faces.

He has done everything he can to help his wife live, and now, finally, he can't escape the simple truth: it is completely and finally out of his hands. He has been brought for the first time and finally to begging, his ragged breath hitching between a gasp and a sob, the looming sky tilting and plunging as he turns his face to the rain, chanting, "God, give me this. Never again I swear to you. God, God, God. Just give me this."

Here is absence once again, hovering, like a sledgehammer in a slaughterhouse, huge, implacable, pitiless. What must he do, what can be done, what prayer has he not prayed, into what echoing emptiness? His hand lifts and clutches at his hair, his pulse jars and stutters in his chest. Heat floods his eyes and ears, the smell of the sweet wet earth clogs his throat, choking him.

On his way out with his "Joe to Go," Laraby passes the man in the red sport coat laughing with the teenagers, and pauses a small beat to hold the door as he glances back at Carla, barely seeing the shoulder of the man in the tan windbreaker who slides past him and inside, murmuring, "Thanks."

"You're welcome," Laraby says, too late, and moves on and out of

that place where he will never save anyone, safely out to dream that someone, somewhere, could ever really be his to save.

Jan Laraby shudders, with a breath. A hesitation, and then another. Her eyes slowly flicker open, the dark shape of her husband's face and the gray light of the rainy sky returned to them.

Laraby sobs, and buries his face in her neck, clinging to her, to every secret contrition imaginable, between himself and a God that must hear us after all.

She brings a trembling hand slowly to her temple.

"You'll be fine, I promise." He smiles at her through his tears. "I promise you."

Carla ∽

Carla bursts from a hospital fire exit out into the rain, across a stretch of puddled alleyway, and into the ordinary world down State Street's sidewalk, where shoppers and commuters rush with umbrellas or newspapers held over their heads to awnings and bus stops or back to their cars.

Carla turns her gaze from the Carby's Special burning on the grill and the stinking dark smoke billowing, back to the bright dining area where the guy in the red jacket is dying and the gunman bends to look under the table and pushes his pistol forward at somebody under there Carla can't see, one of those kids the dying guy had with, must be.

Carla slowly looks back at the Carby's Special crisping on the sad to say none-too-sparkling grill. Hans should do better on that, not that it's bad for anybody or really any big health hazard but customers at the counter like to see a little shine or at least a swipe at it—

Kllliiingggg! A klaxon erupts, a buzzing grinding sound between a bell and a saw, as water pours down from the ceiling sprinklers.

The big squares of sidewalk shine and tilt beneath Carla as she runs, dimly aware of a few pale faces in the rain turning as she clears the curb and starts across busy State Street.

Soaked, wedged behind the open pantry door in the kitchen, Carla flinches at BLAMM! a gunshot and watches as the big shy guy in the white short-sleeved shirt lands on his back on the linoleum with his eyes open, and the gunman turns back away again to face the booth where the kids were. He kneels there, soaked by the sprinklers, and then seems to shrug, like he's just tired of trying to figure it all out. Lifts his heavy black-looking gun and BLAMM!! He shoots himself through his own temple, just in front of his ear. It looks like a rope of blood twists away in the air as he falls, gun still in hand, face hitting the floor.

And then there's nothing, just the deafening klllingg of the fire alarm still going as two cops in bulletproof vests burst through the door, stiff arms pointing guns this way and that.

One cop spots the gun in the dead gunman's hand and shouts, "Shooter, here! Anyone else? Check the back!"

But the other cop is busy, bending from the waist and knees, to point his gun sideways beneath the guy in the red jacket's booth.

Outside the sirens peak and Carla flinches again as they suddenly snap off, all at once.

From the doorway, a third cop looks at everything, and then goes down on his knees as if he's praying. Which he is.

Horns blast, tires screech. The little car fishtailing half-sideways on the wet pavement toward Carla is a little boxy Japanese model, almost like the one in the commercial, but this driver's no college student with cool glasses and a smug little smile, but a mom like Carla, it turns out, because when the car halts, rocking for a second with stopped momentum, she's reaching in to the backseat to lift a crying baby from a car seat to hold and comfort and cherish, and then she turns her face twisted with bitterness and an accusing glare to curse at

Carla through the rain-streaked glass, soundlessly, though Carla's best guess is "fucking idiot, you fucking *idiot*."

Carla stands there, midstreet, soaked, lifting a hand that hovers uselessly in the rain, not to calm or point or plead, but to finally touch her face in wonderment at the danger she has little by little but surely become, to any and everyone, others and her own.

"I'm sorry," she whispers, unheard. To the woman, to her son, and to herself: "I'm so sorry."

Back at Hunt Landing Memorial, raindrops in Carla's lashes make stars of the entrance lights, like a gauzy photo of a Paris or London or New York hotel, warm and lit from within as evening falls. Why can't it be a destination to be dreamed of, a place where strangers are welcomed to rest in comfort, after so much rushed confusion?

The cold is so wet, her clothes stuck to her shivering skin, her teeth chattering and bones aching as she stands before those wide glass doors, not deciding, because it has all been decided, but forestalling the start of the weeks or months or years without her sweet Davy, whose trust in her was so pure and perfect it could only, inevitably, eventually be diminished.

Through the doors and across the linoleum, under the bright fluorescent lights of this place, she's almost just a young woman caught in the rain, a little amused and breathless from running splashing through sudden puddles for shelter, flicking her hands and blowing on them and rubbing them together, smiling a little at the others crowding her elevator.

As the elevator lifts, the moment of weight pulls on her and makes her nearly sway, nearly reach out her hand to grasp the railing that lines this ascending little room. She watches the LEDs brighten and dim, counting the floors, one by one, to raise her back to her truer nearly forgotten self.

When the doors slide open to her floor, more faces turn to regard her, from the hall and nurse's station just there: a policeman's, and the long pale face of the woman with the clipboard, not unkind, really, and the dark crowded face of that man with the nervous voice and that brochure from that day, with his smudged glasses and dark intense look, smiling a sad hopeful sort of smile that makes him seem nice.

Charlie ∼

Traffic blurs by, flashes of color bright against the gray of the cyclone fence and the vast Powatan casino parking lot. Charlie shuffles across, tears leaking unnoticed, dazed.

There are shifts in the continuum, he knows, in what he's heard described as the nexus of cause and effect from one moment to the next, sea changes of momentum that begin at the molecular, and can be divined only through the coded language of omens.

But what good can the soft sudden screech of tires, the slamming of car doors, the footsteps behind him possibly presage?

"Mr. Charlie. You don't look like a winner," Rain Coat says.

An awkward choreography of shifting positions ensues, one that Charlie knows is prelude to pain, even before the short bagman in the leisure suit leans him against a car and slaps him.

"You don't have to do that. It's okay. I know why you're mad, I get it," Charlie says, almost cheerfully.

The tall man in the raincoat shakes his head, disagreeing. "You don't get it. You don't got it. You lost twenty-five and change in an afternoon. And now it's payback hour. You're not lucky. So fuck you."

For an instant Charlie's gaze holds a cold glimmer of defiance, and then he closes his eyes and waits, because he knows his predetermined good fortune will intervene any second: a meteorite will land in the parking lot, a lightning bolt will strike close by, a trucker will lose control of his semi out on the highway and it will burst through cyclone fences and guardrails to come barreling across the Powatan parking lot, and cause Leisure Suit and Raincoat to flee in terror.

Leisure Suit steps up and twists Charlie's arm behind his back, forcing Charlie's face onto the car hood, complaining, "I hate this. The whole fucking thing that's gotta happen here because you were so stupid. I mean, how else are you gonna know we're serious? It's your fault, okay?"

"Okay." Eyes closed, Charlie listens for the sound of the cataclysm, the runaway truck scattering debris, or earthquake beginning, or 747 falling out of the sky, that will create a diversion big enough to ensure his getaway.

Charlie's face twists as Leisure Suit grabs his wrist and pulls upward, until Charlie's arm breaks behind his back.

Charlie stumbles along a concrete gangway out toward an empty adjacent lot, where crows wheel overhead, crying out, diving at litter. From the parking lot, a few tourists and low-rollers slow to gape at him. Out on the highway beyond the rusty chain links and guardrails, semis and cars flash by, shuddering the air with noise and wind.

Charlie's eyes are glazed, focused on nothing.

Spilled iced tea spreads across Charlie's table, soaking his bright paper Carby's place mat. Without moving his head, he shifts his gaze to watch the gunman from behind as the man lowers his gun, watching the guy in the red jacket convulse in his booth.

Brrr, brrr, a phone somewhere begins to ring, softly but insistently.

Past the legs of the gunman, Charlie can barely see the two teenagers, cowering beneath the table of the booth where Red Jacket Realtor begins to die.

Charlie stares as the gunman hesitates and then crouches down to look under the table. Wordlessly, he lifts his gun, and the barrel noses along through bright space and finally comes to rest against the forehead of the kid in the camo jacket.

A tiny click sounds as he thumbs back the hammer. Under the table there, gun barrel against his forehead, the kid just stares, eyes forward, without blinking.

From whatever's burning on the grill, smoke rises up to the smoke detectors in the ceiling. Which suddenly go off, klliiiing—*an ear-splitting metallic blare, like a dozen Skilsaws, grinding.*

For Charlie this moment has somehow become a physical space he can inhabit without anyone noticing, and he barely thinks, who knows what for and why ask, even as he's up with a shrug and a thrust across the dining area, past the jumble of tables and chairs and beige walls tilting, with water like rain spattering everywhere and the blur of the gunman as he begins a quick little quarter turn, his little pink hand bringing the heavy black gun to bear.

No gunshot, but there's a stinging slap that's more than a slap because it lifts Charlie off his feet and spins him as he falls onto his back, flat on the floor and blinking to see the world sideways and bordered by shadowy blackness as the gunman kneels on the wet floor and lifts his gun one more time.

Charlie blinks as the background goes blurry and he focuses on the food ticket he's still gripping, bearing the beautiful miraculous number 7 over the Carby's logo: a winged pig, the goofy motto written above, "In a Jiffy, to Enjoy."

Charlie stumbles to his knees, the pain in his broken arm like a blade in his shoulder, stealing the air from his lungs as he gasps and slowly lays his cheek to the wet earth.

At the edge of the parking lot, two gum-chewing crew-cut kids in camping-style rain ponchos, from someone's RV probably, point across the twenty yards of drizzled dirt and dead weeds at him. A spry elderly woman in sweats with an umbrella has joined them, to shake her head in mildest dismay at the plight of the homeless. A tiny dog yips and yanks at the leash held by a teenaged girl, and she hesitates near this group to look out and across, too, her vague surprise forming a squint and a murmured half-syllable, "Wha?"

Arriving, Kathy has just turned her car down this aisle of cars to park, but this group standing and staring off at the edge of the tarmac in the rain slows her, unaccountable fear tightening her throat, making her ears and neck hot. She stops, already knowing, somehow, but refusing to imagine the worst as she climbs from her car and strides by RVs and mini-pickups, to see if whatever tragedy there is in fact hers, or just some briefly pitiable drama beyond our lives and beyond remedy, to be gazed upon in a moment of abstract wonderment before we turn away to what can be helped. And then she sees it: a pile of wet, filthy clothing in a hollow of dirty snow and dirt and dead weeds and litter, flown by raucous crows. The clothes stir, a moan sounds, and it's Charlie, barely, but whatever he has done or whatever has been done to him, always her Charlie.

She lifts a hand to her mouth, and runs for him, stumbling onto her knees and hard on one hand, scrambling sobbing to her feet again to reach him and kneel there to hold him, rocking him like a child, as if she will never let go.

Charlie's eyes close and slowly open again, glassy and streaming tears, as he twists and moans in his wife's arms.

In a clean hospital gown over his pants, Charlie sits upright on an exam table, submitting, childlike, as a rushed young resident finishes bandaging the graze wound on his forehead.

The resident is speaking soundlessly and shaking his head in awe, and finally a sound penetrates the silence that has blanketed everything, a word, in fact, and then others, following others, but none more important in the end than the first and last: "Lucky," the resident says. "Just a concussion. You may sleep a few days, have some blanks and blurs. Someone should keep an eye on you. There's a guy from County to see you, and then you're out of here. You are some kind of lucky, Mr. Archenault. Beyond lucky."

Another moan escapes Charlie as he reaches, reaches far as he can, into the distance between now and the future always meant to be, to his shoe to slip his fingers between his soaked dirty sock and the chill wet skin of his heel, to pull out the cashier's check there: "Powatan Big Spin Winner, Charles L. Archenault, $100,000.00!"

Bloody teeth, torn lips, he smiles down at it, through tears of triumph.

The Children ～

After Jimmy has ducked the crime scene tape and smashed the plate-glass door with his gun-butt into sagging spider-webbed folds to step between, he wander the dimness within, gun in hand. The security alarm is blaring, but it's an unimportant sound, meaningless really, since covertness will never be an issue again, since he has reached the end of hiding.

At the edge of the Carby's Restaurant dining room floor, he pauses, looking around.

Anne and her father are laughing.

An older guy in a tie and short-sleeved shirt like a teacher but with a little earring is sitting down at a table with his iced tea and ticket.

At the register, the cashier lady or girl totals a bill, and looks up as the tall tired-looking guy in dusty jeans and Peterbilt baseball cap steps up to the counter to order. Muzak plays, an instrumental version of some big swoony pop ballad, and the brightness of the place makes your eyes move from surface to surface and keep on moving, nothing here to look at for long, anyway.

Jimmy turns, surveying the empty littered room, lit by the grayish light of the rainy day this day has slowly become. He sees it, one of the many, but not, because this is the booth he and Anne hid beneath and where her father was shot, a lifetime ago, longer.

Jimmy's foot crushes a paper cup as he steps toward the booth, wary, looking around.

He quickly ducks under, slides himself back beneath the tabletop, clutching the gun. The sirens continue in the distance, wailing, but he has arrived at his last waypoint now, and no countermeasures can prevent him from achieving his objective, which he now realizes remains as it should be, the last and best defense of loved ones and their loved ones, Anne and her father, but which can and must also contain and convey all truths, forever, finally.

A skid of tires outside, car doors slammed and footsteps running, confirm that his communication has been received and will be acknowledged.

Anne enters first, slowly stepping carefully though the broken glass of the door, forward into the dimness, slowly, looking around. She sees him and takes in a sharp breath, a sound he's heard before but of glad surprise, like the beat before her laughter, or before an exclamation: "Gross," or "Oh my God!" She presses her hands together, and slowly kneels on the floor of Carby's Restaurant.

Behind her, Doris stands there now, too, just inside the broken door, wide-eyed, frozen.

Jimmy trembles, lifting the pistol barrel to his head. He'll be his own hostage now, cornered and prepared to negotiate with his life for the truth that can set them free.

Anne's eyes have a new look, fear and desperate hope, her voice not much more than a whisper. "God knows he was brave, Jimmy. Dad smiled at me, as if he didn't have a care in the world. He said be brave. And you can be brave, too. God wants you to."

Jimmy shuts his eyes, and tears roll down his cheeks as he shakes his head. Now he will, now he has to, and his voice comes out, finally, hoarse from disuse. "Annie, you gotta tell what happened, and I got to. We have to remember. Everything. So we can stop thinking about it all the time."

"Shhh, shhh." She looks at him, all phony pious sympathy. "I can testify for us both—the truth is more than just what happened. Trust God to help you, Jimmy. God can help you see into the hearts of everyone who fell. Like I do. His witness. Which you are, too."

He laughs at her through his tears, bitterly because it's almost funny now, for a weird second, as if she really thinks she can convince him, and by doing that convince everyone else for good, and they would all walk out together again and the world would continue on down the path of that whole other reality of possibilities. "So witness. But tell what you really saw, Annie. Tell it." He moves the gun to his forehead, pressing the end of the barrel in, that cold metal circle, hard enough to make a mark.

Anne's mom lets out a gasp. "Jimmy? Honey, please, put it down. Whatever you two think you have to hide, it can't be—"

Jimmy looks straight at Anne. "Tell."

Now Anne shakes her head, narrowing her eyes. "No. Shut up, Jimmy. I protected you. From having to tell anybody anything, ever. Or even remember."

"No. No, you didn't. Because we have to. Or just go crazy."

"Shut up, okay? Just shut up now."

Fear has made her pretend to hate him, but Jimmy knows that's all it is, an enemy to be slain by the truth. "Uh-uh. No. Tell what you saw."

Anne's mouth open and closes, silently, as if she has now become mute.

Her mom looks at her, and gently asks, everyone is always asking, "Honey? Please. Don't be afraid. I love you. We all love you."

Anne's smile is terrifying. "I . . . I saw Dad smile down at me and tell me not to be scared. He held my hand. He did."

Jimmy thumbs back the hammer of the pistol, with a sharp little click to fully pressure her defenses.

Doris takes a small step forward, offering hopelessly, "Jimmy, please, it's enough, just put it down—"

Jimmy ignores her, moving the gun to his temple, pressing Anne, pity and fury vying. "Do it. Tell."

Anne breathes in short little gasps. She stutters, "I s-s-s-saw . . . saw Dad smile down at me and tell me don't be scared. He was so brave, Mama. He held my hand." Her words pour out in a rush. "And I held his. I did. He— But then he dropped his Coke. It spilled. And the sprinklers came on, and there were more shots I could hear and everything was wet and . . . and . . ."

Jimmy simply shakes his head, wrong answer. He laughs as he weeps, shouting, "No! Tell the truth! All of it! What I did, too! Just like you've been saying you will! Tell what I did right before what happened to your dad! You can't hold it over me if everyone knows. And I don't care if they do anymore! Tell what I did!"

Anne looks from Jimmy to her mom and back, helpless, her face gone a white beyond pale as it all presses in and traps her, no retreat, no escape from her father's life and hers and his each in the end so sad and ugly and scared, until finally she spits the word out like a bitter vile thing, "Nothing! Okay? He did nothing! Even when he could have, he did . . . did . . ." She begins to wail, a high quavering note, and Doris grabs her, clinging.

Jimmy finishes it for her, a last hoarse whisper as he presses the gun harder to his forehead and closes his eyes, "—nothing."

Doris covers Anne's face with her shoulder, turning her away.

BLAMM! BLAMM! BLAMM!

Sunlight streams through two ragged bullet holes in the rear service door, cutting through smoke.

A third bullet has torn through the shoulder of the life-sized cardboard Carby's Cowboy that stands by the counter.

Beneath their table, Jimmy barely breathes, staring out at the gunman's shadow approaching, followed now by the man's feet, tan suede Hush Puppies that stop one after the other as he half-turns away, his hands fiddling with his weapon, his hands jerky, trembling, busy: reloading.

The gunman fumbles the bullets, and they fall to the floor, clattering, scattering. He bends to retrieve them, his back to Jimmy, not a yard away. He picks up one bullet rolling on the linoleum, and then one more. Oblivious, he steps closer, reaching for the others.

Through the gaps and angles between chair and table legs, Jimmy's eyes meet short-sleeved white shirt guy's at the other table, but just as fast and with no acknowledgment they both look away, afraid and ashamed, because opportunities to advance and engage will always depend on coordinated support and ample ordnance.

Jimmy turns to Anne huddled beside him.

Still gripping her father's hand, Anne watches the gunman reaching unaware for the bullets. And then she looks at Jimmy, nearly but not asking the unspoken question, which hurts to even think about, because what would she do, what would her dad or anyone do, what is there to be done that might not go wrong and kill everyone, when maybe otherwise they would have all lived?

Jimmy stares back at her, face twitching, eyes wide.

And then she simply gives up and turns away to look out the little bit of window beside her, waiting. Beyond the glass, a lone sparrow pecks at the dirty snow, at nothing. And then it's strange because it seems to lift its tiny head to look right at her, before flying off to join a flock, turning this way and then another, and another in the wide white sky, all together, as if frightened, which can't really be, because they don't ever know, do they, that they are as earthbound in the end as all of us?

Into her ear, Jimmy whispers his secret, "Shut your eyes, Annie. Pray."

And she does. Because prayers are truly winged things.

Facing out the window, she trembles there, clinging to her father's hand. From above, she hears him. "Please. What do you want? My wallet? Please. Please, don't."

Still gripping her father's hand, her face twitches as she cowers away from the dark stain that spreads from her dad's crotch, down his pants leg, because who wouldn't at first be grossed out? But what's too much to imagine, really, is his knowing. Animals, birds like those flown by, they never know, so in their minds don't they live forever, fearlessly? Until the very second they don't?

BLAMM! A shot sings out. In her hand her father's hand squirms as he begins to die.

BLAMM! Another gunshot.

She flings his hand away. Blood runs into his striped shirt-cuff as his hand scrabbles along, frantic, feeling for hers, like a desperate blind living thing. She shrinks back as far and small as she can, her hands fluttering helplessly on either side of her face, unable to touch his hands because then she will become like him, or even have to stay with him, and go wherever he goes or become what he becomes, no matter what.

BLAMM!

Under the table, Anne's eyes spring open and she sees water hissing down like driven rain from the ceiling sprinklers.

The gunman lies there, gun in hand, bleeding from his head. Across the room, the guy in the white shirt also lies on the floor.

Out across the floor, the boots of SWAT team cops come into view. Pausing, stepping lightly, turning this way and that.

Beneath the table of their booth, Jimmy looks at her.

And she looks at her cup of Coke she must have put down still somehow unspilled, so she lifts it and pours it over her dying father's legs, hiding the stain of his urine, and then she turns back to Jimmy.

She makes her eyes go flat and cold as they stare into his. "Shh. Don't you say anything. Ever."

Can she open her eyes? Because when you close them, for even a moment, how do you know the world will be the same when you open them? How can you ever know it is, until you finally do?

So she does, and Jimmy has only shot into the booth cushion beside him, three ragged holes in the leatherette and stuffing, ugly and torn, like a kind of wounded flesh.

But still he has the gun aimed at his head, his face crooked, and shouting, "Don't say anything, right? Ever? Remember?"

She won't close her eyes again, won't risk it. She stares unblinking as he pulls the trigger.

Click. Again: *click.* Brightness dims, shadows of traffic pass, small sounds return. Through the blur of her own tears Anne sees her hand now, after all this time reaching, under the table across that very same space filled with so much fear and loss and grief, to take the empty gun gently from him. And pull him out from under.

Jimmy's shoulders sag and new tears start from his eyes, and it's Jimmy again, just Jimmy after all, whom she loves and whom she has punished so completely and so cruelly. She helps him up and gathers him into her arms, and Doris grabs them both, and the three of them embrace, swaying, crying.

Words spill, overflowing. "We were all so scared! And Mama, I'm so sorry I sat there with my eyes closed while that man shot Dad! And I couldn't help it, I didn't hold his hand, I let it go! I let go of his hand! And he didn't die brave or save us like I said at all, he was scared, he was just scared and all alone like everybody else and—"

"Shhh. Shhhh, now." Doris's grip is hard, enough to hold them all together now that their hold on one another has changed.

Anne gulps at the air, like a diver surfacing, and it fills her with lightness. Like the shifting and lifting of some crushing inner weight, anger begins, finally. "I can't forgive that man. I can't. Never."

Doris clings, knowing grief will follow at last. She whispers fiercely, "Don't you ever, honey. Don't either of you. Not ever."

doves ❧

Laraby ~

As he waits for Jan to finish dressing or gathering purse or lipstick or sunglasses or cell phone, Laraby idly paces the clean wide maple planks of their new foyer, hearing his steps ring in their two-story entryway. Sunlight spills from the high clerestory windows, sending squares of brightness against the broad stairwell wall where Jan has hung a favorite abstract painting—thin lines of rings and wings and wheels etched in gouache, swimming in palest fading watercolor the color of sand, suggesting a codex or architectural plans for some elaborate mythical edifice.

Outside the Hunt Landing Methodist Church, Jan and Laraby hurry breathlessly up the last few steps to the wide doors. She pauses with a wry face, eyebrows raised in doubt, as always at these last few months of Sundays they have come here at his insistence.

He gives her his little shrug and half-smile, and pulls her gently up the steps, sober and grateful as a rescued castaway, or a man emerged from a coma.

They enter within, to stand with their neighbors and townspeople in the blond-wood pews, beneath the stained glass of the soaring angular chancel, to sing: "On the wings of a snow-white dove, He sends His pure sweet love . . ."

All join with strong unafraid voices, gazing earnestly forward, as if at a future plain and wonderful to see, though Laraby knows it isn't really ever so, and rightfully should never be. Planning is such hubris, though he does for the love of his wife and the child she hopes for. He cannot really heal, no one can, except for a little while at most, which gives people hope, which is beautiful to see.

These days he remembers a scene from a science fiction movie, though not the title or story, just the two men in their space suits facing each other in the cold black void, falling an irrevocable millimeter at a time, ever so slowly and forever, farther and farther away from each other. The living live until they don't, the dying die, Laraby has accepted his smaller place in this massive complicated universe of occurrences, of cause and effect whose endings cannot be guessed and, for which he is here to thank God, lie far and safely beyond his will and ability to control.

He turns slightly as they sing to watch Jan, and when she feels his gaze she turns her quick careless smile to him, a gift, loveliest of all her smiles to see.

In late March the Michigan thaw sends rivulets from soaked fields across this stretch of blacktop, but Laraby's little Mercedes grips with a nimble surge and squares right up, no trace of skid as he hard-lefts into the lot of Carby's, one of almost a dozen of these little fast-food theme spots that have sprung up along 84.

In the ER, the nurses drink some kind of preground stale blend they let sit on a warming plate that never shuts off, and by the time Laraby gets any, it's thick enough to film your gums and tongue with a burned taste that keeps you chewing Tic Tacs and drinking Arrowhead, so when he recognizes the Carby's logo and goofy balloon letters from so many foam cups and take-out bags around the hospital, he'll try their coffee, it can't be worse, and it's another half mile past the hospital to a Starbucks.

He pulls into the lot and sees his spot, and with a yank of the wheel and a tap on gas and brake he's in, between a mom van and a beat-up little Escort. He presses the big round brushed aluminum ignition button he loves so much, because it reminds him that technology has the power to lift us all into a future of new possibility together, and he hops out and strides to the big glass doors of Carby's Restaurant.

Why does he almost hesitate, what sudden infinitesimal shift occurs in the weight of air or color of light or houses or wires or sky, what tiny modulation of pitch in the drone and whine of passing traffic, what is there to nearly ask a kind of question he answers with a half-conscious shrug as he steps to the door?

The glass of the door throws a bright square of reflected world back at him as he pulls it open, of fleeting shapes of colors sliding sideways as he moves past and through and into Carby's Restaurant.

Charlie ∽

Spring and finally summer come to Hunt Landing; trees gush with rich verdure and dappled sunlight as warmer breezes blow off the great northern lakes.

It's Charlie's favorite season, when the lawns smell rich with newly mown grass and the evenings stretch out long and languorous with birdsong and the buzzing of deerflies and crickets, while kids in shirtsleeves linger in the fading light to toss a few last desultory pitches.

On a late July weekday morning like any other, a small crowd has gathered outside the boarded-up Carby's Restaurant to watch a rusty wrecking ball smash the place into drywall dust, bits of glass flying and sparkling like confetti in the sunlit air, nails groaning and creaking loose from splintered studs.

A black-and-white sign bears a golden sunburst, explaining, SOON TO BE ANOTHER DAYS INN—YOUR HOME AWAY FROM HOME.

Behind a sawhorse barricade, among the others watching idly, Kathy stands by Charlie. A soft cast and sling cradles his broken arm, and little Beth hangs on his other good arm, leaning away with all her weight, swinging a little as she stares entranced at the ugly little restaurant jerking and folding in upon itself.

Kathy floats her hand out to gently touch Charlie's broad back, and he knows for certain again that his own ultimately undeniable good fortune has never left him, though it may have seemed so, for a few moments.

Just past the six-lane gray ribbon of Interstate 94 after it straightaways out of Ypsilanti, there's a mile or so of weedy lots, struggling bare woods, and salvage yards before it begins: the Township of Hunt Landing's row of fast-food parlors, aproned by dirty snow and dead shrubs, traversed by sagging power lines.

Charlie navigates this stretch of county road as always, with a foot hovering near the brake, since this time of year it's patchy with wet and kids on lunch hour from Hunt Landing High will dash out from one greasy gyp joint and run across all four lanes without a glance to join their "posses" and "homies" in another—Wiener schnitzel to Subway and back again.

Charlie signals and turns his Taurus with the ARCHENAULT DRIVING SCHOOL sign on top into the McD's on 84, his stomach grumbling. He's early enough that there's no one between him and the Ronald McDonald kiosk and speaker, but with a few yards to go he spots it: stuck and flapping in the dead shrubs right alongside the drive-up lane—a newspaper page of bright fast-food coupons. He checks his rearview for anyone he might be holding up, and then stops and hops out and snags it.

It's all Carby's, where Charlie has been on occasion, a pastel stucco-and-glass sandwich franchise half a block away, clean and bright enough, with a busy grill and a late-lunch rush from the nearby hospital and junior college that Charlie thinks he can beat to the counter. For free iced tea and half off the special, which isn't very, Charlie checks his rearview again, looks back arm-over-seat, slips her into reverse, and backs out onto Route 84.

A horn behind him blares and Charlie brakes, waving sheepishly at the little beat-up compact zooming around him and on ahead.

In the Carby's lot, Charlie finds a spot between a big late-model pickup with a nice chrome lockbox bolted to the flatbed, and funny, that same worse-for-wear little Escort with bondo on the side that almost ran him off the road. Everybody's in a hurry. He does the textbook over-shoulder check and backs in between the two, but ends up a little too close on the left, and so pulls back out to readjust and repeat.

Charlie climbs out of his car and walks to the water-stained stucco facade with the big balloon letters. He yanks open the door to the warmth and the smell of coffee and bread and meat, and the faint sounds of laughter and murmuring, and heads for the order counter with his discount coupon.

Carla ⌒

Surrounded by children's crayon drawings and worn stuffed animals, Carla laughs as Davy crawls across the Star Wars blanket they've laid on the worn carpet of the visitation room; his look is so intent and serious, his focus so concentrated, that he seems ever so slightly, comically cross-eyed.

She lifts him and holds him in her lap, cooing. He coos back, smiling, unafraid, reaching out a tiny hand as always to grasp her finger, which brings fresh tears, stinging again, to her eyes.

Suddenly, "It's time, Carla," the woman from Social Services says. She reaches for Davy. "He'll be fine." In the doorway, a new different Social Services trainee, young enough to gape at the scene, finally looks away.

A tear slides down Carla's cheek, because she doesn't know how to even imagine more senseless hours of no one but herself to fill somehow, when there will be no faces turned toward her, waiting, like Davy's, or even like the people who came in to Carby's Restaurant and looked at her while she totaled up their bill and made change and handed their tickets to them. No faces will look expectantly at her, because she has nothing anyone can be permitted to need, not anymore, not until she finishes the weeks of court-mandated counseling, one on one with Ron Abler, who waits now in the hall, and in group with others who have experienced other "upsetting events" and need a hand "getting back on track."

She clings a moment longer to Davy. And even though she can't, never in this life or any after, she lets him go because she must, whispering, "I'm sorry, little man. I'm so sorry. Can you say bye-bye? Say . . . bye? See you tomorrow?"

The woman reaches out a hand and touches Carla's, briefly but not unkindly. And then she walks out with little Davy, followed by the silent trainee carrying Davy's infant toys in a cardboard box, leaving Carla to silently wait until tomorrow and the day after, for the long weeks of days to be over and for Davy to be returned to her, because she will have learned how to be forgiven and deserve him once again.

Carla loves this little cell phone she has saved for and finally bought just yesterday with a nice sixty-dollar activation rebate: a trim Nokia with an old-fashioned fake "rotary" design. She can check on Davy anytime from almost anywhere and her babysitter, Jenn, can reach her anytime also, if Jenn could ever remember the number or where she wrote it last.

Carla drives and dials, getting the day-cook, Hans, to reassure him that she's a block away and that he can send Susie home now if she's so sick, although Carla knows Susie is way more likely hungover from her usual Sunday night Chardonnay and HBO binge.

"If she's so sick just send her home already. I'm a minute away, okay?" Carla tells him.

"Yahh, hokay." Hans sounds rushed already.

Before she can hang up, she hears the sad little melody of beepy tones that means she's hit that sometimes dead spot in her cell coverage, and she pulls the phone from her ear to see the message blinking there: "signal faded." Wouldn't you know it, iffy connections from the place she works, meaning spends like eighty percent of her life in. Good thing Hans doesn't mind her using the restaurant landline now and then when she needs to, for sure.

Carla lowers the little cell to hang up, which is when she has to hit her horn at this jerk backing up out of McD's into her lane. In a driving school car, how funny is that?

Carla shakes her head and slaloms her little Escort around and steps on it, speeding the last mile along Route 84 to her fill-in shift at Carby's.

The lot's pretty empty when she pulls in, just a mom minivan with a realty sticker on it and a giant new pickup kind of truck, and as she rushes to the big doors, no time to zip her parka, she shivers a little at a gust of March wind, and at least shuts the front against the cold, gripping the zippers, don't want to bring anything back to Davy.

She pulls on the door and feels the damp warmth on her face, and puts up a nice busy little smile as she hurries inside, where it's not so bad, just a few waiting by the order counter, but the rush isn't far off.

The Children ~

Juggling file folders and car keys, Abler slows on his way from his session with Carla Davenport to glance at the little black-and-white TV the parking lot attendant watches in his little gatehouse, under his counter, in his clutter of Lucky Strikes and hard candy and drugstore novels. It's usually tuned silently to a ball game, but this morning it's got the sound on low and the morning newscast, the anchorman intoning, "Police unable as yet to establish a motive or any connection to the shooting victims in local Carby's Restaurant, and doubtful that they ever will . . ."

The attendant shakes his head in wonderment and swivels his chair a quarter turn to meet Abler's eye. "Used to go in for the special, back when they opened." He raises an eyebrow and lets out a soft whistle. "Right there."

Abler ignores the man as he imagines the faces of Anne Hagen and her mother and her friend, mute Jimmy Jaspersen twisted in tearful fury at him, as if he were the one entrusted with explaining deaths that day. We cling so hard to reasons why, they're like shining stones in a child's fist, because reasons allow us to righteously blame, always easier than grief. Now those families are denied even that refuge. No business deal, jealous lover, revenge for a real or imagined slight, will be unearthed, and no adage, "do unto others," or "think twice before you speak," or "try to put yourself in the other guy's shoes," will be reaffirmed, no useful perspective gained. It is all a hard bitter waste, beyond any consolation.

He has seen Anne and Jimmy in follow-ups, finally, since the implacable force of what they hid from themselves and the world burst through every wall and locked door of denial and defense, and memory and emotion began together again for them. Beginnings are nearly all, Abler knows, almost enough to ask only that they begin to become the hopeful, glad, complaining children they once were, yet again.

On the attendant's little TV, the news anchorman continues earnestly, "Hearts go out to the families as they continue to seek closure in the coming days and weeks."

Silently, Abler leaves the man who once ate in the same place where those men were killed for no reason on earth, and he walks the aisles of empty cars back to his own.

How we struggle with our voices, to manage beyond the shaped idea of each word our timbre and pitch and rhythm, plunging and veering, betraying and redeeming, and in a child's speech even sanctifying, through the sheer innocence of accident. Lydia smiles to watch her son speak, his lips careless and even clumsy in their rush at consonants, sibilance that nears a lisp, vowels swallowed by haste in midword. His hands move restlessly against each other, and then part to spread in the air like a benediction, or surrender, or a prelude to an embrace, as his breathless narrative stumbles blindly into gleeful digressions, the gist a wry snarky observation, or exclamation of guileless disbelief, or suspicion confirmed.

At their little Formica table, surrounded by countertops cluttered with their rows of glass spice jars and wooden-lidded vases of pasta and rice and coffee, Jimmy talks his mile-a-minute blue streak, no word as important as the very fact they exist as sounds in the air, in this little kitchen where they have lost each other so completely, until these last few months, when their family has found itself again, if only as mother and son.

Lydia dries dishes, hanging on his every word. And together they burst into laughter, also an important sound.

Jimmy has at last achieved a safe position, supported and defended by loyal allies, here in their bright kitchen in the middle of a weekend day, home from school and making his mom laugh out loud. It doesn't matter at what, he realizes all at once; it never has, because what's important is only to see her head tilted back and her eyes flashing to watch him speak as if nobody else on earth could ever as well, though he knows that lots of kids definitely could, and probably better.

Trust has returned slowly, as the edges of objects everywhere seem to soften and light becomes less glaring, sounds less sudden. Moments fit simply and easily against one another as hours and days pass dependably, and in his room or in class or at this kitchen table Jimmy has become willing once again to live in each and look forward to the next.

Silence has been his bridge to Anne, but now it simply measures the distance they will need to keep awhile, as it should be. So he will remember her, rolling her eyes and sighing in annoyance at him, or pretending to, at least when her hand wasn't floating helplessly in the air and her bony shoulders swaying as she leaned forward and back again, forward and back, also laughing.

Today a few of the P-Ball squad are set for a lunch-hour game of touch capture the flag out in the thin woods behind the bleachers. He has his book bag slung on his shoulder and is almost to the doors in his camo jacket when he sees her, narrow shoulders and blond hair and the way her ears show through a little and her eyes that take him in shining and her mouth that almost smiles. Light behind her darkens and her dad is there in his red sport coat she hates.

Jimmy slows and goes for the cockney accent. "Mr. and Miss H, 'ow are we?"

Anne's dad likes him, he knows. They always exchange dry witticisms and maintain a stubbornly straight-faced, politely blinking demeanor that began as a sort of contest but is now just a riot all by itself.

"James. Care to join, spot o' lunch?"

Anne's already rolling her eyes, meaning nothing, since she does it a few hundred times a day like the Quad Squad and basically all of them do. But then she shrugs and makes a little show of grabbing the shoulder of his camo jacket and yanking him along as they turn and head out.

They pass up Wendy's, too crowded, and maybe Howard was there, who Anne most definitely doesn't want to see, not with him or her dad, and they drive on down 84 to see where else is empty enough, since lunch with Anne has to be all so stealthy.

Her dad turns them into Carby's. The lot's pretty much empty, and as they climb out she goes first, sliding the heavy door back with a clunk to open on brightness they step down into, her dad yawning, Anne straightening her bulky parka, Jimmy a step behind, watching.

No small distance has been crossed, Doris knows, when she has heard her daughter's sobs again and again from the still hall and peered into her room to find her perched on the edge of the bed with her face in her hands, rocking, and Doris has entered so carefully, and slowly put her arms around this stricken girl-child who is now hers, her breath hot with tears, her eyes reddened and leaking, her shoulders twitching with her stuttering gasps. So much of a child's first true grief is bewilderment, but Doris has stopped asking why; no part of her wants to be shocked over and over again that no reason will be found, ever, or that no reason ever found will suffice.

Anne is hers now, which is all, which they shyly discover together, as moments accumulate through the days: a movie at the mall; a glance at each other laughing; reprising a line on the way home and laughing again; a comment on a girl's shoes or the color of a blouse; a bowl wordlessly passed while prepping dinner; conversations resumed, exactly where they left off, interrupted days ago. Joy is simple to take, finally, from Anne's sleepy whining at being rushed to school when she's running late, to her momentary sullen teenaged glare at being denied an iPhone, or even these her tears, so long due, for her father who loved her and whom she loved, so completely fearlessly.

⁊

Anne thinks of Jimmy less and less; she has glimpsed him among his new friends, with their book packs and cargo pants and choppy hair, taunting one another, shouting and high-fiving in the school halls. She has heard from her mom, who ran into his somewhere, that he's doing well and says hi, but they both understand that to ever really move beyond what happened they have had to move beyond each other.

Through the kitchen window into the yard, Anne glances out to see the pigeon coops, rusted and empty, piled haphazardly, as they have been for months, their tenants long fled, finally, it seems.

And then she hefts a cardboard box of plates and silverware and follows her mother, who carries her own box of kitchenware, to the front door. With no rugs or curtains to muffle sounds, their voices ring out and return to them from the bare walls and scuffed hardwood floors, hollow.

Out in the drive their van is already nearly packed solid with boxes of other belongings, from other rooms now empty. After Anne and her mom rearrange these boxes and the stray belongings they have stuffed into the places between, to find the last places left for these their last belongings, they climb into the front seat to sit side by side.

There will be classes and boys and music and goofy laughter again somehow, and girlfriends this time around, Anne knows, because nothing exists in all of that to ever fear as much as what's already behind her, back at the end of the time that was hers and her father's together.

Anne and her mom share a small sad smile, and Doris pulls them slowly out onto and down the shaded street that has been theirs for so many years, to pass beyond the old familiar roads of their town, to others more deserted and strewn with early autumn leaves, past straight rows of stubble in fresh-cut fields flown by crows, all the long way to another town, with its supermarket filled with bright aisles of cans and boxes in perfect rows, and its new high school with identical rooms of neat columns of desk-and-chairs, and the playing field where the marching band practices in formation.

Slowly the reflection of this world slides across their windows as they pass, and Anne understands that even here she will keep a little of her strangeness, always, but no one will ever know, because they trust in where things belong, that everything has a place, and it makes them innocent.

Anne's dad has swung by the high school to drop a forgotten check for her PE supplies and pick her up, since he has a showing nearby and he's free for lunch and they have the same hour today.

And of course Jimmy has to horn in.

But today what can she say, she knows his lunch is the same hour as hers, and Dad always likes Jimmy, and they'll go somewhere off campus and hopefully unpopular, where nobody else will be, so it won't matter anyway.

She tucks a strand of limp blond hair behind her ear and touches the blemish on her chin, nervous as Dad drives by the Wendy's and brakes to turn in. But she glimpses the gaggle of kids in parkas and book bags just in time, among the jumble of dim color a set of stooped bony shoulders and a pale profile, and quickly says, "Not here. Too greasy, deforesting the world."

From the back, Jimmy smirks. "Ohhh, did I see Howard back there?"

Anne cannot believe it. She goes red. The little creep.

Beside her, her dad signals and pulls back into the center lane. Of course, now he can't resist, "Ohhh, Howard? Do I know about Howard?"

Anne gives him her look of mild reproach. "Dad. You can't know everyone."

Dad gives her a sideways big-eyed goofy look, like, "whoa, deep." And she giggles.

"So, eating where? Carby's, right here? Home of the Special."

Jimmy opines, Jimmy-style: "Always a tasteful and nutritious repast, rich in sodium nitrates."

Anne: "Not if it's crowded, please, okay?"

They look, trade nods, and Dad lefts into the near-empty parking lot, no turn signal, so typical. And yes, he's going to wear the jacket, and no, she's not going to say a thing.

Together they climb out of the minivan.

Acknowledgments ～

This novel results from a fortuitous combination of factors. In no uncertain order: the inspiration of my lovely, often patient and indulgent wife; dependable and fundamental but never obvious advice from mentors; the faith of family and friends; a suspension of disbelief sufficient to take myself seriously; and long, uninterrupted hours in which to do so.

First, I thank my wife, Debrah. Aside from her many invaluable suggestions for specific revisions, she has provided an indispensable touchstone of honesty for the writing by reminding me that the quieter my own voice, the more easily my characters' voices may be heard. She has guarded their humanity and dignity at every turn and taught me Percy Bysshe Shelley's point: Imagination enables compassion. Any man in love with his wife is lucky—and I am—but to have married another writer as perspicacious and tirelessly generous as Debrah exceeds good fortune.

My sister and her husband, Amy and Paul Curtis, never failed to encourage my progress, and with my other siblings and their spouses, Stefanie and Gordon Taylor, and Jeff and Digna Freirich, accepted my dedication to this novel unquestioningly and without much evidence of likelihood of success. There were times I doubted more than they did, and I've been fortunate to have their belief to take heart. My father and mother, Jerry and Connie, helped me focus more consistently on this endeavor, as did Alan and Hilla Benson.

My dear friends David Angsten and Brett Conrad both led by example, writing their own excellent novels.

My wife's sister, Robyn Brady, posed thoughtful questions, which prompted clarifications, and I thank her.

To me, writing well will always seem to be the result of acquired skills, perhaps driven by innate love of language and its challenges, but instilled nonetheless, by endeavoring to follow the example of *il miglior fabbro,* and the best lessons of committed teachers. Among those whom I thank too late but no less earnestly: Professors Marion and David Stocking of Beloit College. I will not recount their lessons here; it is enough to say I depend on one or two in particular, daily, decades later.

It may or may not be Buster Keaton I'm thinking of, but nothing recalls struggling with a troublesome sentence so much as a man unfolding a cot. One end springs up, and when it's finally wrestled into position, the other end rebels. When both ends are level, a corner of the bottom sheet can always be trusted to spring free. Copy editor Jane Herman helped me hold one end down while I attempted to straighten the other, and for that I thank her.

My estimable agent, Svetlana Katz, never wavered, remaining preternaturally calmly convinced. If she worried, she did so secretly, and I thank her for that, as well as for her dependably keen observations and suggestions.

I'm a bit dismayed to realize how many years Ron Levin and Lindsay Williams contributed faith-based efforts, with abiding good humor, for meager rewards.

Author and psychiatrist Judith Herman probably didn't intend her profound study *Trauma and Recovery* to suggest a central conceit and unity for ensemble drama, but her clear and heartfelt insights into the subject guided me to both.

Film producer Robert Salerno's enduring advocacy of the screenplay encouraged me to revisit and improve this novel, and I thank him.

Post-traumatic stress is a shape-changing nemesis that exploits pre-existing vulnerabilities in a psyche, a family, a community, or a nation; it remains my hope that by understanding its effects, we will be moved to recognize it more readily, and perhaps inflict it less often.